CHERISH ME

Book Seven in the Holmes Brothers Series

FARRAH ROCHON

wandering
road
press

Wandering Road Press, P.O. Box 990 Gramercy, LA 70052

Cherish Me

FARRAH ROCHON

Chapter One

Wincing from the ache that thrummed throughout his sore body, Harrison Holmes deduced that the persistent throb pulsing behind his eyelids meant one of two things: a miniaturized rock band had taken up residence inside his head overnight, or after forty-three years on this earth he was in the midst of his very first hangover. The effort it took just to lift his eyelids guaranteed that he would never put himself in the position to experience a second hangover. Ever.

With a groan, he sat up, clipping his head on the wooden arm of the small, uncomfortable futon.

Son of a bitch.

That would leave a mark.

He swung his legs over the side of the futon, but nearly tipped over when he attempted to stand. Plopping back down on the thin mattress, Harrison lowered his head into his hands and sucked in several deep breaths. Of all the days to wake up with a hangover.

Through bleary eyes he peered out at the sparsely furnished third story attic-turned-studio-apartment above the law office he shared with his law partner, Jonathan Campbell. The stark space had served as his temporary home for the past three weeks. At least he *hoped* it was only temporary.

"It's temporary," Harrison grounded out through a mouth that felt as if it had been scrubbed with sandpaper.

He kneaded his temples in an effort to stave off thoughts of the home he *should* be in right now. The comfortable bed he *should* be waking up in. The warm, caring, alluring wife who *should* have been lying next to him last night.

He braced himself for the shooting pain that was sure to pierce his chest. It happened with increased regularity these days. Just the thought of the wife he missed with every single fiber in his body brought about a physical ache—an ache he had no idea how to curb.

That wasn't true. He knew one way to curb it. He could go home.

If only he could figure out just where in the hell he and Willow had gone wrong, maybe then they could fix whatever was broken in their marriage and he could move back into his house with his family. That's what this "break" was supposed to be about, after all. Willow's insistence that some time apart would help to clear the air and make it easier to talk things through was the only reason he'd agreed to move out in the first place. But, so far, they hadn't talked about anything.

This limbo they were currently living in wasn't sustainable. They had to do something about their marriage.

However, right now, he needed to do something about this hangover.

Harrison checked the watch he wore twenty-four/seven and offered up a prayer of thanks that he still had three hours before he was due in front of the Honorable Wilber

Rubin. He would need every single second to get himself ready to face the arbitration judge.

He stood, taking a couple of seconds to steady himself. This was why he didn't drink. Why in the hell would anyone purposely put themselves through this?

Once he was certain he wouldn't fall flat on his ass, he crossed the two or so yards it took to make it to the bathroom. The space was barely big enough for his six-foot-three frame, but Harrison refused to complain. He'd rather sleep in the cramped apartment above his office than in some hotel, or worse, take his dad up on his offer for Harrison to move into his old room. For some reason, that felt like admitting defeat.

This wasn't the first time he'd spent the night on the futon in the three years since he'd joined Jonathan's firm. There had been times when he'd worked so late into the night that it made more sense to sleep over than to drive out to his home in Lakeview. If he tried hard enough, he could convince himself that he'd spent every night of the past three weeks sleeping on that lumpy, uncomfortable excuse for a bed because he was working late on a big case, and not because he was no longer welcome in his own bed.

Harrison sucked in a painful breath.

That wasn't fair. Willow hadn't thrown him out of his bed. But he hadn't felt all that enthusiastic about being there these last few months either.

Harrison grimaced at the scruffy face he encountered in the mirror. He didn't recognize the person staring back at him. He didn't recognize the life he was now living.

How had he gotten here? His seventeenth wedding anniversary was two short weeks away, and he could probably count on one hand the number of arguments they'd had in that span of time. And not one of those had been *real* arguments.

How had a couple who hadn't had so much as a single major fight in seventeen years of marriage land themselves in this predicament? His inability to come up with a reasonable answer had kept him up an untold number of nights these past six months.

The chime of the antique doorbell on the 18th Century colonial that housed the law practice knocked Harrison out of his recriminating musing. He waited for a moment, wondering if Jonathan would answer it. He figured his partner had spent the night on the couch downstairs. But after a couple of minutes passed and the doorbell rang again, he realized Jonathan must have gone home last night. Apparently, his law partner was better at handling his liquor than Harrison was.

He decided to ignore the doorbell—well, as best as he could ignore it with this ringing still going on in his head. It wasn't even eight o'clock yet. The office didn't open until noon on Mondays, given that both he and Jonathan usually spent most Monday mornings in court or meeting with clients outside the office. Whoever was out there would just have to wait until their receptionist arrived in another half hour.

The doorbell chimed for a fourth time, followed by the ding of a text message on his phone. He went back into the bedroom and picked up the phone. It was his sister, Indina.

I'm outside. Open up.

"Shit," Harrison cursed. He didn't want anyone to see him looking this ragged, especially his sister, the Queen of Unsolicited Opinions. But he also knew Indina would not be ignored.

He hurried down the stairs and, thankfully, spotted the

decanter and half-filled tumblers of bourbon still sitting on the coffee table in the parlor where they'd been drinking last night. Yesterday had been a rough day for Jonathan. His friend had needed him. Hell, they'd needed each other.

Harrison picked up the evidence, balancing the two glasses against his chest so he could hold the expensive decanter with both hands. Just as he was setting the crystal globe on the bar, Indina rang the bell again, and followed up with three hard knocks.

Harrison jumped, spilling the leftover bourbon from one of the tumblers onto his shirt.

"Would you open this door?" his sister called, knocking again. "I can see you in there."

"Give me a minute," Harrison called back. He looked down at his shirt. Damn. He looked even worse than he had a few minutes ago.

"Harrison Clark Holmes, open this door!"

Knowing she would go ballistic if he took the time to go upstairs and change his T-shirt, Harrison prepared himself for the judgment he would no doubt receive. True to form, the moment he opened the door his sister frowned and scrunched up her nose.

"You smell like cheap liquor and disappointment."

Harrison cocked a brow. "Shows how much you know about bourbon. There's nothing cheap about this liquor."

"I don't care how expensive it is, it still stinks. And you look like hell. Go take a shower."

"I was about to," Harrison said, moving aside so she could enter. "But someone wouldn't stop ringing the damn doorbell. As if my head isn't hurting enough."

Indina sized him up, her eyes roaming over his disheveled clothes. "Let me guess, you have no idea what to take for a hangover?" she asked, a smile lifting one corner of her mouth.

Harrison didn't bother to answer as his sister let out a peal of laughter. And, just like that, it once again felt as if someone had struck the rim of a Tibetan ringing bowl in his head.

Why'd he let her in? Oh, yeah, because her nosy ass probably would have called the fire department and had them break down the door if he hadn't.

"Did you drive all the way out here just to make my headache worse, or is there a purpose for this visit?" Harrison asked.

She held up an envelope. "I brought the caterer's contract so you can look it over. They emailed it yesterday."

"Is this 1985 or something?" He snatched the envelope from her hand. "You could have just forwarded the email instead of driving across the city during Monday morning rush hour."

"Yes, I could have," she said, following him into the parlor. "But I wanted to see how you were doing." Her voice took on a cautious, serious edge as she stopped him with a hand on his arm. Her eyes teemed with concern. "How *are* you doing?"

Harrison tilted his head back and rolled it from side to side, trying to release the built-up tension in his shoulders.

Despite his repeated insistence that there was no need to worry, he knew his entire family was concerned about the state of his and Willow's marriage. That's what close-knit families did when someone was going through a rough patch. They couldn't help but be concerned. And when it came to his sister, she couldn't help but *voice* her concern.

"I don't know how I'm doing," Harrison answered honestly. Indina would have seen straight through a rote *I'm fine.* "It's been three weeks and nothing has changed. I've been to the house four times since I moved out, but the only thing Willow and I have talked about are the kids."

"The two of you need to talk about your *marriage.*"

"You don't think I know that?" He ran a hand down his face. "I'll see if she will agree to at least set aside some time for us to talk when I go over there this morning."

"You're going this morning?"

He nodded. "I need to pick up my blue herringbone tie."

"What does a tie have to do with anything?"

"I'm going in front of Judge Rubin today and everyone knows that Judge Rubin's favorite color is blue."

His sister rolled her eyes. "That's asinine, but if it gives you and Willow an opportunity to talk, take it. I've tried to talk to her about what's been bothering her, but whenever I do she changes the subject."

Harrison wasn't surprised at either revelation. Indina couldn't help sticking her nose in where she shouldn't and Willow's unwillingness to open up about this rift between them had been a thorn in his side for months now.

Desperate to get the focus off the state of his marriage, he held up the envelope he'd taken from her but still hadn't opened. "What kind of damage are we looking at for the catering?"

"Fifteen thousand. Eighteen if we want to serve beer and wine," she said.

The gala to celebrate the start of the foundation they'd established in their deceased mother's honor was less than a month away. Last week, the caterer they'd hired for the event had abruptly closed up shop and skipped town, taking the two thousand dollar deposit they'd paid with him. Eating that loss, along with the extra money they would have to pay for hiring a new caterer at the last minute, was going to make a huge dent in their fundraising profit, but there was nothing that could be done about it now. Shit happened. He was learning that more and more every day.

"At this point we have no choice but to cough up the money. I'm just grateful they're willing to take the event on at this late date, no matter what the cost," Harrison said.

"I'm not as concerned about the cost as I was just a few days ago," Indina said.

Harrison's brow arched. "Really? And why's that?"

A sneaky grin curled up the corner of his sister's mouth. "Because we're officially sold out."

His head snapped up. "Sold out!"

"Yep! Two hundred fifty tickets sold, at five hundred dollars a ticket. And that doesn't count the pre-gala event."

"Well, damn. At least something's going right these days."

"Yes, now the only thing that would make it perfect is if you and Willow can get your shit together before the kickoff party." She tapped his shoulder. "Get to work on that."

"I'll try," Harrison said, unable to drum up much enthusiasm in his voice.

He saw Indina to the door and then went upstairs to finish getting ready. He was tempted to bring his clothes with him so that he could shower in his own bathroom instead of this cramped, dollhouse-size shower, but he couldn't show up stinking of bourbon. What would Willow think? What would his kids think?

Instead, he quickly showered, ran the electric razor over the lower half of his face, and packed up everything he needed for this first appearance before Judge Rubin.

Twenty minutes later, Harrison pulled into the driveway of the two-story Lakeview home he and Willow had moved into when Liliana was just two months old. His baby girl would make sixteen next month. It was amazing how quickly the years flew by. It was amazing how quickly his ideal life had crashed down around him like a ton of brittle bricks.

And there was that pain again. Sharp and breath-stealing. Relentless and unforgiving.

"You didn't come all the way out here to stare at the house," Harrison muttered from behind the wheel.

Acknowledging the apprehension inching up his spine for what it was, he alighted from the car and started for the front door. Over the past three weeks, Harrison had done all he could to convince himself that this separation wasn't a big deal. It wasn't even a formal separation. It was just a break. Sooner or later, he and Willow would sit down and talk this thing out and everything would be back to normal.

But with every hour that passed, normal seemed to stretch more and more out of his reach. Nothing about living apart from his family felt normal. And figuring out how to fix this was harder than Harrison could have ever imagined.

He arrived at the door and stood there for a moment, debating the best way to handle this. The last few times he'd come over Willow knew he was on his way, but he hadn't thought to give her a head's up this morning. Should he call and tell her he was outside? Should he ring the doorbell? Should he just use his key?

Doorbell. He would ring the doorbell.

For a moment, Harrison just stood there, stunned. Was he really about to ring the doorbell to enter his own damn house? How in the hell had it come to this?

Just as he reached for it, the door opened, and a startled Liliana jumped back in surprise.

"Holy shit," she yelped. She clamped a hand over her mouth. "Sorry, Daddy."

Harrison chuckled. "That's okay, baby girl. I didn't mean to scare you."

He'd seen her yesterday, when they'd all gotten together for church and Sunday dinner at his Dad's, yet Harrison felt as if he hadn't seen her in ages. He was used to seeing her *every day*. He missed her.

They didn't have that much time left in this house together. In less than two years she'd be off to college. She'd already started talking about going out of state to Spelman. He wanted to be here with her, soaking up every minute he could while she was still living at home.

"On your way to school?" Harrison asked unnecessarily. Of course she was on her way to school. Where else would she be going on a Monday morning?

"Uh, yep," Lily answered him. "I'm going over to Amina's and her mom is driving us to school."

"Is the car okay?"

"I guess. If you can call a fifteen-year-old car with a broken heater and no Bluetooth okay," she said with a shrug.

His brother, Ezra, had offered Lily his old Toyota Corolla. At first she'd passed on it, but apparently vanity was no match for the freedom of having your own ride. She'd accepted the car the very next day, even though she could only drive it down the block to her friend Amina's. And even that was giving her more leeway than she deserved, seeing as she was still operating with only a learner's permit. She would move up to an intermediate driver's license in just a few weeks, when she turned sixteen.

He and Willow planned to surprise her with a new car for her birthday, but her attitude of late had put that plan in jeopardy. His sweet little girl's disposition had turned markedly sour over the last few months.

"Just be grateful you have a car," Harrison told her as he kissed her forehead and moved aside so she could leave.

After waiting at the door to make sure Lily made her way safely past his car as she backed out of the driveway, he went inside.

It was all so familiar, yet in just three short weeks it had started to feel...different. From the TV mounted on the wall in the kitchen he could hear the babble of a local morning news anchor droning on about the latest developments in the case against two ex-city councilmembers. The sound of muffled voices drifted from somewhere upstairs, and then moments later, the shower in the kids' bathroom started running.

The bathroom door closed, and seconds later Willow appeared at the top of the stairs, her arms filled with laundry. She took one step, then stopped short when she noticed him.

"Oh. Hey," she said.

Harrison stared at her from the base of the stairs and tried to swallow past the painful lump that instantly formed in his throat.

God, but his wife was beautiful. After all these years, she still had the ability to snatch the air straight out of his lungs with just one look.

"Hey," he answered. "I, uh, need a blue tie."

She nodded. "In front of Judge Rubin today?" she asked as she continued down the stairs.

"Yeah. Presenting due diligence findings." He stopped her as she approached. "I know you have to get the kids off to school, but I was hoping—"

"Wait. Is Lily still here?" she interrupted him.

"No, she was leaving when I got here."

"She'd better have gotten out on time. She's been tardy twice in the last two weeks. One more time and I'm taking away her driving privileges."

Harrison followed her as she continued toward the laundry room, just beyond the kitchen. He snatched a slice of bacon from the plate on the counter.

"Do you need me to have a talk with her?" he asked.

"No. She's doing better now that I had her to delete Snapchat from her phone. I told her she can only use it on the weekends."

Harrison nodded. It seemed as if she had things under control. For some reason, that triggered a stab of anxiety down his spine. He didn't want chaos, but he didn't want to see his home running like a well-oiled machine without him either.

"Willow, we need to—"

She cut him off. "So why are you in front of Rubin?"

Harrison tamped down his frustration. He didn't want to talk about work. She always did that. Brought up every subject except the one they needed to talk about.

But at least they were talking.

"It's for the Bayou Land Dredging acquisition," he answered.

"So that's going forward?" Willow asked.

He nodded. "Largest single acquisition Campbell & Holmes has ever seen. And I get to bring it home."

Genuine admiration shone in her eyes. "Congratulations."

"It's too soon for congratulations," he said, buoyed by the pride he heard in her voice. "We're just getting started. Phillip MacMahon is going to give me a run for my money."

"Phillip's the one who should be nervous, not you." She

stuffed the load of dirty laundry in the washing machine, plopped her balled fist on her hips and looked around. "I need to find Athens's gym shorts so he doesn't have an excuse to miss out on Phys. Ed." She looked up at him. "Do me a favor, when you go upstairs to get your tie, knock on the bathroom door and tell your son not to take forever in that shower. It was a pain waking him up this morning. He's two seconds away from losing Xbox privileges during the week."

"I thought he *had* lost Xbox privileges during the week?"

"He did, but I...I felt bad about...you know." She looked away.

Harrison didn't need further explanation. He'd felt like shit since the moment they sat Liliana and their ten-year-old, Athens, down to explain to them that they were separating.

Taking a break. Willow had decided that describing it as taking a break was gentler.

It didn't feel gentler to him. Whatever way you sliced it, he was still living apart from his family. He was still going to bed alone at night instead of next to his wife. His world was still in shambles.

And they still hadn't talked about what needed to be done to fix their broken marriage.

Harrison stopped her before she could walk past him, capturing her wrist. "Wills," he said. "When are we going to talk about *us*? We have to talk, baby."

She looked down at his hand, and then up at him.

"Mama!" Athens hollered from upstairs.

"I—I need to go see about him," Willow said. She wrested her wrist from his grasp and left the laundry room in a hurry.

Harrison dropped his chin to his chest.

He was at a loss. How was this break supposed to help if they never addressed the problems that had precipitated it? How were they supposed to mend whatever was broken between them if they didn't talk about it?

He had no idea what to do. He just knew this not doing anything bullshit they had going on right now wasn't working. He and Willow were growing farther apart by the day. He had to figure out how he was going to repair whatever was broken in his marriage.

Before there was no marriage left to repair.

As she unnecessarily straightened the bedspread in the guest room, Willow checked the clock on the nightstand. She only had a few more minutes before she would be forced to go back out there. If she waited much longer, she would be late in getting Athens to school.

But if she went back downstairs while Harrison was still there, he'd try to get her to talk again.

A combination of grief, regret and shame coalesced in her stomach. She was hiding from her own husband. Willow pulled her trembling lip between her teeth, resolute in her vow not to cry about the state of her marriage. She didn't have time for tears. She had to get her ten-year-old to school on time, and she had to pick up the dry cleaning, and go to the grocery store, and fill out the forms for Lily's field trip to the state capitol, and a thousand other things. Tears would have to wait.

She listened as Harrison told Athens he'd see him at his doctor's appointment later today, and a few moments later, she heard the front door shut.

Willow breathed her first full breath since she'd spotted Harrison standing at the base of the stairs this morning. He hadn't told her he was coming over, which meant she'd had zero time to prepare herself for the onslaught of emotions that overwhelmed her whenever she saw him these days.

A wave of arousal washed over her as she recalled the image of him in that smoky gray suit. The constant tug of war being waged within her—this pull toward her husband while also wanting to push him away—had her so confused. If only she could wave a magic wand that would wipe away the last few months; maybe then they could go back to being the husband and wife they'd been all these years.

But there were no magic wands. And, if she were being honest with herself, she could admit her discontent had been building for longer than a few months. It would take more than magic wands or wishing upon stars or any other quick and easy fixes to repair what was broken between them.

"He's right," Willow whispered. "You need to finally talk this through."

She missed her husband. She wanted him back. But was she ready to face the potential outcomes that might arise once she and Harrison finally sat down and aired all of this out?

Willow swallowed past the anguish clogging her throat.

"Mama! You ready?"

She snapped to attention at the sound of Athens's voice.

"I'm on my way," she called after clearing her throat again.

Stashing thoughts of her crumbling marriage away for the moment, she sucked in a deep breath and left the sanctity of the guest room. It was time to get started on her day.

But as they made their way to the city's only black all-boys Catholic school—the school Harrison, his brothers, and all his cousins had attended—Willow struggled to keep thoughts of the conversation she knew she and Harrison needed to have at bay. As Athens chattered on about the comic book his uncle Reid's new girlfriend, Brooklyn, had dropped over at the house, Willow's mind returned to that image of Harrison gazing up at her from the base of the staircase.

The mixture of love and remorse and confusion she'd seen in his expression mirrored what she'd been feeling since the moment he moved out. She wore a mask for her children's sake, pretending as best she could that she was okay, but Willow wasn't naive enough not to recognize what this separation was doing to her kids. Lily had been more withdrawn than usual, while Athens had been the complete opposite. He'd started to cling to her, as if he could hold on to the one parent still in the house.

A hiccuping cry slipped from her mouth.

"Mama, you okay?" Athens asked.

She swallowed. "Yes, baby." She reached over and smoothed a hand down his face. "So, have you thought about which superhero you'll be for the gala?"

When Athens learned that the kickoff party for his grandmother's foundation would have a superhero theme, he'd begged Willow to let him attend. She'd granted him permission, with the caveat that he stay at the table in the far corner for most of the party.

Athens spent the rest of the drive going through the litany of various superheroes he was considering for the gala. It seemed her son would require several wardrobe changes a la Diana Ross at an '80s music awards show.

As they merged into the school drop-off line, Athens asked, "What was Daddy doing home this morning?"

"He...uh...stopped over to get a tie he needed for work."

Her son nodded. "I hope he needs another tie tomorrow."

How she managed to squelch the sob on the brink of escaping, Willow would never know. She pulled up in front of the school, leaned over and gave Athens a kiss on the cheek.

"Have a good day, honey."

"You too," he said, accepting her kiss with zero shame. How much longer would she be able to enjoy moments like this? Not long enough. If she recalled, it was around age twelve when Lily decided it was uncool to get kisses from her mother in public.

"Wait one minute," Willow said as Athens exited the car. "Hand me that backpack."

His light brown eyes grew wide, a clear sign of a kid who knew he was caught. He reluctantly peeled the bag from his shoulder and stretched it across the empty passenger seat. Willow unzipped the front compartment, where the rectangular delineation of one of his handheld gaming devices strained against the black nylon.

"You need some lessons from your sister when it comes to sneaking contraband," Willow said. "Next time hide it between two books in the main part of the backpack, not in the front where it's so easily visible."

"What's contraband?" he asked, his pudgy little nose scrounged up in that adorable look she loved so much.

"Never mind," Willow said. She blew him a kiss. "Have a good day at school, baby. Remember, I'm picking you up a few minutes early so we can go to your doctor's appointment."

Athens's shoulders deflated. "I don't wanna go. He's going to stick me with the needle again."

Just like that, Willow's heart broke in two. She absolutely hated that he had to go through this. She hated it even more when she thought about how this could have all been prevented if she'd done a better job of monitoring his health.

It's not your fault.

The doctor's words played once again in her head, but as much as she tried to take them to heart, the notion that she'd failed her son continued to weigh on her, suffocating her with guilt.

"I promise it won't be bad," Willow said, making a promise she knew she couldn't keep. The person in the car behind her blew their horn. "I gotta go, baby. I'll see you later."

She blew him another kiss and quickly made her way out of the drop-off lane. She tried to fill her head with her list of duties for the day, but only moments after leaving the school grounds Willow had to pull over into the parking lot of a florist shop. She could barely see past the tears streaming down her face.

Now that she no longer had Athens's incessant chatter to distract her, the impact of Harrison's surprise visit this morning hit her like a strike to the chest. Seeing him standing there brought home just how much she missed him.

It wasn't as if they'd never been apart. She and her two sisters took at least one trip a year, and Harrison had several conferences he attended annually. But this felt different. This *was* different. The past three weeks had given her a glimpse into a world she didn't want to live in, a world without her husband at her side.

There *was* no world without Harrison. The mere idea of it was too ridiculous to fathom. The two of them had been one body for going on twenty years, practically inseparable from the first time he'd finally convinced her to go out with him, after asking a half-dozen times.

A small smile managed to whisk across her lips despite her tears. If she closed her eyes Willow could still see him strolling up to her as she sat underneath a tree on the quad at Xavier University. He'd been so damn cocky. He'd thought all it would take was an invitation and she would just fall into his lap.

She'd wanted to. God knows it had taken every ounce of strength she possessed not to pounce on his offer of dinner and a movie, but even as a younger sophomore Willow had known that if she'd given in that quickly he would think he could get his way every single time.

So she'd made him work for it. And in the end, it had been worth it.

She'd gotten the guy. They'd gotten each other. And for twenty years had enjoyed the kind of relationship most people could only dream about. She and Harrison had never once gone to bed angry throughout their nearly seventeen year marriage. They'd barely had a major disagreement. They'd shared the rarest of rarities, a nearly perfect marriage.

But the glass on their picture perfect marriage had suffered a devastating crack, and she had no idea how they were going to fix it.

What if they couldn't fix it? What if this break turned into a separation?

You already are *separated.*

She was kidding herself, thinking if she just slapped another word over it, it would change the reality of what she and her husband had allowed to happen to their marriage.

Willow still had a hard time wrapping her head around the fact that he'd left at all. When she suggested they take some time apart, she honestly hadn't expected Harrison to agree to it. She wasn't sure what she'd expected.

No, that wasn't true. She'd expected her husband to fight for their marriage. She'd expected an impassioned tirade, for him to demand they work out their problems then and there. She'd expected him to start the conversation she just couldn't bring herself to start.

What she hadn't expected was for him to pause for a couple of seconds before going upstairs to pack a bag.

The memory of that moment slammed into her like a physical blow. She bent over, wrapping her arms around her stomach. She'd never felt so lost. Her idyllic life had come crashing down around her, and the reality was too much for her to deal with.

She was tired of pretending everything was okay. She'd held it together for the sake of her kids, but there was only so much she could do. The ability to catch her breath escaped her, the weight of the past three weeks pressing down on her chest.

"How did we get here?" Willow called out between hiccuping sobs.

But she knew how they'd gotten here. *She* was the reason they were here. *She* was the one who'd pulled away.

She was the one who'd done wrong.

Now she had to figure out a way to fix it.

And she would. She had to. She would find the courage to own up to her role in all of this, and bring her family back together. She would not allow her marriage to end this way.

But first she had a household to tend to.

"Get it together," she said, sitting up and wiping the tears from her face.

She knew better than to get back on the road before she was one hundred percent certain she wouldn't lose it again, but Willow also knew she couldn't spend the morning sitting in this parking lot either. She had a to-do list a mile long waiting for her, and last time she'd looked *have a break-down over your broken marriage* wasn't one of the bullet points.

She would give herself another five minutes, and then she would suck it up and continue on with her day. She would pull it together and do what she had to do. It's what she always did.

Chapter Two

"I won't even entertain that suggestion," Harrison spoke into the phone. "Get back to me when you have a realistic offer for my client to consider."

He listened with half an ear as Phillip MacMahon countered yet again. They'd been playing this game for the past four months. The boys over at Bossier, Guidry & Associates were inching closer to that magic number his client had agreed upon, but they would never know how close until they actually hit it. This was the part Harrison lived for. The fact that he'd heard a slight edge in Phillip's normally cool voice was a bonus.

"No cigar," Harrison said when his former coworker finished laying out his follow-up offer. "I think it's better for both parties if we continue with the arbitration. The Delmonicos would like to get this business squared away as soon as possible. If Bayou Land Dredging isn't willing to make a fair offer, there are other companies out there who are. See you in Judge Rubin's chambers," Harrison said, ending the call.

He returned to his iPad, where he'd been scribbling

notes for this afternoon's summons before the judge. He made it a point to be as prepared as possible whenever he went to bat for a client, but this time his normal preparations wouldn't cut it. Harrison wanted to be more than just prepared. He wanted to stomp the opposing council in the ground and walk all over his head.

Hard feelings were to be expected when a ten-year professional relationship blew apart like one of those controlled building demolitions on TV. Getting the best of his old firm wasn't just a desire, it was a *necessity*. He wanted those bastards crying at night. He wanted each and every one of them to go to their graves wondering why they'd ever made the mistake of not giving Harrison Holmes his full due.

There was a knock at the door a second before Jonathan poked his head in. "You done with MacMahon?" his law partner asked.

Harrison nodded and motioned for him to come in. "Yeah, we're done."

"What'd he offer?" Jonathan asked as he took a seat in the leather wingback chair that faced the desk.

"Fifteen million," Harrison answered, unable to curb the excitement in his voice. He could see Jonathan doing the math in his head. Thirty-five percent of fifteen million dollars was more than Campbell & Holmes had cleared all of last year. It would provide enough capital to bring in at least four new associates, a half dozen support personnel, and lease office space on the Northshore.

Even better? *He* would be the one bringing this one home. It was his chance to thank Jonathan for taking a chance on him. A way for him to prove to his law partner that he'd made the right choice.

"What's Luca Delmonico's price?" his partner asked.

"Fifteen," Harrison answered. "But I can get them to offer more."

Jonathan's brows rose. "And what makes you so sure?"

"Because Bayou Land Dredging just leased the rights to dredge more than ten thousand acres of marshland, but the new coastal restoration guidelines require they use a specialized hopper, one that's half the size of the smallest they currently use. Delmonico Machinery has the proprietary rights to the design.

"Once Bayou Land owns it, they can do more with that hopper than a small outfit like Delmonico's could ever hope to."

"But they have to own it first."

"Yep." Harrison nodded. "And it'll cost them."

"Take some advice. When you go in front of Judge Rubin today, don't go in there looking so damn gleeful."

Harrison couldn't hide his smile. "I'll try."

With a chuckle, Jonathan sat back in the chair and rested his folded hands over his chest. "Are you sure you're up to facing the judge today?" he asked. "You were looking a bit shabby when I left this morning."

"So you *didn't* drive home last night?" Harrison remarked. He'd wondered, but he should have known his partner was too responsible to drive home after the amount of bourbon they'd both consumed last night.

"Of course not," Jonathan answered. "I camped out on the couch downstairs. I left around five this morning. I wanted to make sure I was gone long before LaKeisha came in. She always gives me this look if she gets in and finds that I've had to spend the night here, especially if I'm not in the middle of a big case."

Harrison could only imagine what their receptionist thought about him staying here for the past three weeks.

She hadn't said anything, but he'd been the subject of some curious—sometimes even sympathetic—looks.

LaKeisha Lawrence had been with Jonathan long before Harrison had joined the law firm. She kept this place running like a finely-tuned instrument, orchestrating every client meeting and courtroom hearing with the efficiency of a seasoned conductor. Harrison learned early on that it was better to stay on her good side, because a pissed off office manager could make a lawyer's life hell.

Having worked for a big firm for most of his career, he'd been used to asking for something and having it waiting for him within a matter of minutes. That's how things worked when there were over one hundred associates and twice as many support staff on the payroll. But a two-man law firm with a single office manager who also functioned as the receptionist, HR rep, social media specialist, courier and whatever else needed to be done, didn't operate that way.

Despite their rocky start, Harrison and LaKeisha got along just fine now. But, like Jonathan, he didn't want her to walk in one morning and find him the way Indina had earlier today. He was instituting his own personal rule: no more bourbon shots during the work week. Or maybe ever.

He waited to see if Jonathan would bring up any of the stuff they'd talked about last night. Harrison wasn't surprised when he didn't. The only time his partner ever seemed to talk about his ex-fiancée was on the rare occasion when he'd had too much to drink. Like last night.

"I've got my own date with a judge I need to prepare for," Jonathan said, rising from the chair. "Good luck with Rubin. Any hope that it'll get worked out today?"

Harrison waved off that possibility. "That's not happening. Too many big egos in the room—including my own," he willingly acknowledged. "But based on the frustration I heard in Phillip's voice when I ended the call, it should make for an entertaining afternoon. By the way, I'm going straight to a doctor's appointment with Athens once I leave Judge Rubin's chambers."

"Everything okay with him?"

Harrison nodded. "Just a checkup. We're still hoping to stem the tide on his pre-diabetes. Today we find out if the increased exercise and change in his diet have made a difference. At least that's one thing Willow and I have been able to agree on, despite...well...you know."

His throat tightened.

"Look Harrison, I know this shit is hard, but you can't beat yourself up," Jonathan said. "You're good parents. Forget about everything else that's going on. Just know that, if I'd ever had the chance to have kids of my own, I would have looked to you and Willow as the example of parenting that I wanted to model."

The naked regret he detected in the other man's eyes before he walked out of the office made Harrison feel even worse for him than he had last night. That regret, coupled with some of the things Jonathan had said after four fingers of bourbon, left no doubt. The carefree smile his law partner usually wore was nothing but a mask.

Even though he and Willow were going through a rough patch, it was nothing compared to what Jonathan had faced three years ago, when his fiancée all but left him at the altar. Anyone who took the situation at face value would swear Jonathan had put his past with Ivana Culpepper long behind him. Given the amount of women he'd been attached to in the three years since Ivana had picked up and left the country, one would question whether Jonathan thought about her at all.

He did. Based on what he'd drunkenly shared last night, Harrison would say he thought about her a helluva lot.

Yesterday would have been the three-year anniversary of their wedding day. The milestone had left Jonathan in the worst headspace Harrison had ever found him in, and it made him even more wistful for the marriage he and Willow had once shared.

Dammit. He'd tried his hardest to keep thoughts of his own marriage from seeping into his brain for the rest of the morning. The phone call with Phillip MacMahon had helped, but his and Willow's separation was never far from his mind.

He didn't want to be like Jonathan in three years, drowning his sorrows about what might have been in tumblers of bourbon. Harrison knew better than to expect that their problems would get solved overnight, but after three weeks he thought at least *something* would have changed. It was too easy for this to all go sideways on them. Each day he stayed away from his family meant another day of Willow and him not talking about whatever had caused them to drift apart this past year.

Why in the hell had he agreed to leave his home?

The answer to that one was easy. It's what his wife had wanted, and from the moment he'd first met her, Harrison had vowed to make her happiness his top priority. Never in a million years did he think Willow's happiness would one day require him *not* being in her life.

Harrison rubbed the hurt that had taken up permanent residence within his chest.

He picked up the stylus and returned his attention to his electronic tablet, swiping his forefinger across the notification on the locked screen. When he tapped the iPad to open up his calendar, the throbbing in his chest became unbearable.

Pick up the wine and flowers.

Harrison set the tablet back on the desk and ran both hands down his face.

He'd set a reminder months ago to buy a bottle of Italian wine and a bouquet of irises—Willow's favorite flower—to accompany the gift he planned to give her for their anniversary. He'd been so damn excited when he'd booked the weeklong trip to Italy. Willow's heart had been set on visiting the country for as long as Harrison had known her. In fact, their very first date had been a late-night showing of *Roman Holiday* at the Zeitgeist Theater on Prytania Street back when they were both in college.

He'd wanted to take her for their honeymoon, but his fear of flying and the fact that he'd just started law school at the time, had stopped them. He'd considered surprising her with the trip multiple times over the years, but had always come up with an excuse about why it wasn't a good time.

Pictures an old college friend had posted to Facebook from their trip over the holidays had planted the idea in his head once again. He damn near suffered a panic attack at the thought of that flight across the Atlantic, but Harrison was convinced the excitement he was certain to witness in Willow's eyes when he presented her with the plane tickets would make it worth it.

Now here he was, contemplating whether he should even tell her about the trip.

Funny how drastically things could change over the course of one year.

He never would have expected that just a couple of months after booking this trip they'd lose his mother to the heart disease she'd suffered with for years, or that his own marriage would set out on this downward spiral that he couldn't seem to spin them out of.

But maybe this trip to Italy could be the thing to set them back on the right track?

He wasn't naive enough to believe that whisking Willow away on an Italian vacation would solve all their problems, but at the very least they'd have the opportunity to talk. So far, whenever they communicated, it was about the kids, or the house, or something else *not* related to the elephant in the room: the impending implosion of a more than twenty year relationship.

There was something else Harrison knew he needed to consider. This acquisition deal between Delmonico's Machinery and Bayou Landing Dredging was the biggest thing he'd taken on since joining Jonathan's firm. Taking off for a week to flit about Italy wasn't the most responsible thing he could do at this juncture in his career. But when it came down to a choice between this and his marriage, there really wasn't a choice at all. No deal, no matter how lucrative, was worth losing his marriage over.

Harrison pulled up the itinerary he'd sent to the travel agent, where he'd outlined exactly what he wanted them to do while in Italy. He'd planned to give Willow the tickets the day after tomorrow, on the eighteenth anniversary of the day he'd proposed.

He closed his eyes and rested his head against the headrest, ruminating on how he'd envisioned the night going down. He'd planned to prepare chicken carbonara, Willow's favorite Italian dish, and serve it with a nice bottle of Italian wine. After that, he would hand feed her tiramisu and those little Italian wedding cookies she loved so much from Angelo Brocato's in Mid-City. After their feast, he'd tell her to pack her bags because they were finally taking the

Roman holiday she'd always dreamed about. Then they would spend the night making love the way they used to do before they had kids.

A low groan escaped his lips.

God, but that would have been sweet.

Now, Harrison wasn't sure if they would even spend their anniversary together. The thought tore a hole through his very soul. His throat throbbed, his muscles tightened, and a wave of nausea washed over him. The possibility that the woman he'd cherished for more than half his life might actually choose not to celebrate their wedding anniversary with him unleashed a tidal wave of distressing emotions.

"We have to fix this," Harrison said in an aching whisper.

Why couldn't he come up with a damn solution already? He'd always been the fixer. That was his role. If his younger brothers got in trouble, Harrison was the one they ran to for help. Whenever there was an issue at his old law firm that no one else was willing to take on, he was the one who came to the rescue. When he met his soul mate and learned about her rough childhood, he had been the one to promise Willow that she would never want for anything ever again. Solving problems was etched into his DNA.

He saw this trip as a litmus test. If Willow chose not to fulfill her lifelong dream of going to Italy, it would tell Harrison more about the state of their marriage than any words she could ever speak. He wasn't sure he was ready for her answer. Would he be able to handle it if she turned him down?

She wouldn't. The Willow he knew would never pass up this opportunity.

Then again, the Willow he knew would never have suggested they "take a break" from their marriage either.

She wouldn't have stood by as he walked out of that house three weeks ago. The Willow he knew wouldn't allow him to continue sleeping on a futon above his law office while his kids got ready for school in the morning without their father there to wish them off.

Maybe he didn't know his wife as well as he thought he did.

Harrison cradled his head in his hand. He wouldn't make a decision on the trip just yet. He needed to make certain his wife's answer wouldn't be the first nail in the coffin where their marriage potentially resided.

On a day when her nerves had already been put through the wringer, Willow could think of a dozen other things she'd rather be doing right now than sitting in the doctor's office. Anxiety danced along her skin like someone auditioning to be an extra in a Rhianna video. She figured it was due in equal parts to waiting for the doctor to return from the exam room with Athens, and the fact that her husband was sitting in the chair next to her.

Okay, so maybe not in equal parts. Her concern over Athens far outweighed anything else, but being in this room with Harrison while he sat there looking like an afternoon snack was not helping matters. She'd always loved the cut of that gray suit. The way it accentuated his broad shoulders and fit waist had a mouthwatering affect. Hours later and her body was still trying to recover from the shock of this morning, when her knees had turned to the consistency of banana pudding after she'd first noticed him standing at the base of the stairs.

But the enticement of that dark gray suit, and the man

who resided underneath it, had only served as a distraction to stop her from obsessing over the true matter at hand, the fact that Athens was in with the doctor and she was out here. Willow couldn't find the words to describe the emotions that swelled inside her when the nurse came in to escort Athens in the back for his blood work, and her son had told her he was big enough to do it on his own. She hadn't been ready for that little display of independence.

Her baby didn't need her.

Okay, she was being ridiculous. He was only ten years old. *Of course* her son still needed her. Both of her children did. Although Lily would gnaw her own foot off before she ever admitted it.

Yes, Lily and Athens still needed her, but for how much longer? Willow could have sworn she'd just taught her little girl how to tie her shoelaces yesterday. Yet, here Lily was, a soon-to-be sixteen-year-old who'd just gotten her first mailer from a college asking her to submit for admission.

A mournful gasp escaped her lips before she could stop it.

"What? What's wrong?" Harrison asked.

"Nothing," she said, glancing over at him with a sheepish smile. Concentrating on her husband seemed to be the safer bet at the moment.

Willow studied him under the guise of examining the model airplanes displayed on the doctor's desk. He'd only arrived a few minutes ago, and immediately had to take a work call. But at least he'd taken the time to text, letting her know he was running late. The fact that he was here at all was a demonstration of the type of father Harrison had always been. Many of the wives in her little circle of quasi-friends couldn't count on their husbands to cut their workday in half in order to show up for a doctor's appointment. With Harrison, it hadn't been a question. When it came to their children, there was never any doubt that he would be right here at her side. Even if he was a little late getting there.

Without thinking, Willow reached over and smooth her thumb under his eye. "You look tired," she said.

She felt him stiffen, as if shocked by her touch. It shocked her too.

How could something that had come so naturally to her suddenly feel so...not natural? It had been weeks since either one of them had shown any kind of overt affection to the other. The impact of that, of how far they'd grown apart, startled her.

Touching him was a good thing. It's when she got used to *not* touching Harrison, or not craving his touch on her own body, that she should be worried.

After a moment, he visibly relaxed, and then shrugged. "I didn't have the best night's sleep," he said, rolling his shoulders. "The futon at the office isn't the most comfortable thing I've ever slept on."

Guilt and regret battled for dominance in Willow's psyche, with guilt winning out over the other emotion by a landslide. He shouldn't be sleeping on that miserable futon. Three years ago, when Harrison started working for Jonathan, they'd updated the furniture in their master suite, spending weeks shopping around for the perfect mattress. She was the one who posited that a good night's sleep was essential to his success. They'd spent more money on that mattress than she had on her first used car.

Now neither of them were sleeping on it.

Willow hadn't been back in their bed since Harrison moved out, choosing to sneak into the upstairs guest bedroom after both the kids fell asleep. She just couldn't face that huge, empty bed without her husband. Not knowing when, or if, he'd ever lay next to her again was too much for her battered soul to withstand.

If he'd ever lay next to you again?

Of course Harrison would be back in their bed. *Of course* he would, dammit! She refused to acknowledge this break as anything more than a minor speed bump. A brief interruption so she could take some time to get her head together and face a few issues that had popped up, issues that had been lingering just under the surface. It definitely wasn't a signal to the end of her marriage.

She would eventually straighten things out with Harrison. What other choice did she have? Live without him?

No. Impossible.

The ache of living without him had been constant these past three weeks. She could not—*would not*—live the rest of her life like this.

Just as she lifted her hand to reach for his, the door opened and Athens walked in, followed by his doctor. Willow hopped up from her chair and went to him. He wore a brave face, but she knew he'd cried when they'd taken blood. He always did. Her heart ached just thinking about him facing that alone. Why had she listened when he said he didn't want her in there with him?

"How'd it go, honey?" Willow asked, wrapping him up in a hug.

"He's a champ," Dr. Leroy Fudge said with a playful tap on the top of Athens's head. The pediatric endocrinologist had been recommended by the kids' longtime pediatrician, and despite the chuckle she always had to suppress at the thought of him encouraging his patients to give up sweets with a name like Fudge, Willow could not be happier with the care Athens had received thus far. With Dr. Fudge's help, they would nip this thing in the bud before full-fledged juvenile Type 2 diabetes was ever able to take hold.

"It'll be a few minutes before we get the results of the blood tests back," the doctor continued. "But in the meantime, let me say how pleased I am with this young man's progress since his last visit. He's down six pounds and his BMI is inching closer to what it should be for a child his age." Dr. Fudge looked to Athens. "Playing basketball outside is better than playing it on an Atari isn't it?"

Athens's mouth scrounged up in confusion. "What's an Atari?"

"It's the Xbox back when your old man was young," Harrison piped in.

"Oh. Well, no," Athens said. "I'd still rather play against Steph Curry on the Xbox."

"But he *does* play outside and he will *continue* to do so," Willow said. "We've also been taking walks around the neighborhood. You've enjoyed those, right?"

"No. It's kinda boring."

Apparently, her son had zero concern for her feelings.

"Boring or not, it's been good for you, so keep it up," Dr. Fudge said. He turned to Willow and Harrison. "I can't stress enough how beneficial it is for Athens to have such a strong support system behind him. The two of you should pat yourselves on the back. He still has some work to do, but with the family working together as a unit, I have no doubt we'll see the results we've been looking for in just a few months' time."

"Thank you," Willow said. She deserved an award for the way she successfully managed to smile past the guilt she was suddenly drowning in. She'd never felt more like a fraud than she did at this very moment, accepting the doctor's praise for being a healthy family unit when they were anything but. She looked over at Harrison and caught the edginess in his tense smile.

They were both frauds.

It left her with a bittersweet ache. It didn't have to be this way.

Because the doctor was right, she and Harrison *did* work well together. They always had. The fact that they were apart now, when their son needed them the most, was beyond shameful.

If only she could find the courage to talk to her husband. If only she didn't fear what his reaction would be if she told him about that damn dinner date—a date she regretted with every fiber in her being.

But why should she regret it? Because it opened her eyes to what had slowly been eating away at her for years? Because she'd finally realized that her perfect little life wasn't the idyllic existence she'd convinced herself it was?

Willow gave her head a mental shake.

She couldn't think about this right now. Her focus needed to be on Athens.

"Why don't we head out to the family area," Dr. Fudge said, slipping his electronic tablet into the wide front pocket of his lab coat. "Nurse Bautista will meet you all there with the results of Athens's blood tests soon."

They exited Dr. Fudge's office, and Willow went straight to the restroom across the hall. She needed a moment to herself. Despite the doctor's encouraging outlook, an unsettled feeling remained in her gut. The weight of the past forty-five minutes bore down on her, crowding her brain with the multitude of matters that were currently amiss in her world. If only she could blink and have her life return to the way it was a year ago, before everything began to collapse.

When she finally made her way to the family waiting area, she found Athens and Harrison sitting next to each other on one of the low, cyan-colored couches. Harrison had taken his suit jacket off and laid it next to him on the armless couch. Willow steeled herself against the torrent of thoughts the sight of his muscled shoulders triggered. That's something she didn't need to concentrate on right now either.

One of Athens's favorite programs played on the flatscreen television mounted on the wall, but her son paid it no mind. He was entirely focused on whatever game he and his father were playing. It was probably the car chase game. They both held phones out in front of them, motioning the devices from side to side, as if turning a steering wheel. Athens made a crashing sound, and then doubled over with laughter.

Willow swore her heart swelled to twice its normal size. It had been weeks—three weeks, to be precise—since she'd seen such a carefree smile on her son's face. Athens was a mama's boy to his core, but he loved his daddy just as hard. She'd tried not to think too much about the toll this separation was taking on her kids, but it was impossible to ignore when the evidence was staring her right in the face.

Athens missed his father. Harrison missed his son. They shouldn't be apart.

She pressed her quivering lips tightly together, willing her emotions to remain in check. Goodness, but she was a mess today.

Who was she kidding? She'd been a mess for weeks. *Months.*

Willow cleared the emotion from her throat as she continued on toward them.

"Who's winning?" she asked. She stood just over Athens's shoulder.

"I always win," her son said, cocky as all get out.

"Only because I let him." Harrison playfully elbowed him on the arm. He looked over at her and their eyes locked. The enthusiastic grin he'd shared with Athens softened into something more subtle. Tender.

Willow's chest tightened with awareness as warmth flooded her insides. Her heartbeat hammered in her ears. Excitement fluttered in her stomach as her husband's sweet, soft gaze traveled over her like a gentle caress.

The moment was broken by Nurse Bautista's jovial greeting. "The Holmeses are here! How is my favorite family?"

Athens hastily set his phone aside and perked up. He had the most adorable crush on the pretty, petite nurse.

"I have good news," the nurse teased, wiggling Athens's patient folder in her hand. "Why don't we go into the consultation room so I can make your day?"

And make their day she did. Relief cascaded through Willow's bloodstream as the nurse ran through the panel of test results.

"His blood sugar levels were down by twelve points. Even better, his A1C level is at 5.9 percent. That's as close to normal as he's been since he started seeing Dr. Fudge."

"That's awesome, dude," Harrison said, holding his hand up for a high five.

"Where's mine?" Nurse Bautista asked. Athens hopped out of his chair and slapped his palm with hers. "Whatever you're doing, keep it up. Pretty soon you won't have to come in and see me at all."

Willow had to hold in her laugh at the way Athens's

smile immediately faltered. She'd have to watch him. Her son might sneak some chocolate just so he could see the pretty nurse again.

"Or, maybe we can *still* drop in occasionally, but you wouldn't have to get stuck with the needle anymore," Willow suggested.

"Oh, yes," the nurse said. "I like that even better. I would be crushed if I didn't get to see you once in a while."

Athens's light brown skin turned as red as a ripe strawberry.

"Keep up the good work," she said, holding her hand up for another high five. "You too, Mom and Dad," she said, giving both Willow and Harrison high fives as well. "You both should be proud of what you all have been able to accomplish. It's not easy to reverse the tide on a pre-diabetic diagnoses, but if you all keep up what you're doing, I have no doubt Athens will be just fine."

The nurse provided her with a new list of foods they could now incorporate into Athens's diet before seeing them out of the consultation room.

As they made their way to the parking lot, Harrison said, "Well, it sounds as if we're at least doing one thing right." He rubbed Athens's head. "I'm proud of you, Little Man. Good job."

He opened the SUV's driver's side door and held it while Willow climbed in. Instead of closing it, he leaned one hand against the rim and said, "That goes for you too, Mom. I know it hasn't been easy. His progress shows just how badass you are."

"No cursing," Athens called from his side of the car.

"Sorry," Harrison replied.

He smiled. So did she. It felt...nice. Comforting.

If someone had told her just a year ago that receiving a

simple smile from her husband would have this kind of effect on her, Willow would have laughed herself into a choking fit. She'd spent nearly half her life on the receiving end of those smiles. For the past seventeen years, Harrison's subtly sweet and sexy grin had been the first thing she saw when she woke up in the morning and the last image she saw before she closed her eyes at night. She'd taken for granted just how lucky she'd been to have that charming smile in her life. She'd taken *so many* things for granted once she'd found Harrison, like how well they worked together as husband and wife, as the parents to their children. As a family.

Without giving much forethought to her words, Willow said, "Why don't you come to the house for dinner tonight?"

She understood the surprise widening Harrison's eyes on an elemental level. It's exactly what she was feeling on the inside. Where had that even come from?

"Yes, yes, yes," Athens yelled. Thank goodness the seatbelt was there to restrain him. He would have hit the car's ceiling with all that jumping around. "We can play basketball before dinner. We can, right, Mama?"

Well, there was no taking the invitation back now. Not that she wanted to. They needed this.

"Sure can," Willow said. She turned to Harrison. "So?"

"Yes. Of course," Harrison said. "Of course I'll come to dinner." He peered down at his phone. "I need to get back to the office, but only for a little bit. I'll come over to the house as soon as I wrap up my notes from this morning."

Willow nodded. "Good. We'll see you then."

"Thank you, Wills." The gratitude shimmering in his light brown eyes nearly caused her own to well with tears.

She nodded. The fullness in her throat wouldn't allow her to speak.

Harrison closed her car door, then walked over to his own. He waved as he drove past them.

As she watched the black Mercedes turn onto St. Charles Avenue, back toward downtown, Willow had one goal in mind. To make a meal her entire family would enjoy so that they could feel whole again, even if only for a short while.

Chapter Three

As she unwrapped the fresh salmon steaks from their butcher paper packaging, Willow couldn't stem the nervous excitement buzzing inside her head. She was cooking dinner for her family, something she'd done thousands of times for nearly two decades. It shouldn't have been a big deal. But it was. It was the most important meal she'd cooked all year.

After leaving Dr. Fudge's office, she and Athens drove straight to Whole Foods. Willow tossed aside her original dinner plans. There would be no spaghetti and meat sauce tonight. Instead, she'd decided to prepare one of her family's favorite meals, grilled salmon with garlic and herb butter sauce, sautéed asparagus, and roasted sweet potatoes. And for dessert, a diabetic-friendly cherry-apple crisp.

Not her typical Monday night meal, but this wasn't a typical Monday in the Holmes household. There was something markedly different in the air. Tonight felt special, more meaningful.

Tonight, they would be a family again.

Willow caught movement out of the corner of her eye

and turned to find Lily standing before the open pantry door, a backpack slung over one shoulder.

"Why are you wearing your backpack?"

"I'm going over to Amina's," her daughter said from inside the pantry.

"No. Not tonight." Willow shook her head. "Your dad is joining us for dinner."

Lily came out of the pantry holding a bag of kettle corn. There was a spark of surprise in her eyes before she changed her expression back to the dull, disinterested facade she'd been wearing so well for the past few weeks. Willow was *sooo* over that look. She wouldn't be the least bit sorry if she never saw it again.

"What's so special about that?" Lily asked with a shrug.

"Liliana."

"What? Just because the two of you decided to separate, now it's a big deal that he's coming to dinner?"

Willow pulled in a breath and counted to five, reminding herself that teenagers were not demons and that her daughter had a right to be upset.

"First of all, it isn't an official separation," Willow pointed out. "We're just—"

"Taking a break," Lily said with her signature eye-roll. "Yeah, I know."

"Okay, so here's what we're not gonna do." Willow dropped the bundle of asparagus onto the counter and turned fully so that she was facing her daughter. She wagged her finger. "You and that tone? It's not happening."

Lily's expression brought Surly Teenage Girl to an entirely new level. Willow wiped her hands on a dishtowel then walked over to her.

"We've talked about this," she said, rubbing the shoulder that didn't have a backpack slung over it. "Your dad and I just need to figure some things out. You're older, I expected you to have a better understanding of all this."

The sheen of contriteness and shame glimmering in Lily's eyes triggered yet another wave of guilt. It was unfair to expect a teenager to handle something that she, at forty two, had struggled with for the past three weeks. This had all come out of left field for both Lily and Athens.

Well, maybe not *totally* out of left field. She and Harrison had tried their hardest to shield their kids from the issues they'd been having in their marriage, but Willow wasn't foolish enough to think they'd hidden everything. Lily had sensed something was going on between them for several months now, but she doubted her daughter had anticipated seeing the day when her dad would pack a bag and leave. Even *she* hadn't seen that one coming.

When she looked back on it, Willow realized they'd probably done their children a disservice by keeping them in the dark. It had to have been a shock to go from seeing the loving couple they'd always known their parents to be, to two people now living apart. Was there any wonder her sweet, loving daughter had turned into a salty little shit over the past few months?

Willow ran a hand down Lily's hair and cupped her cheek.

"I know this is difficult. It's difficult for all of us."

"So why...why are you doing it?" Lily asked. The hiccup in her voice rent Willow's heart in two. "Why did Daddy have to move out in the first place?"

She didn't know how to answer her daughter's extremely legitimate question. At least not without revealing more than she wanted to reveal, more than she even wanted to acknowledge.

There were so many factors that had led her to the place

Willow now found herself in. Little things that had been building, piling one on top of the other, until it had all come crashing down. In the weeks since she and Harrison decided to give themselves some space, she'd chosen the utterly ridiculous tactic of not thinking about why they were apart, as if ignoring the issue could miraculously cure all that ailed them.

She wasn't a stupid person. She knew nothing would change until she and Harrison sat down and talked. A lack of communication was one of the reasons their marriage was in the state it was now in. But Willow wasn't sure she was ready for that conversation. Just the thought of opening up to Harrison, of revealing the truth about how sitting across the table from another man had opened her mind to all that she'd been missing; it made her heart rate escalate.

She ran her hand along Lily's braided hair. "It's like we said when we sat you and Athens down a few weeks ago, your Dad and I want to see if a little time apart will help us clear our heads. That's all. It's not uncommon when people have been married for as long as we have to take a little break and assess their relationship. As a matter of fact, it can be a good thing. It gives us both a chance to reflect on how important we are to each other, and to our family as a whole."

Willow struggled to believe a single word of the bullshit coming out of her mouth right now, but her words seemed to put Lily at ease. Her daughter nodded.

"Well, since I'm part of this family I guess I need to be here tonight, huh?" Lily asked.

"Yes, you do. This is a chance for us all to be together. Your dad would be crushed if you were not here. I know he misses you."

A small, reluctant smile lifted up one corner of Lily's mouth. "I miss him too."

There was that guilt again, pressing against her throat like two giant thumbs, choking the life right out of her. She swallowed past it and patted Lily's cheek. "If it isn't too late you can go to Amina's after dinner, but only for a little while."

"I'll just text her later," she said. "What time will Daddy be here?"

"He had to run to the office for a little while after Athens's doctor appointment, but he'll be here soon," Willow said, returning to her dinner preparations. "By the way, your brother lost six pounds. The doctor is very encouraged by his progress."

"You know that little booger came bragging to me about it," Lily said with a smile. She leaned an elbow against the kitchen counter, the bag of kettle corn seemingly forgotten. "I was thinking that I may buy him some skates with my first paycheck."

Willow whipped around, staring in astonishment.

"What?" Lily asked.

"*That's* what you want to do with your first paycheck?" Willow asked.

Lily had just started working her first part-time job, tidying up the new offices at Holmes Construction, the company owned by Harrison's cousin, Alex. It was only two days a week, and basically a favor from Alex, but it was a great way for Lily to start learning about what it felt like to earn an honest day's wage.

"Yeah. So?" she said with a shrug. "Athens likes to watch rollerblading on YouTube. And it looks like good exercise. Maybe we can all get some skates and go out rollerblading together."

"I like the sound of that," Willow said, trying her hardest not to burst at the seams with excitement. Her daughter actually wanted them to do something as a family.

Lily smiled before taking off for her room, and for the first time in longer than she could remember, Willow felt a small glimmer of hope begin to coax its way around her chest. It had been so long since she'd felt anything like this, she wanted to bottle it up to preserve it for when she needed a little pick-me-up.

She heard the front door open just moments before Athens's rapidly growing feet bounded down the stairs.

"Daddy's here!" her son called out.

That fissure of excitement cascaded down her spine again. It was such a weird feeling, but Willow welcomed it. When she and Harrison were first married, her heart used to skip a beat whenever he came home from work. She'd lost that. She missed feeling this way about her husband. She didn't realize the feeling of anticipation hadn't been there until it...wasn't.

Harrison came into the kitchen, still wearing the gray suit and blue tie he'd been wearing all day. She'd thought he would have changed into something more casual while still at his office.

"Hey," he greeted.

"Hey," Willow returned.

Good Lord, but he was handsome. That smooth brown skin and those stunning dimples had taken her breath away from the moment she met him. He'd only grown more handsome with age, maturing into the quintessential family man slash professional slash all-around perfect catch.

Yes, she'd caught the *perfect* catch.

So why in the hell did she feel so unfulfilled? How

could she possibly justify the discontent that had over-whelmed her this past year?

There were scores of women who would give anything to be in her shoes. She'd noticed the way some of her fellow PTA members—both single and married—looked at Harrison when they attended meetings. She'd gotten together a few times with the mothers of Athens's fellow scouts, and heard the stories of husbands who virtually ignored their wives, or openly carried on affairs with coworkers, and even one with their longtime nanny. It was a reminder of just how lucky she was to have a husband who respected her *and* their marriage.

Yet, Willow couldn't deny that she'd become disillusioned.

Something was missing. Not necessarily in her marriage, but inside *her*. Somewhere along the way, her ambitions had fallen by the wayside.

No, that wasn't true. They hadn't just fallen by the wayside, she'd made that choice all on her own. She'd willfully compromised her dreams for the sake of marriage and family. It wasn't until earlier this year, when faced with a glaring example of what could have been, that Willow started to question some of the roads she'd chosen to travel, and those she'd allowed to remain untrodden.

"It smells good in here," Harrison said as he came around the kitchen island. He picked up the extra virgin olive oil and poured several ounces into the glass bottle on the shelf. He added red wine vinegar and French vinaigrette spice blend, and then shook the bottle.

It was just as it had always been. She never had to ask him to help her in the kitchen. Even on those evenings when he wouldn't get in until it was almost time for them to eat, he'd set down his briefcase, roll up his sleeves, and do whatever he figured was needed, without her having to ask.

He was perfect.

She had the perfect freaking husband! Why in the hell wasn't that enough for her?

Willow put the brakes on that thinking. Harrison was wonderful, but he was *not* perfect. Neither of them were.

But perfection had never been a requirement for a fulfilling, healthy and happy marriage. What she had should have been enough for her. Getting to the heart of why she'd started to feel so dissatisfied with her life was something she owed her entire family, but most of all she owed it to the man standing next to her, a man who'd done everything he could to provide a happy life for his wife and children.

At least this dinner was a step in the right direction.

Or, maybe not.

When they all sat at the table twenty minutes later, the awkwardness was palpable. It was as if they'd never sat down together for a meal. Before the kids got involved in every after-school activity under the sun, and Harrison joined Jonathan's law practice and became busier than he'd ever been, Willow had made it a point to gather the family together every night for dinner. It's something she'd learned from her mother-in-law, Diane Holmes, a woman she'd loved as much as she loved her own mother. In Diane's words, a group of people became a family while at the dinner table.

But this tension-filled air didn't feel like her family at all. She felt a physical ache when she thought about how much of that was her fault.

Lily had reverted back into sullen teenager mode, a sour frown on her face while she looked longingly at the phone she wasn't allowed to use while at the table. Athens, on the other hand, had turned into a chatterbox, trying to fill the uncomfortable stretches of silence by gleefully filling Harrison in on every single second he'd missed, with Willow occasionally chiming in when her son's recollection was a bit off the mark.

Harrison tried to draw Lily into the conversation, asking her about school, the drill squad and the upkeep on the used car she'd gotten a few weeks ago. Her daughter's monotone, single-word replies grated along Willow's nerves. What happened to the sweet girl who'd just suggested they buy skates and all go skating together? Was she locked in a closet upstairs or something?

After several painful exchanges, Harrison finally gave up and they finished out the meal in silence.

"Okay," Willow said, a few minutes later. "Let's clear these dishes. It's time for the two of you to get your things together for school tomorrow. We will not have a repeat of this morning," she warned, looking pointedly at Athens.

He had the decency to look ashamed.

Both kids brought their plates into the kitchen, with Willow following them. Harrison came in behind her, balancing the platter that held the salmon on top of the salad bowl.

"Well, that was painful," he said once Lily and Athens left the kitchen.

"I'm sorry," Willow said.

"What are you apologizing for? You didn't tell Lily to treat me like I'm some kind of disease, did you?"

"Of course not," she said. "I just... I don't know what to do about her. I keep reminding myself that she's a teenager. Being a pain in the ass is a part of the job description. But does she have to be this damn good at the job?"

A hint of a smile lifted one corner of his mouth. "At least we know she has a good work ethic."

Willow laughed. She couldn't help herself. If there was one thing Harrison excelled at, it was making her laugh even when she didn't want to.

Their laughter faded as they stared at each other; a sense of foreboding sucked all the oxygen out of the room. Harrison closed the few feet that separated them. He dipped his head and looked her in the eyes.

"Wills," he said, his voice low. "We need to talk."

Dread tightened her throat. They'd needed to talk for some time now. It was time she stopped running away from it.

Willow swallowed and nodded. "I know," she said. She glanced up at the ceiling. "Why don't you give me some time to make sure the kids are both squared away for the night."

He looked at the Baume & Mercier watch she'd bought him when he left his old firm and joined Jonathan's. "Why don't I come back in an hour. I'll meet you out back?"

She nodded. "That sounds good. I'll see you in an hour."

He took a step forward and leaned in slightly, but stopped himself before he could give her the peck on the lips her body automatically readied itself for. It had come naturally to her—to both of them, apparently. Having them both pull back cast a glaring spotlight on how odd this all was. How could a simple kiss between husband and wife elicit this much anxiety and awkwardness?

"I'll...uh...I'll see you in an hour," Harrison said. He took a couple of steps before he pivoted. He walked back to where she stood, reached down and captured her hand in one of his. With a gentle squeeze, he said, "Thank you, Willow."

"For what?"

"For this. For inviting me over for dinner. For taking this first step. We needed this tonight. I needed to be here with you and my kids."

Once again, she had difficulty swallowing. Finally, she answered, "Yes. We needed you here too."

A tormented spark of hope flashed across his handsome face. "I want to be here permanently. Maybe when I come back in an hour we can finally talk about what we need to do to make that happen."

She didn't want to make any promises. She couldn't. She sensed Harrison's hurt when she failed to respond.

But she still had too much to work through before she could make any promises. If they tried to just go back to the way things were, they would find themselves right back in the morass of pain and longing and confusion they'd been bogged down in for all these months. Instead of answering, Willow simply nodded as she followed him to the door.

"One hour," she said.

His smile was sad, but sweet. "I'll see you then."

As he walked up the driveway, Harrison allowed his eyes to roam over the front of his house. The soft glow from the solar lights illuminated the foliage growing along the cypress fence. Those damn weeds were back again, entwining with his wisteria. Maybe he could come over on Saturday to pull them. Could he do that? Or would that infringe on the still undiscussed terms of his and

Willow's so-called break? Maybe he should just hire someone to start taking care of the yard.

Harrison immediately rejected that thought. He'd be damned if some random landscaper put his filthy hands on his begonias.

He entered the front door and walked through the living room to the kitchen, and then out the French doors that led to the backyard. He stood at the edge of the brick patio and looked out over his pride and joy.

He loved this yard. It had taken two years of working every available weekend he had off, along with dozens of trips to The Plant Gallery and Home Depot, to get it exactly the way he wanted. But he'd eventually achieved the quintessential backyard paradise. He looked over at his newest toy, the four burner natural gas grill with an attached rotisserie that he'd had installed just a few months ago in the outdoor kitchen. Stainless steel. Corrosion resistant. All around badass.

The ache that had become a regular part of his existence settled even more deeply within Harrison's chest. He'd envisioned grilling out here every weekend while Willow lounged in the hammock and Athens and Lily enjoyed the swimming pool. Instead, it all sat here untouched, like an abandoned amusement park longing for someone to put it to use.

He heard movement behind him and turned to find Willow coming through the French doors.

"I didn't know you were back," she said in a lowered voice, as if she was afraid she'd wake the kids, who definitely weren't sleeping this early in the evening.

"I only got here a few minutes ago," he answered.

They stood there for several awkward moments before Harrison gestured toward the pergola he'd built with his dad's help. A wooden swing hung from the teak crossbeam overhead.

Willow sat on one side, a few inches farther to the right than she would have this time last year. She wrapped her arms around her chest and rubbed up and down her forearms.

"You cold?" Harrison asked as he sat closer to the center. He didn't want to add to her discomfort, but he refused to be out here like a couple of teenagers afraid to get caught sitting too close.

"Not really." She looked over at him. "I'm nervous. How weird is that?"

"Pretty weird, but understandable. I'm nervous too," he admitted. He rubbed his hands back and forth over his thighs, wrinkling the crease in the khakis he'd changed into. "It feels as if we're about the have one of the most important conversations of our lives."

She shook her head. "No. Don't put that kind of pressure on me, Harrison."

"But it *is* important, Willow. We have to talk this out. We need to figure out why in the hell we're not working."

"But we're not going to figure it out in one conversation, so don't think of this as a make or break thing." She turned toward him, pulling one leg up on the swing and resting her chin against her knee. "Just talk to me right now. It doesn't have to be about us. Just talk about life. How'd it go in front of Judge Rubin today?"

"You don't want to hear about Judge Rubin."

"I do." Her nod was more enthusiastic than the situation warranted.

Harrison knew exactly what she was doing. It was the same thing she'd done whenever he so much as hinted at them talking about the issues plaguing their marriage.

The main one being that there *were* no concrete issues, and least none that he could point to. They'd just gradually found themselves in this place where they hardly spoke to each other about anything outside of their kids. And then, after his conference in Philadelphia earlier this year, that chasm suddenly grew into a canyon he hadn't been able to bridge.

No, he didn't want to talk about work right now. But if that was what Willow needed in order to ease into the heavier conversation he was determined to have tonight, he would oblige.

"I know you've been putting in a lot of hours on this case," she continued. "Do you think the merger will happen anytime soon?"

"Based on where we stand right now, I doubt it," he answered, not correcting her on calling it a merger instead of an acquisition. After all these years of them discussing his work, she still got the two confused. Harrison gave her a brief summary of what happened today in Judge Rubin's chambers. "We're in the more advantageous position. My client has more than one company interested in their machinery designs, which gives them the upper hand."

"How does it feel going up against Phillip?" she asked. "Does it seem weird?"

"Not a bit." Harrison shook his head. He looked over at her. "But seeing him makes me even happier that I left the firm when I did. I'd be miserable if I'd stayed there."

She'd encouraged him to make the move to Jonathan's firm long before Harrison had finally gotten the nerve to do it. He'd been too afraid to lose the seniority he'd assumed he'd built at Bossier, Guidry & Associates. It had taken him too long to recognize that his old bosses didn't appreciate what he brought to the table. He doubted they would have ever made him a partner.

"It was the right move," Harrison continued. "I work my ass off, but it'll be worth it in the end."

"Of course it was the right move. The hours you put in actually *mean* something at Campbell & Holmes. Your name is on the door."

He deliberated for the barest moment before he reached over and took her hand in his, brought it to his lips and pressed a gentle kiss to the backs of her fingers.

"Thank you," Harrison said. "You still know the right thing to say, exactly when I need to hear it."

"You're welcome," she said. Her warm, affectionate smile caused his heart to swell.

He loved this woman so much it hurt.

"What happened to us, Wills?" His whisper came out harsher than he'd intended, but Harrison couldn't keep the emotion from his voice. It was the question that had plagued him more than any these last few months. "How did we get here? Why am I not living with you and the kids? Why am I not in that bed with you every night? That's where I belong, Willow."

She slipped her hand from his hold and wrapped it around her updrawn leg. Several quiet moments passed with only the occasional chirp of a stray cricket interrupting the stillness.

Finally, Willow spoke.

"I've been thinking about that a lot over the past few weeks." She tilted her head to the side, looking up at him from her slight crouch. "You know what I came to realize? We don't fight."

Harrison shook his head. "No. We don't."

"Do you know how odd that is for two people who have

been together for as long as we have?" She lowered her leg and sat up straight. "I tried to remember the last fight we had, and it was back when Lily was in the seventh grade and played us against each other to go to that slumber party. Remember?"

"I remember that," Harrison said with a gruff chuckle. "You told her she couldn't go because she'd spilled nail polish in the bathroom and tried to blame it on Athens. I didn't know you'd already told her no, and brought her there without asking."

"She played us like a fiddle," Willow said, shaking her head. "But that was it, Harrison. Four years ago. That was our last big argument." She turned to him. "One of the reasons this has been such a shock to our marriage is because we're not used to there being any tension. We've always gotten along so well."

"Like peanut butter and jelly," he said. "At least that's how the great Diane Holmes thought of us."

It had been his mother's collective nickname for them from the time they'd become engaged.

Willow smiled, but then her expression sobered. "She would be so disappointed in us."

"Not in us. In the situation, yes, but I doubt there's anything we could do that would have disappointed her." Harrison angled his head back and looked up at the sky through the slats of the pergola, studying the wispy clouds that partially obscured the moon. "I think, more than anything, it would have hurt her to see us hurting." He brought his gaze back to his wife's. "Because this hurts, Willow. It hurts so damn much."

"I know." Her voice trembled. "It hurts me too."

"So what are we going to do about it?" Harrison asked, wincing at the raw desperation cloaking his words. But, dammit, he *was* desperate. He wanted to fix this—to fix them. He softened his voice before he asked, "Do you want to go to marriage counseling?"

Her eyes shifted to his before she cast them downward again. "You'd be willing to do that?"

Harrison took hold of her chin and lifted her face up so he could look into her eyes. "I'd be willing to walk through fire if it meant figuring out what's broken between us. I can't go on like this, Willow. It's not fair to either of us."

He caught the single tear that escaped, using his thumb to swipe it from her cheek. Harrison thought about the plane tickets in his back pocket. He'd slipped them in there before he left the office, still unsure whether he should even bring it up. But it was time to pull out all the stops. His marriage was on the line here, he would do whatever he could to ensure its survival.

Lifting up slightly from the swing, he retrieved the envelope and held it out to her.

"What's that?" she asked.

"I'm supposed to give this to you tomorrow, but now's as good a time as any."

Willow looked at the envelope, then back up at him. "What's in it?"

"Your anniversary gift. Take it," Harrison encouraged, nudging her hand with the envelope.

She finally accepted it and gently untucked the flap. Harrison watched as her eyes roamed over the tickets. He recognized the exact moment when she comprehended what she was looking at.

"Are you serious?" she whispered.

He hunched his shoulders. "You've always wanted to go."

"But you don't fly. You won't even take a forty minute

flight to Houston." She paused. "Wait a minute. This is for next week!" She swung her head around to look at him with wide, shocked eyes. "Harrison, did you buy last minute tickets to Italy?"

"I bought these almost a year ago," he said. "Just after the holidays."

A gasp escaped her lips as she flattened her hand over her heart. "You've been planning this for a year?"

"I've been owing you a honeymoon for *seventeen* years. I figured it was finally time we take it."

Her expression softened with gratitude. "You've always been the sweetest man I've ever known," she said, returning her attention to the tickets. But then her shoulders wilted. The corner of her mouth tilted downward. When she looked over at him again, her eyes were filled with reluctance and warning. "Harrison, you know this isn't a magic pill, right? It wasn't that long ago that we tried to just pretend everything was okay, and you saw how that turned out."

"I know," he assured her. "I'm not expecting us to go to Italy and have everything suddenly return to the way it used to be."

No matter how much he wanted that to happen.

Harrison reached over and took her hand in his again. "I just want to spend some time with my wife. With *only* my wife. No kids. No brothers, or sisters, or clients. Just you and me in this place you've always wanted to go. Let me do this for you, Willow."

"Do you really think you can disconnect for"—she glanced down at the tickets—"an entire week? We haven't taken a single family vacation without you having to steal away at least a day for work."

Harrison shook his head. "Not this time. This trip will be about you and me, and no one else."

Anxiety gripped his chest as he waited for her answer. The fear he now felt was one of the main reasons he'd been so reluctant to give her the tickets in the first place. The threat of her turning him down loomed over him like a menacing cloud. If she was able to say no to this trip, especially after the way her eyes had lit up at the first sight of those tickets, it would tell Harrison exactly how far gone things were between them.

"What about the kids?" she finally asked.

He released a breath he hadn't realized he'd been holding. She hadn't responded with an outright no.

"I've already talked to my dad. He's going to come stay over here for the week."

"Wait! The foundation's kickoff party! It's next month. It wouldn't be fair to leave all that work to your sister and brothers."

"Are you kidding me? Indina would love nothing more than to be given carte blanche over the last minute decisions for the kickoff party. There isn't all that much left to plan anyway. Indina can handle it." He was seconds from falling to his knees and begging. "Come on, Willow. Let's do this."

She stared down at the tickets for a moment before asking, "Can I have a day to think about it?"

A twinge of disappointment pinched his chest, but Harrison quickly squashed it. He hadn't expected her to jump into his arms and agree right out of the gate, had he?

Okay, so maybe he had.

He'd give anything for this to be the magic pill she'd referred to, but there were no magical solutions. Figuring out just what had gone wrong in their marriage and finding a way to repair it would take work. This trip was only a start. The fact that she hadn't said no—that she was willing to consider it—was a win.

"When would we leave again?" she asked, looking at the tickets again.

"Saturday. Everything is all planned out. The only thing you have to do is have the time of your life."

She nodded and sent him a brief smile, too brief to decide whether or not it actually reached her eyes. Several quiet moments passed before she clamped her palms over her thighs and pushed up from the swing.

"It's getting late. I should probably go in."

His mind recoiled at her suggestion. He didn't want their night together to end so soon. But Harrison knew better than to push. He stood, took her hand and gave it a squeeze. "Thanks again for inviting me to dinner."

"Thanks for coming, both to dinner and back here to talk. We needed this."

They needed more than just this one talk. So much more. But this was more than they'd managed to do in the three weeks since he'd left. It was a step in the right direction.

Still holding hands, they walked back through the softly lit backyard, along the stone path leading up to the patio. Harrison slowed his steps as they approached the French doors. He didn't want to go inside just yet, because he knew it would gut him when he had to continue out the front door instead of joining his wife in their own bed.

God, why couldn't he go in there with her? Why couldn't they be in a place where it felt natural to go in their master bedroom, step into the shower together, and wash each other's bodies before slipping underneath the covers and making love? When did *that* scenario become something he could only wish for?

Apparently, not sensing his reluctance—or maybe she did sense it and just didn't care—Willow continued into the house, through the kitchen and into the living room. At least she hadn't let go of his hand.

She still held on once they arrived at the front door. She looked up at him, a tender smile gracing her lips. It was a smile that reached her eyes.

"Goodnight," she whispered.

"Goodnight," he returned, his voice just as soft.

Taking a chance, Harrison leaned forward and placed a gentle kiss on her lips. His body flooded with warmth at the delicate contact, a cascade of endorphins surging through his brain as he immersed himself in the familiar feel of her mouth.

The kiss ended much too soon, but Harrison knew he would dream about it for the rest of the night.

He thought he sensed some reluctance when Willow started to let go of his hand. What would she say if he asked her if he could stay? After that sweet, tender kiss they'd shared, he was tempted. But Harrison knew if she turned him down it would devastate him.

Unless she *offered...*

She didn't.

"Be careful driving back to the office," she said.

Disappointment assailed him once again. "I will," he answered. He leaned forward and snatched another kiss. Leaning his forehead against hers, he whispered, "I love you, Willow Elizabeth Holmes."

"I love you, too, Harrison Clark Holmes," she returned.

He thought about how many times they'd ended the night with those exact words. How could they say those same words to each other with the way things currently stood between them? Did the words not mean what they used to mean?

They meant the same thing to him. He loved his wife with every bone, every fiber, every single cell of his being. Whether it was the same for Willow, he could no longer be sure.

But Harrison refused to ask her what she meant when she told him she loved him. Because if he didn't like her answer, he knew the anguish he'd face would be so much worse than anything he'd felt up to this point.

With a final kiss upon her forehead, he unlocked the front door and walked out of the house, hearing the click of the deadbolt as Willow locked up behind him.

Chapter Four

W illow craned her neck as she searched through the sea of students emptying out of the building on the campus of Loyola University in New Orleans's Uptown neighborhood. The prestigious school sat adjacent to Tulane University, another of the city's illustrious institutions. And her baby sister had been invited to speak at both of them. Willow could not have been prouder.

"Hey! You lookin' for me?"

She turned at the awful Robert De Niro impersonation and a smile broke out over her face. She rushed over to her sister and wrapped her arms around her. "Where'd you come from? I thought you said to look for you in the building facing Freret Street?"

Jade, who stood a full foot taller than her, leaned over and returned the hug, holding on longer than usual.

"My lecture ended early, so I went to visit a colleague who used to work with me in the Psych department at Rice. I thought I'd be done before you got here, but, as usual, you're on regular time instead of CP time."

Willow rolled her eyes. "Better than leaving you here

waiting for me," she said. "Oh, by the way, the line from *Taxi Driver* is 'You talkin' to me,' not 'You lookin' for me.'"

"Yes, I know." Her sister laughed. Then, after finally letting go, she rubbed Willow's upper arm and asked, "So, how're you doing, honey?" Jade's apprehension was evident in her concerned eyes as they roamed over Willow's face.

"If I lied and said I was okay you'd see right through it," she said. "Let's just say that I've been better, but I've also been worse."

"I've lived through your worse with you. That's not something any of us ever want to face again." Her sister squeezed her arm, a sad smile tugging at her lips. But then, in typical Jade fashion, her eyes brightened and she clapped her hands together. "Guess what? I'm done with my lectures for the day, so it is officially wine o'clock. Let's get on over to your house and drink every bit you have."

Willow burst out laughing. She could always count on her younger sister to put a smile on her face. Even during some of their roughest times, when the Carter girls had absolutely no reason to smile, Jade's endearing sense of humor would make an appearance and cheer them all up. There were so many nights she'd cried herself to sleep when she was younger, but Willow knew that number would have been much higher if not for her sister.

They made a stop at Martin's Wine Cellar and picked up a couple of bottles of Jade's favorite cabernet sauvignon before heading to her house. The parent of one of Athens's scout mates would pick the boys up from school today, so Willow had hours before either of her kids would be home.

She popped popcorn and broke out the box of Godiva chocolates she kept stashed in the freezer. Plopping on the sofa, she accepted the wineglass Jade handed to her before putting her feet up on the oversized ottoman and leaning her head against the cushioned back of the sofa.

"Are we really about to drink wine and eat popcorn and chocolate at two in the afternoon while we discuss my crumbling marriage?" Willow asked.

"Yep, I think we are." Jade took a sip from her glass. "Ahhh. I do love this wine." She looked over at Willow and asked, "Is it really crumbling?"

Willow took her own healthy sip before answering. "Crumbling may be a bit too harsh. Gradually deteriorating maybe?"

"Do semantics really make a difference here?"

"I guess not," Willow said. She sighed. "It's just... I don't know, Jade. I never thought we'd be here."

"When did this even start? I mean, damn, you and Harrison are like the poster children for the sickeningly in love. I didn't think anything could put a stop to that."

"We're still in love. I love my husband more than anything. That's what's so crazy about this. My love for him hasn't changed at all, but it seems as if everything else has." Willow lifted her shoulders in confusion. "I was just fine with driving the kids to practice, and baking brownies for the church bake sales, and leading the community action team meetings and all the other stuff I'm require to do. But it just isn't enough anymore. I don't feel...fulfilled." Willow groaned. "I can't believe I just said that. Like someone in the middle of a midlife crisis. I'm such a fucking cliché."

Jade gasped. "You said fuck."

Willow winced. "Don't tell Momma."

Her sister laughed so hard she nearly fell off the sofa.

"I'm serious, Jade." She pitched a throw pillow at her head.

"You're forty-two, Willow. Momma can't punish you for saying the word fuck."

"I'm not talking about saying a bad word. I'm talking about my marriage. I don't want her to know about the chaos in my life right now."

Her sister twisted on the sofa so that she could face her, bringing one leg up and settling the bowl of popcorn on the sofa cushion between them.

"I'm still trying to figure out when the chaos started. What is it about your life that has you not feeling fulfilled? What's wrong?"

"That's the thing. There's nothing that's really wrong. My life should be perfect. I have everything a woman is supposed to want." Willow ticked the items off on her fingers. "I have two beautiful children. I have an amazing house to raise them in. And a gorgeous husband who bends over backwards to provide everything I need."

Her sister frowned at her before saying, "Bitch, you *do* have it all. Why are you complaining?" Jade caught her by the wrist before Willow could toss a second pillow at her head. "I'm just messing with you. Look, I get what you're saying, honey, but just because you have what society tells us is the idyllic life, it doesn't mean you have everything. Something's missing in here." Jade tapped Willow in the center of her chest. "What is it? What's missing?"

Willow should have known better than to open up to a trained psychologist. Jade saw past the surface. She always had. And she knew the exact questions to ask to get to the heart of the matter.

But Willow wasn't ready to face those questions. She knew she wouldn't like the answers.

And her sister definitely wouldn't like the answers, because, although it wasn't fair, Jade played a part in the dissatisfaction that had been stuck in Willow's craw for nearly a year. Both her sisters did, along with their mother.

Life had not been easy for Rachel Carter or the three daughters she'd raised on her own. As a child, Willow watched her mother struggle to keep food on the rickety tables of the pay-by-the-week motels they'd lived in during those early years after she escaped their abusive father. Often times, her mother had only been able to scrounge up enough food for her daughters, choosing to go to bed hungry herself.

But despite those hundreds of small bumps in the road, and quite a few rocky mountains along the way, Rachel Carter had prevailed, managing to claw them all out of poverty. She'd done so by going to night school while working at low-paying jobs, earning her bachelor's degree, landing an entry-level job with a Fortune 1000 company, and eventually working her way up to head of Human Resources. Not to mention getting herself two master's degrees on her climb up that corporate ladder.

Willow's sisters had done the same, with Jade going on to earn her Ph.D. in Psychology, and their eldest sister, Rain, opening her third yoga studio in the Houston area just a few months ago.

And here sat Willow, a suburban housewife.

A cliché.

She'd had aspirations of her own, the same as the other women in her family. She'd finished college and filled out applications for graduate school. She'd had all intentions of becoming a biochemical engineer who would one day make a medical discovery that could save millions of lives. Not only that, she'd also planned to teach younger kids about science so they could enter the field and work on making medical discoveries of their own.

But she hadn't done any of that, had she?

Why not? It was a question Willow had asked herself countless times since the dinner she and Harrison had attended with some of their old college friends earlier this year. It wasn't as if she hadn't had the opportunity. Her husband had encouraged her to continue with her education. Even a few years into their marriage, after landing the job at Bossier, Guidry & Associates, he'd looked into the on-site daycare and secured a spot for Lily so that Willow could go back to school if she wanted to.

She was the one who'd said no. *She* was the one who'd decided she could better support her family by taking care of house and home. The truth, when she chose to face it, was an ugly one. The only person Willow had to blame for the regrets she'd felt since that dinner was herself.

But she couldn't share any of this with Jade. Willow knew her sister too well. Jade would feel guilty and apologize for her own success, when she had nothing to apologize for. As far as telling her about the dinner? Well, if Willow told her about the first dinner, then she'd have to tell her about the second one—the one that Harrison hadn't attended. The one none of the others had attended, only herself and Marcus.

It was only dinner.

Yes, it *was* only dinner, but her guilt over keeping it from her husband continued to eat away at her.

"It's a combination of things," Willow finally answered, intentionally keeping her answer vague. Knowing Jade would jump on this next tidbit, Willow added, "Honestly, I think I may be a bit depressed."

"Well, I already suggested that," her sister said. "Not that I would ever try to diagnose you, but the signs are there.

You know depression is nothing to sneeze at, *and* it's nothing to be ashamed of."

Willow had done enough research on Situational Depression to know that she had likely fallen into one. Considering the combination of losing her mother-in-law, anxiety over Harrison's hectic work schedule, Athens's health issues, Liliana's pissy teenage mood swings, and her feelings of inadequacy when she compared her life to other people around her, and there was no doubt she was a walking case for a situationally depressed person. She also knew better than to think it was something she could somehow work her way out of on her own.

"I've been thinking about seeing someone," Willow admitted. "A therapist."

Jade set her wineglass on the side table and picked up her phone. She tapped on the screen a few times, then put the phone back down. "I just sent you the number for one of the best in New Orleans. Dr. Abraham Rosen. He and I went to Stanford together."

"Thanks," Willow said. She blew out a tired breath. "I guess my days will be filled with therapists and doctor visits for the foreseeable future." She looked over at her sister. "Last night Harrison suggested we start seeing a marriage therapist."

"I highly support that," Jade said. "Of course, I'm biased, but it's a smart decision. Again, nothing to be ashamed of. Often times the people in a relationship have too much of an inward focus. It may take someone from the outside to see what you and Harrison *can't* see. "

"Yeah, well, seeing a therapist wasn't the only thing we talked about." Her sister looked over at her, one brow lifted in inquiry. "He gave me my anniversary present," Willow said.

She pushed herself up from the sofa, walked over to the built-in bookshelves, and pulled the printed airline tickets from the Jesmyn Ward novel she'd tucked them in this morning. Then she walked back over to the sofa and handed them to her sister.

Jade unfolded the papers and nearly choked on her wine. "Rome? You're going to freaking Rome?"

Willow hunched her shoulders. "I haven't decided just yet."

"Haven't decided? What's there to decide?"

"I don't know if this is the right move, Jade. I'm afraid Harrison will expect this to be some kind of cure-all for all that ails our marriage. We can't fly off for a week in Italy and then expect everything to be normal once we get back home. That's why I'm not sure if we should even go."

"Do you hear yourself right now?" The incredulousness in her sister's voice was so thick it was practically another occupant in the room.

"What?" Willow asked. "You're the psychologist here. You know it's a possibility that's what he's thinking."

"I'm not speaking as a psychologist right now. I'm coming to you as a sister. If that fine-ass man offers to spend a week with you in one of the most romantic places on God's green earth and you even consider *not* going, you can forget about seeing Abraham. I'm going to have you admitted to the psych ward."

Willow rolled her eyes.

"Wait." Jade held the tickets up closer to her face. "You leave *Saturday*?"

"I told you it's for our anniversary. We make seventeen years next week."

"Why are we just sitting here? You should be packing! Let's go."

"No." Willow shook her head. "You're only here for a night. I'm not going to spend it packing."

Of course, her sister completely ignored her. She set her wineglass on the side table and hopped up from the couch.

"You don't have to pack, but we can at least pick out what you're going to bring."

Willow knew any complaints would continue to be ignored, so she followed Jade to the bedroom. She stood to the side while her sister searched her closet, pulling out dresses and holding them against her front.

"I wish I lived closer. I would totally borrow some of these. Of course they would look like mini dresses on me, but I'd still look cute."

"Is that a short person joke?"

"You'll know when I'm making a short person joke." Jade gestured toward Willow's pocket. "Grab your phone and see what the weather in Rome will be like next week."

As Willow did as directed, her sister continued her closet browsing, picking out several outfits and dresses she deemed suitable for an Italian vacation.

"Okay, now for the important stuff. Where's the lingerie?"

"Really, Jade?" Willow rolled her eyes. "Lingerie isn't going to help my marriage."

"It can't hurt." Jade headed for the other side of the walk-in closet.

"Uh, hello!" Willow raced over to where her sister was rummaging through the built-in drawers.

"A bunch of granny panties and ratty T-shirts?" Her sister asked, that incredulous tone making a reappearance. "I know you don't want any more kids, but there are more effective forms of birth control, you know?"

"Shut up." Willow jerked her favorite, threadbare T-shirt from Prince's 2004 Musicology Tour from her sister's hand. "After nearly twenty years together, sexy underwear isn't that important."

"Says who? And I'll repeat: it can't hurt." Jade stuffed the T-shirts back in the drawer and took Willow by the arm again. "Come on. We have some work to do."

"What are you up to?"

"Just follow me."

Jade marched them both out of the house. Twenty minutes later, Willow found herself walking into the Victoria's Secret Boutique in Lakeside Shopping Center.

She was a grown woman with two children, yet could still feel her face heating as her baby sister methodically moved from one rack to another, debating everything from aesthetics to ease of removal. When they left the store an hour later, Willow was armed with five new pieces of clothing. All things she never would have considered buying on her own.

She climbed behind the wheel of her SUV and turned over the engine, but then left it idling as she peered over at her sister.

"Look, Jade, this was fun and all, but you know a few pieces of sexy lingerie won't repair my marriage, right?"

"I never claimed they would. However..."

"It can't hurt," Willow droned, rolling her eyes yet again.

"Don't go out there expecting drastic changes. You're not going to fix your relationship in a single week. The important thing here is spending time together. Go and enjoy your husband. Leave the expectations at home."

"But there *are* expectations," Willow argued. She thumped a fist against the steering wheel. "I know my husband. Harrison will—"

"Forget what you *think* you know. I repeat: Go and enjoy your husband, Willow. Enjoy the hell out of him. Fuck each other's brains out, then eat some gelato."

Willow burst out laughing despite her misgivings.

"I mean it, honey," Jade said. She reached over and covered the hand that now clenched the steering wheel. "You and Harrison mean too much to each other not to give yourselves the best possible chance. But if you try to force something to happen, it may backfire. Just enjoy it. And whatever happens, happens."

Willow sucked in a slow, cleansing breath. "Okay." She nodded. "No expectations. I will go to this place I've wanted to visit my entire life and have the best time ever with my husband."

"There you go. And don't forget that whole fucking his brains out thing," Jade said. "That's important. Do it for all of us who don't have fine ass husbands with thighs that look as if they're made of steel."

Willow slid her a look. "You've been checking out my husband's thighs?"

"Hell yes," her sister said. "His and those fine ass brothers'."

Willow chuckled, shaking her head. Maybe Jade was right. Maybe the key to enjoying this time away with Harrison was to let whatever was going to happen just... well...happen. It wasn't as if she was going with a stranger. She was going with the man she considered her one true soul mate.

She and Harrison deserved this chance. They deserved *every* chance when it came to salvaging their marriage.

It was time she allow them to have it.

"Are you sure we shouldn't just take what they're offering and move on?"

As he sat across the conference table from Michael Delmonico, Harrison resisted the urge to bat the twenty-something away from him like a pesky gnat. It wasn't the way one conducted oneself when dealing with a client, no matter how much the client deserved it.

Of course, Michael wasn't their official client. It was his father who sat at the helm of Delmonico Machinery. If Harrison had any say in the matter, he would deal directly with Luca Delmonico every single time. Luca was a shark, not afraid of a good bluff. Michael was afraid of his own shadow. The younger man didn't realize how weak it would make them look if they caved to Phillip MacMahon's latest demands.

"No, we should not," Harrison answered him. "Trust me on this."

It was a good thing the company was being sold. If Luca had decided to pass the company he'd built on to his son, Michael would run it into the ground within a couple of years.

Thankfully, he would never have that chance, because Harrison was going to get the Delmonicos more money than they could have possibly dreamed of for their small, family-run machinery business. This deal was, by far, the most important he'd taken on since being made partner. Possibly the most important of his life. Luca had come to him back when he was still with Bossier, et al. If one wanted to be a dick about it, they could argue that Harrison had stolen the client from his old firm. And if ever there was one who prided himself on being a dick, it was Phillip MacMahon. It was just one of the reasons his former coworker was out for blood.

Harrison didn't give a shit.

Campbell & Holmes's fee for negotiating this acquisition was small potatoes to the guys at his old firm, but for a two-man outfit like the one he and Jonathan shared, that was life-changing money.

And young Michael here wanted to just take what was being offered and move on? Get the fuck outta here!

As enticing as thirty-five percent of an eight-figure payout was, for Harrison, this was about more than just the money. This was about pride. And doing what he thought was best for his client, of course. The Delmonicos would benefit from these hardcore tactics just as much as he would.

Harrison had started at Bossier, Guidry & Associates not long after finishing law school and had reached legend status his second year at the firm by stepping in when a senior associate came down with food poisoning in the middle of a heated contract negotiation. He was the young, hotshot lawyer all the others in the firm talked about around the water cooler. He was the one his fellow junior associates envied. Harrison had figured it was just a matter of time before the powers that be took notice. If he worked hard enough they would eventually give him his due.

But that was never going to happen. He knew that now. He had the evidence thrust in his face whenever he sat across the table from Phillip MacMahon. Phillip, who had been brought into the firm three years after Harrison joined. Who didn't have nearly the track record Harrison did. But who'd made partner, when Harrison had been told "maybe next year" for five years in a row.

He didn't need anyone at Bossier, Guidry & Associates

to validate him. But he could still relish the look on Phillip's face when he was forced to tell his client that he would have to pay eighteen million dollars if he wanted to acquire Delmonico Machinery.

Was it too much to ask to see a few tears? That would be sweet.

A knock on the door jerked Harrison out of his vengeful daydreams. Their office manager, LaKeisha, poked her head in. "Sorry to disturb you, Mr. Holmes, but your wife just called. There's an emergency with one of your kids."

Harrison's heart immediately jumped into his throat. In the span of two seconds his overactive brain had conjured a scenario of Athens falling into a diabetic coma, despite the positive feedback they'd received from Dr. Fudge yesterday. Or what if he was hit in the chest with a baseball during Phys. Ed? Hadn't he just read about a kid dying during a Little League game from that very thing?

"I can come back later," Michael said.

Harrison had forgotten the other man was in the office. "Yes. I'll be in touch." He called Willow before Michael Delmonico even left the room. She picked up on the first ring.

"I'm getting my stuff. I should be at St. Aug in another ten minutes."

"No, come to St. Katherine's."

Harrison stopped short. "St. Katherine's? This is about Liliana?"

"Yes," Willow said, weariness saturating her voice. He heard another voice in the background. "One minute, Harrison." Muffled voices continued on for a few moments before Willow returned to the line. "How quickly can you get here?"

"I'm leaving now. I can be there in ten minutes tops," he said. "What happened? Is she okay?"

"She's okay. Just get here."

Harrison made it to the all-girls private school that cost more per semester than what he'd paid for his undergraduate degree twenty years ago in eight minutes flat. Moments later, he walked into the main office.

"Hello Mr. Holmes," the school secretary greeted before he had a chance to speak. "They're in Dr. Saul's office. You can go right in."

"What's this about?" Harrison asked, but the secretary simply motioned toward the frosted glass door with Dr. Evelyn Saul, Ed.D. etched in block letters. He entered the office and could have sworn there was a difference in the air's molecular makeup. A weightiness existed within these walls that he hadn't felt on the other side of the door.

Willow sat across from the principal's sleek, steel and glass desk. Liliana sat in one of three chairs against the wall.

"Sorry I couldn't get here sooner," Harrison said as he took the seat next to Willow's. He looked over at her. "What's going on?"

Willow turned to Lily. "I'll let your daughter tell you."

All eyes turned to Lily, who slunk lower in her seat. "I got in a fight," she mumbled.

Harrison's eyes bucked. "A fight?"

Dr. Saul cleared her throat. "Do you want to correct that misstatement, or should I?"

"I *provoked* a fight," Lily said.

"Wait. You *started* a fight? *You?* About what?"

"Does the reason really matter?" Willow asked. "The school has a zero-tolerance policy. Liliana knows this."

Dread oozed down Harrison's spine. Zero tolerance?

Did that mean they were throwing her out? After all the money they'd spent sending her to this school? Couldn't be. There had to be a couple of steps between a fight and getting tossed out of school.

"Our policy calls for expulsion," Dr. Saul said, as if she'd read his mind and wanted to confirm his fears before any inkling of hope could set in. "We will still have the disciplinary hearing, of course, but in the ten years I've been principal of this school there has only been one exception to that rule. And because Liliana has already admitted to being the instigator, and because the drama teacher, Mrs. Calder, witnessed it..."

The principal hunched her shoulders in a *what else is there to say?* gesture.

Harrison ran a hand down his face. Talk about a damn nightmare.

"So, is that it?" he asked. "She's out? Just like that?"

"That's the way zero tolerance works, Mr. Holmes. The rules are clearly stated—"

"Whatever happened to detention? Hell, even a couple of weeks' suspension? There has to be *something* less drastic than kicking her out of school. These are kids. They're allowed to make mistakes."

"Harrison," Willow said in a cautionary voice.

"I'm sorry," he said. He released a frustrated breath.

The principal, whom he'd always liked, folded her hands and placed them on the desk. Her eyes held more understanding than he deserved.

"Policy states that the student is first suspended until a disciplinary hearing is held. That will likely take place on Friday, but may be delayed because of testing, which Liliana will be allowed to go through with. However, she will be tested separately from the student body.

"Pending the outcome of the hearing, a decision will be made within the next week. But understand that the likelihood of that decision being anything other than expulsion is minimal.

"This is a difficult situation," Dr. Saul continued. "And, believe me, Mr. Holmes, I take no pleasure in the thought of losing a student like Liliana. She has been a model Golden Eagle for most of her years at St. Katherine. It's only these last few months that things have taken a turn." She directed her attention to Lily. "I wish you would have come to me, Liliana."

Guilt overwhelmed him as he took in his daughter's sullen expression. Lily had pulled a few hijinks over the years, but she'd never been a problem child. In fact, compared to most teenagers, she'd been exceptional. Good grades, no back talk, a willingness to pitch in and help Athens with his homework. She even helped with housework outside of the chores she was assigned.

But things had started to change a few months ago. Well before he moved out, Harrison sensed that Lily had known that something wasn't right between him and Willow. Her attitude had turned snotty, and she'd started spending more time at her friends' or in her room.

But fighting? He never would have expected this from the sweet girl they'd raised.

Dr. Saul ended the meeting and Lily was allowed to go to her locker to clean it out—in case she wasn't allowed to return after the testing.

Goodness, his daughter was getting kicked out of school!

"I can't believe this is happening," Harrison said as he stood outside the main office with Willow.

"This is our fault," she whispered. She looked up at

him. "You know that, don't you?"

"No." Harrison shook his head. "Lily is almost sixteen. She knows better than this. She knows fighting is not how you solve your problems."

Walking away and not talking wasn't how you solved them either, but this didn't seem like the time to bring that up.

"She's acting out," Willow argued. "She's been doing it for weeks, and it has just gotten worse since you left." She shook her head. "I should have seen something like this coming."

"How could you?"

"Because she's my daughter! It's my job to notice these things, Harrison!"

"Willow—" He reached for her but she took a step back. A knife to his gut couldn't have hurt any worse than her reaction to his near touch. It felt as if someone had reached into his chest and wrapped a vise around his heart.

Willow hugged her upper body, rubbing her arms as if cold. "I should have seen it," she repeated in a soft murmur. "I've noticed her changing. I just didn't think it would escalate into something like this." She closed her eyes and sucked in a deep breath. "We're going to have to sit her down and talk to her."

"That goes without saying," Harrison pointed out.

She looked up at him. "And we'll have to really pay close attention to her these next few weeks."

Her words caused a sickening feeling to immediately settle in his gut. He didn't have to tell her that it would be difficult to pay close attention to Lily from thousands of miles away next week. Unless...

"Don't do this, Willow."

"Harrison, we can't—"

"No."

She held her hands out in a plea. "How can you expect me to take off on some last-minute vacation when my daughter is clearly going through issues that *we* caused?"

"Don't!" He clamped his hands on her shoulders and locked eyes with her. "I won't let you use this as an excuse to back out of this trip, Willow. You said it yourself, our separation is the reason she's acting out. Going to Italy together and figuring out what went wrong between us is exactly what we *should* do."

Her head jerked back, accusation flashing in her topaz eyes. "I thought you said this trip wasn't some magic pill?"

Harrison let go of her shoulders and took a step back. He noticed Lily walking toward them out of the corner of his eye.

"We can finish this later," he said.

"No, let's finish it now." Willow crossed her arms over her chest. "Tell me the truth, Harrison, is that the reason you booked this trip? Are you expecting us to go to Italy and miraculously fix everything broken in our marriage?"

He leaned in close and, in a fierce whisper, said, "I already told you I booked this trip a year ago, well before you decided being married to me was the worst fucking thing in the world."

She flinched and he immediately regretted ever opening his mouth.

"Shit," he cursed. "I'm sorry." He ran a hand down his face.

"You're right," she murmured. "We can finish this later."

"Willow." Her name tore from his throat in a desperate plea.

She took several steps back. "You need to get back to

work. And I need to get Lily home."

"We're going to talk about this, right? You're not just going to shut me out?" Harrison hastily asked as Lily approached.

Willow's gaze darted toward their daughter. "Everyone is coming to the house tomorrow to talk about the kickoff party," she said in a low tone. "We'll talk then."

What else could he say? It's not as if he could force her to talk to him. And they didn't need to hash any of this out in front of Lily anyway. His daughter had enough to worry about.

"Okay," Harrison answered with a simple nod.

But the sinking feeling in his gut told him that everything was definitely not okay.

Chapter Five

As she held the butterfly pose—soles of her feet together and knees spread apart—Willow stared down at her cellphone, eyes focused on the text she'd received a few minutes ago. She read it for what had to be the fifth time in the last sixty seconds and still had no idea how to answer.

No, she definitely knew how she *should* answer. She just wasn't ready to type out the words.

Hey! Will be in town next week. Dinner again?

It was an innocent invitation from an old friend, as innocent as the last invite he'd extended. Marcus Ewing undoubtedly had no clue how much anxiety those nine words had whipped up inside her. He had no earthly idea how the aftermath from their last dinner had upended her world. The profound way it had affected her, turning a simple meal between friends into one of those milestones she would likely look back upon decades from now and pinpoint as a watershed moment along her journey through life.

Months later and Willow was still trying to decide if that was a good thing or a bad thing. In ways it had changed her for the better, kindling long-buried hopes and dreams she hadn't thought about in years. But in the same way that night had shone a light on what had been missing, compelling her to question the choices she'd made and invoking an unjust resentment toward her husband and marriage.

So why was she so tempted to say yes?

She set the phone on the floor and covered her face in her hands. "My God, Willow," she breathed.

Had she not learned anything? She'd spent the past eight months drowning in guilt over the feelings that first dinner had sparked. How could she possibly consider putting herself in that situation again?

Her phone dinged with another text message. It was Marcus again.

Is Harrison in town? Maybe he can join us this time?

Willow released her yoga pose and sat up straight. Would she suffer the same guilt if Harrison was there?

No, probably not. The problem was that she *didn't want* Harrison there. His presence would ruin the fantasy. If he joined them, her husband would be a constant reminder that she was nothing more than a suburban housewife.

When she'd had dinner with Marcus eight months ago, she hadn't felt like a wife and mother. She'd felt like someone with a brain that was good for more than figuring out after-school schedules and putting together weekly shopping lists. There had been little talk of the things that normally occupied her day-to-day existence. Instead, they'd talked about Marcus's work as a research scientist. He'd sought her advice on how to tackle issues he'd faced in the lab, and engaged her in a discussion about new technologies that were being developed.

That's why she was tempted to say yes. It didn't matter who sat across the table from her. It could be Marcus, or Sonia, or Nyesha, or any of their old college friends who'd attended their group dinner last year. She wanted to experience the feeling of being something other than Harrison's wife, or Liliana and Athens's mother again.

Of course, the fact that it *was* Marcus Ewing asking her out added another sticky layer to the situation, since he was the only one of their group of old college friends who'd seen her naked. She and Marcus had broken up well before she'd even met her husband, but she could tell Harrison wasn't Marcus's biggest fan.

None of that mattered because she wasn't going out to dinner with him or anyone other than her husband. She loved her husband more than air. She loved being a mother to her children. She'd spent the past year contemplating how different her life would be if she'd finished grad school and entered the workplace, but this was the path she'd chosen, and she refused to regret it.

Picking up the phone, Willow replied to her former college mate's text.

Leaving for our anniversary trip to Rome this weekend! Sorry, not sorry.

She added a smiley face emoji before hitting *Send*.

It wasn't until she noticed her expression staring back at her on the phone's screen that Willow realized she was smiling. With that text she'd made her decision. She and Harrison were going to Italy.

As she rolled up her yoga mat and put it back in the closet, her excitement about finally coming to a decision about the trip gave way to exhaustion over the night to come. In less than an hour her house would be filled to the brim with Holmeses. She *soooo* was not up for that tonight.

She loved the family she'd married into as much as she loved her blood sisters and mother, but the Holmes clan could be...well...a lot. And after the last twenty-four hours, the thought of a houseful of boisterous Holmeses was enough to make her head hurt.

But she would just have to deal. Because tonight's gathering was important. They were getting together to discuss last-minute details regarding the kickoff party for the Diane Holmes Foundation. If there was anyone Willow was willing to do anything for, it was Diane Holmes.

"God, how I wish you were still here," she whispered.

The connection they'd shared went far beyond the typical mother-in-law/daughter-in-law relationship. Diane Holmes opened her arms and accepted Willow from the very first day they'd met. She'd been a confidant and a counselor, willing to listen and offering her opinion with a kindness few people possessed. Having to say goodbye to that gentle soul was, without a doubt, the hardest thing Willow had ever done in her life.

And that was saying a lot, because this life of hers hadn't always been sunshine and roses.

But those rough times had ended a long time ago. She'd been blessed with a big, nosy, affectionate family that had folded their arms around her and welcomed her into their loving brood. No matter what she was going through personally right now, she owed it to her family to be there for them. For Diane.

Willow showered, then went downstairs to whip up a quick spinach and artichoke dip they could snack on while finishing up the final preparations for the upcoming gala.

She was just about to go back upstairs to check on Athens when she heard the click of the front door's lock disengaging. A moment later, Harrison walked in.

"Hey," he said, his voice tentative.

"Hey," Willow answered, hating the way her own voice wavered on the single word. She thought they'd gotten past this tension, but yesterday's clash in the hallway at St. Katherine's had given rise to another dose of uncertainty between them.

"I wasn't expecting you this early. You said you were running late." His text had come just before Marcus's.

He held up his phone. "I texted again to say that my meeting had been cancelled."

"Oh."

They remained in the foyer. Neither spoke. They didn't so much as move an inch. They just stood there, staring at each other.

"Well, I—"

"Maybe I can—"

There was a brief knock on the front door before it opened again.

"Hey, hey, hey. What's up, people?"

Her brother-in-law, Ezra, and his fiancée, Mackenna Arnold, walked in.

"Well, hello, you two" Willow said, breathing a sigh of relief that they'd broken up the awkward moment between herself and Harrison. "I didn't expect you to make it tonight," she said to Mack as she greeted her with a hug. "I thought you'd be preparing for your interview with WWL-TV tomorrow."

"I've prepared enough," Mack said. "I don't want to come off as too rehearsed."

"Good idea."

Mackenna had recently announced her candidacy for mayor of New Orleans after serving two terms on the city council. Early polling had her so far ahead of the rest of the pack that Willow doubted she had to campaign at all, but Mack wasn't letting up. It was an exciting time for the entire city, but especially for the Holmes clan, who had known Mack since she and Indina roomed together as undergrads.

Ezra handed Harrison a plastic food container. "I found this recipe for buffalo cauliflower bites online. They're supposed to be a good substitute for hot wings. Figured they were better for Athens."

Willow's heart melted like an ice cube in the desert. From the moment they'd learned of his health issues, the entire family had taken an active role in helping Athens get back on track.

"Thank you," she said, taking the container from Harrison and motioning for everyone to follow her into the kitchen. "He's doing really well. His last doctor's appointment was the best he's had since the pre-diabetes diagnosis."

The front door opened again and Indina called out, "Where is everyone?"

Moments later, her sister-in-law joined them in the kitchen, accompanied by her new husband. Indina and Griffin had shocked everyone last week when they returned from a work trip in San Francisco with the news that they'd stopped over in Las Vegas and gotten married. Willow was still a bit sad over it. She would have loved to see her in a wedding gown. But her sister-in-law was over-the-moon happy, and that's all that mattered.

Indina set a shopping bag on the counter and drew a white cardboard cakebox from it.

"I've got food," she announced. "The new caterer put together a sampler box of some of the goodies they're serving for the gala. Sorry, but I already ate the mini crab cakes. Take it from me, they're to die for."

"We should have gone with this company from the beginning," Ezra said as he lifted a puffed pastry stuffed with some kind of meat from the box.

"It's those twin girls, right?" Mackenna asked.

"Yep. Tyra and Tomeka of Sassy Sisters Catering," Indina said. "They have been a dream to work with this past week." She turned to Harrison. "The price in the quote I showed you? It includes all the table linens *and* the waitstaff."

"No way," Harrison said.

"Did the other caterer expect us to hire our own wait-staff?" Ezra asked.

"Yes, he did," Indina answered. "Which means Sassy Sisters will cost less than the caterer who skipped out on us, even though they took the job at the very last minute."

"Let me try this food," Mack said, reaching into the box. "I'll have a lot of campaign functions that I'll need catered."

"Should we take this into the living room so we can get started?" Willow asked. "Wait, where's Brooklyn and Reid?"

"I talked to him on my way here," Indina said. "He was stuck in traffic on the bridge, but that was at least twenty minutes ago. They shouldn't be too far out. Oh, and Dad won't make it. His bowling buddies had to change their game because of some tournament at the bowling alley this weekend. He wanted to cancel, but I told him to go. Now that he's finally going out again, I think it's important that we all encourage him to get out of the house whenever we can."

"I agree," Willow said. "It's good for him."

Clark Holmes may have been seventy according to his

birth certificate, but he was still young at heart, as handsome as his three sons, and the picture of health. The last thing Diane would want is for him to wither away, mourning her death for the rest of his life.

Brooklyn and Reid arrived a few minutes later, and they all settled in the living room. They passed around the samples from the caterer while waiting for Brooklyn to set up everything for the big reveal of the commemorative comic book she'd drawn as a keepsake for those attending the comic book-themed gala.

Reid's new girlfriend, who'd instantly stolen the hearts of everyone in the family, was an aspiring comic book writer and illustrator. She'd created a new character, Dynamo Diane, expressly for the foundation's kickoff party. The superhero she'd drawn in Diane's likeness had brought tears to Willow's eyes when she'd first laid eyes on her.

In her opinion, the foundation, which would work to raise awareness of heart disease in the black community, was the perfect way to honor Diane. The plan was to offer scholarships to young women who wanted to study medicine, and provide health screenings and education about heart disease to those in underserved communities. It touched Willow's science-loving heart to know that their family would help draw young black girls to STEM-related fields.

"Don't reveal the comic just yet," Willow said. "I know Athens will want to see this."

She went upstairs and knocked on her son's door before opening it. Even ten-year-old boys needed their privacy, as Willow discovered last week. That reminded her, Athens and Harrison needed to have THE talk. She'd done so with Lily, it was Harrison's turn.

Thankfully, her son had his face in a comic when she opened his bedroom door.

"Brooklyn is downstairs with a comic book I know you'll want to see," she said.

Willow laughed as Athens shot off the bed, whizzing past her on his way downstairs.

She stopped at Lily's door, debating whether or not to disturb her. Things had been tense since yesterday's meeting with Dr. Saul. The effort it took not to lash out at her was a test to Willow's willpower. When she thought about how much Lily had gambled away over a stupid fight —how she would very likely be kicked out of school and how hard it would be for her to get into another good school with a mark on her disciplinary record—she became even more incensed. But she didn't want Lily to feel left out of tonight's gathering.

Willow rapped on the door a couple of times. She opened the door at her daughter's tentative, "Yes?"

One upside to yesterday's debacle was that her stank attitude had all but dissipated. Hard to play the surly teenager when your ass was sitting in hot water.

"Everyone's downstairs," Willow said. "Brooklyn is about to show us the finished comic book. Why don't you come and join us?"

She closed the magazine she'd been reading and set it next to her on the bed.

"Do they all know?" Lily asked, her voice laden with apprehension. "About what happened yesterday?"

Willow shook her head. "I didn't tell anyone, and I don't think your dad did either." She gestured with her head. "Come on."

Lily scooted off the bed. When she joined her at the door, Willow wrapped her arms around her and kissed the side of her head. As much as she wanted to strangle her for that stupid fight yesterday, she knew it wouldn't help matters. Lily needed her understanding right now.

This was the reason to turn down Marcus's dinner invitation. This was why months of musing about what life could have been like if she'd pursued those long ago dreams of becoming a scientist were dangerous. She had a job. *This* was her job. Making sure her children knew they were loved and cared for—that they understood that they were the most important part of her existence—should be her sole focus.

Being a wife and mother was not a sacrifice. After witnessing how hard her own mother struggled to raise she and her sisters on her own, she should be thankful that she and Harrison were in a financial position that allowed her to stay at home and care for their children.

It was easier said than done, but Willow vowed to work on it.

When she and Lily returned to the living room, everyone was going crazy over the final sketches for the Dynamo Diane comic book.

"These are even more amazing than I thought they would be," Indina said. "This can't be all there is to it. You have to continue the adventures of Dynamo Diane."

"Well, I'm hoping I can," Brooklyn said. She looked over at Reid, her big, bright smile taking up the bottom half of her face. "I was accepted into a comics writing consortium in Hot Springs, Arkansas today!"

"You got in!" Reid jumped up from the sofa and ran to her, wrapping Brooklyn up in a hug and spinning her around. Then he captured her mouth in a kiss that had Willow shielding Athens's eyes.

"Not in front of the young and impressionables," Willow said.

Yet, as she watched them, Willow couldn't hide her own smile. She was thrilled that her brother-in-law had found someone like Brooklyn. Reid had floated from one girl to another from the time he'd hit puberty. Brooklyn LeBlanc was settling down material. And she would knock his cockiness down a peg or two.

"Congratulations," Willow said, giving Brooklyn a hug.

"It's a good thing we got you to draw Dynamo Diane before you become some hotshot comic book writer that none of us can afford," Ezra said.

"Never." Brooklyn laughed. "I have a comic I've been working on for ages, but I would love to continue drawing Dynamo Diane. I wanted to make sure I had permission from all of you first before I move forward."

The room erupted with a chorus of *of course* and *yes* and *absolutely* from the Holmes clan.

"Wait!" Ezra said. "I forgot about the stuff Aunt Margo gave me. I'll be right back." He returned a few minutes later with a cardboard banker box. "Aunt Margo sent these for the pre-gala comic book event. She said Uncle Wesley bought a bunch of comics for Alex, Eli and Toby when they were little, but they never really got into it. She found these in that old footlocker Uncle Wes kept in the attic. They're in pretty good shape to say they've been locked away for more than thirty years."

When Ezra uncovered the box, Brooklyn dropped the mini quiche she'd been eating, along with her jaw.

"Oh. My. God." Her eyes were as wide as silver dollar coins.

"That means it's something good," Reid translated.

"Oh my GOD! This is The Punisher Limited Edition. Wait!" Brooklyn picked up another magazine. And another. "Is this the entire 1986 series? Do you have any idea how rare these are? And they were just in a box in the attic?" she screeched at Ezra as if he was the one who'd kept them locked up all these years.

The abject horror on her face made Willow want to burst out laughing, but she understood what it was like to feel passionate about something that others just didn't get. She'd felt the same way when trying to explain her science experiments to her sisters as a kid.

Brooklyn was lost to the rest of the discussion as she and Athens went through the old comics, but the rest of them dove into the remaining details, going through the list of tasks that needed to be done in these next few weeks before the gala. Every time Willow tried to offer up a hand to do something, Indina informed her that it was already taken care of. Her sister-in-law was great at her job, but if Indina ever wanted to give up being an industrial interior designer, she could definitely set up her own event planning business.

She noticed the box from the catering company was empty, so Willow offered to get the artichoke dip she'd made.

"I'll help," Indina said, following her into the kitchen.

"It's only one bowl of dip and a bag of pita chips," Willow said once they'd reached the kitchen. "Pretty sure I can handle it."

Indina swatted at the air. "You know that's not why I'm here." In a lowered voice she asked, "What's going on with Lily?"

Willow strove for a confused expression. "What do you mean?"

It didn't work. Indina crossed her arms over her chest

and laid that *don't even try this bullshit with me* look on her. Willow sighed as she poured the pita chips into a separate bowl.

"She got into a fight at school."

Indina's eyes grew wide. "What li'l heifer had the nerve to pick a fight with my niece? Whose ass do I need to kick?"

"If you want to kick the ass of the person who started the fight, you need to go right out there and give your niece a swift one," Willow answered.

Her sister-in-law's mouth dropped open. "Lily started it?"

"Yes. And, because that very expensive school has a zero-tolerance policy when it comes to fighting, there is a high probability that she'll be expelled."

"Oh, my goodness." Indina put a hand to her chest. "What was she fighting about?"

"I can't get a straight answer from her. All she's said so far is that something has been building between her and this other girl. Apparently it started online. Lily is the one who brought the disagreement to school." Willow rested her elbows on the counter and covered her face in her hands. "I thought I was doing the right thing by giving her space. She's almost sixteen. It would be unreasonable to monitor what she's doing online, right?"

"Well, I guess you have your answer."

"Yeah," Willow blew out with an exasperated sigh. Folding her arms over her chest, she leaned a hip against the counter. "It makes me hesitant about this upcoming trip."

Indina's expression softened. "He finally told you about Italy."

She wasn't surprised Indina knew about the trip. There's no way Harrison had kept it away from his sister all this time.

"I wondered if he would still give you your anniversary gift. Seeing how things are...well, you know," Indina's voice trailed.

Seeing how they were now separated.

Taking a break.

"He did," Willow confirmed. "We're supposed to leave on Saturday. But how can I, Indina? It was bad enough when I thought I was only leaving Athens with his health issues, but now that I have this thing with Lily..." Willow pulled her bottom lip between her teeth and looked over at her sister-in-law. "I thought I could, but it would be irresponsible to go."

"No." Indina shook her head. "No way. You do *not* get to use your kids as an excuse to back out of this trip, Willow."

"I'm not using them as an excuse."

"Yes, you are. The kids will be fine. Didn't Harrison ask Dad to look after them?"

Willow nodded. "He's supposed to spend the week here. But I can't ask Clark to deal with a sulking, moody teenage girl."

"He helped raise me. He has plenty of experience with sulky, moody teenage girls. And it doesn't matter. *I'll* handle Lily."

"You have enough on your plate with work and the kickoff party. I can't ask you to look after Lily too."

"Are you asking, or am I offering?" Indina reached over and took both of Willow's hands in hers. "You and Harrison need this time away. I'm afraid if you don't take it, the two of you will just drift further apart."

"But—"

"But nothing. There's too much at stake here, Willow. You're fighting for your marriage. There is *nothing* more important than that. You have enough family here to watch over the kids. Go to Italy with your damn husband and remember what made the two of you fall in love all those years ago."

It was exactly what her sister suggested to her yesterday. Willow wrapped her arms around Indina.

"Thank you," she whispered in her ear.

"Any time," Indina said. "Just promise me you'll fight for it. The two of you are my biggest role models. If you and Harrison can't make a marriage work Griffin and I don't stand a chance in hell."

"Oh, please," Willow said. "Yes you do. I've never seen two people more in love."

Indina smooth a hand along her hair. "I used to say the same about you and Harrison all the time. The two of you need to find that again."

"It's still there," Willow assured her. "I love him so much, Deenie."

Her sister-in-law winked. "Then show him."

I t was almost nine o'clock by the time everyone cleared out of the house. Willow lingered in the living room, straightening the sofa cushions and throw pillows. She was stalling. She knew it. Harrison knew it too. Yet he was giving her some space while she collected her thoughts.

He'd want to pick up where they'd left off in the hallway at St. Katherine's yesterday, but Willow wasn't up to rehashing things they likely both regretted ever saying. Besides, there was no point to it. She no longer needed to debate whether or not they should go to Italy. They *had* to go. She saw that now.

Indina was right, they were fighting for the soul of their marriage. She would not allow herself to take the coward's way out by using Lily's fight as a reason to back out on this time away with her husband. They needed this time together. Wasn't that one of her issues, the fact that he worked so much and that they never had any time together anymore for just the two of them?

She'd been so intent on making sure Harrison didn't look at this trip as some magical panacea that would cure all their problems that she'd closed her eyes to all the possibilities that *could* come out of it. A week in Italy wouldn't mend everything that was broken in their marriage, but it could be a start. It would give them time to focus on each other, without the dozens of obstacles everyday life threw at them on a constant basis.

"Need some help?"

Willow jumped at the sound of Harrison's voice. She turned to find him leaning against the wall in the shadowed entryway that led from the living area to the kitchen, one hand casually stuffed in his pocket. She loved him when he looked this way, relaxed and unstressed. And sexy.

"No. I'm done in here," she said.

He pushed away from the wall and quietly sauntered over to where she stood. The way his big body loomed over her should have felt intimidating. Instead, she felt comforted. She'd come to rely on the reassurance and protection that large body had provided over the years.

"So," she said. "Are you ready to tell the kids about the trip?"

His brows arched. "We're going?"

"Yes, we're going," she said. Hugging her upper body, she leaned into him, resting her cheek on his solid chest. His warmth surrounded her even before he wrapped her up in his arms. "We need this, Harrison."

He kissed the top of her head. His softly whispered, "Thank you," rustled her hair.

She looked up into his handsome face. "There's a catch," she said. She felt him suck in a breath, as if bracing himself. A smile slowly crept across Willow's lips. "You have to promise that we'll have gelato every single day."

A low laugh rumbled from deep in his chest. "I think I can handle that."

"Good," she said, still smiling.

"Daddy? You're still here?" They both turned at the sound of Lily's voice.

She stood at the base of the staircase, staring at them in confusion. Willow realized it had been a while since her daughter had witnessed the two of them embracing.

"Yes, your dad and I want to talk to you and your brother."

"About what?" Lily asked, the caution in her voice matching the concern in her eyes.

"Have a seat," Harrison said as he released Willow from his hold. "I'll go up and get your brother, then we can all talk."

When Harrison left them, Lily turned to her. "Are you two getting a divorce?"

"No, no, no," Willow said. "It's nothing like that."

"The last time you sat us down to talk it was to tell us Daddy was leaving."

"You're way off-base, Liliana. Wait until your dad and Athens get here. I promise, it's nothing like what you're thinking."

Lily settled on the sofa, bringing both feet up and

clutching a throw pillow to her chest. Her pretty brown eyes brimmed with a wariness Willow had seen much too often these past few months. Her daughter's lack of trust was disheartening, but, unfortunately, understandable.

"Someone was up reading comics when he should have been getting ready for bed," Harrison said as he and Athens came into the living room. He rubbed him on the head. "I guess we can blame Brooklyn and Dynamo Diane for getting him all riled up."

"Okay, so, what's going on?" Lily asked the moment Athens sat down. Despite Willow's attempt to put her at ease, her daughter clearly didn't believe there was nothing to be concerned about. Harrison walked over to the accent chair where Willow was sitting and sat on the arm of it, casually slinging his arm across the back of it and resting his hand on her shoulder.

"Your Dad and I are going on a little vacation together. Actually, it's a big vacation," Willow said. "Our wedding anniversary is next week and your Dad surprised me with a trip to Italy!" She reached over and took Harrison's hand in hers.

Willow recognized her error when Athens's and Lily's eyes followed the gesture. She didn't want to get their hopes up. She released Harrison's hand and stood. Walking over to the sofa, she sat on the ottoman and tried to come up with the best way to manage their expectations.

"Now, I don't want you kids to get the wrong idea. Just because your father and I are going away together, it doesn't mean everything will drastically change once we return."

Lily folded her hands over her arms. "So, what you're saying is that Daddy is still going to live above his office."

That little spark of hope on Athens's face immediately vanished. But it was better he understand it now than spend the next week thinking his world would return back to normal when they got back from Italy.

"Yes, maybe. Probably," Willow clarified.

"So why go at all?" Lily asked. "What's the point?"

"Because it's our anniversary," Harrison said. He rose from his perch on the chair and came over to where Willow sat. He put his hands on her shoulders and gave her a light squeeze. "This hasn't been the easiest year—for any of us—but it's a big deal to be married for seventeen years and we should celebrate it."

"So you're going just because you think you should celebrate being married, even though you're not living like a married couple? Do you guys even still love each other?" Lily asked.

"Yes," Harrison and Willow answered at the same time.

"Of course we do," Willow said. She reached over and clasped her hand over Lily's. "Sweetie, I know this is confusing. It's confusing for us too."

She slid her hand free. "Yeah, it's pretty confusing when you say you love each other and you're going on some big trip together, yet Daddy has to sleep at his office. Like Auntie Indina said, you two need to get your shit together."

"Liliana," Harrison said, his voice hard.

Willow looked at him over her shoulder. "Why don't you put Athens to bed?"

One brow arched. "You sure?"

She nodded.

Lily blew out an exasperated breath and pushed up from the sofa. "I'm going to bed too."

"Lil—"

Willow caught Harrison's hand, halting his forthcoming reprimand. "Go on," she said. "I'll handle this."

His eyes following Lily as she bounded up the stairs, he

clamped a hand on Athens's shoulder, urging him to follow. Willow remained on the ottoman, pressing her folded hands to her lips. She needed some time before she approached Lily.

Harrison returned to the living room, a subtle smile on his face.

"He went out the minute his head hit the pillow," he said.

Willow grinned. "Tonight was a lot for him." She stood and walked over to her husband. He stroked her cheek with the backs of his fingers.

"Are you sure you want to handle things with Lily by yourself?"

She nodded, closing her eyes and savoring his gentle caress. She missed these sweet, incidental touches.

"I should probably head back to the office," he said. "I've got a long day tomorrow, and I need to start packing." He lifted her hand and placed a kiss on the back of it. "I'll see you Saturday. Our flight leaves at five in the afternoon, so we should head to the airport no later than two."

"Okay," she said. "See you then."

She waited until Harrison left the house before going upstairs. She knocked, even though she planned to enter no matter Lily's reply.

She barely heard the strained, "Come in," through the wooden door. When she opened it, Willow's heart broke in two. Lily sat on the edge of the bed, her eyes closed, rivulets running down her cheeks. Every ounce of frustration she'd had in her withered and died at the sight of her daughter's tear-stained face. What did she expect of a teenage girl who was afraid her parents were on the brink of divorce? How could she expect Lily to fare any better than she had?

Willow closed the door behind her and leaned back

against it, her hands clenching the knob.

"We need to talk," she announced.

Lily didn't open her eyes. She simply nodded.

Sucking in a bolstering breath, Willow walked over to the bed and sat beside her daughter. "First things first," she began. "You have every right to be upset about what's going on between me and your dad."

Lily looked over at her as she wiped her cheeks. "What *is* going on between you two? Why'd you stop talking to him?"

"I didn't."

"Yes, you did," she said. "I remember exactly when you did. It's when he went to that conference thing in Philadelphia earlier this year. You wouldn't take his calls, and when he came home things just...changed," she said.

Oh, God. Willow hadn't realized it had been so obvious.

Lily swiped at her cheeks again, before asking in a small voice, "Did Daddy cheat on you when he was in Philadelphia?"

"What?" Willow screeched.

"I'm not a little kid, Mom. I can handle it."

"No," Willow said. "Of course he didn't. Why would you even think that?"

"Oh, I don't know." She flailed her hands dramatically. "Maybe because that's usually why people get a divorce."

"We are *not* getting a divorce, and your father did not cheat on me," Willow said. She took her hand. "Lily, I wish I had a simple answer, but I don't. It's something your dad and I need to figure out."

"Figure what out? I don't get what you guys need to figure out!"

"I don't know how to answer that." She felt like such a fraud. Here was her daughter, thinking Harrison was the one who'd caused this rift, when it was Willow's own actions that had changed things those many months ago. But this wasn't something she could discuss with Lily.

"Couples just...they drift apart," Willow continued, her throat aching with the guilt she tried desperately to swallow. "The stress of losing your grandmother, and Athens's health issues, and your dad becoming a partner in the law firm. And some personal issues I've been dealing with," Willow tacked on in a feeble attempt to own up to her own culpability in the mess their family was now mired in. "It just became too much." She cupped her daughter's cheek. "And I realize that you've gotten lost in all of this. I understand why you would act out."

"I'm not a little kid looking for attention," Lily groused.

"Really? So what was that fight about?"

"Valeka called me a ho on Snapchat."

"That's it? Some girl called you a ho?"

"You don't think that's enough!"

Willow rubbed her temples, her eyes falling closed as she took a moment to grasp what little calm she could muster. "Lily, do you realize what this may do to your school career?"

"I wasn't thinking about that," she said.

"No shit!" Willow retorted. "I'm sorry." She sighed. "It's just...that is a very expensive school, Lily. You've been on the waiting list to get in since you were five. Every single graduate goes on to college—many of them to the top schools in the country. You don't throw away the opportunity you've been given over some girl calling you a name."

"I'm sorry, Mom. I really am. I didn't think about getting thrown out of school. I was just tired of dealing with that bitch. She always has something to say."

Willow let the use of the word bitch slide. Her daughter

was talking to her. It's something she hadn't done lately, and Willow needed it to continue.

"Are you sure this had nothing to do with what's been going on here at home?" Willow asked.

"I'm sure," Lily said. "If she wasn't being such a coward and walking around with an entourage outside of school, I would have kicked her ass when I saw her at the movies last weekend."

Willow put her hands up. "Okay, so that's one too many curse words. I'm all for being a cool mom, but I'm not *that* cool. And there will be no more fighting, in school or out of it. You know fighting doesn't solve anything."

"I'm sorry," Lily said. "I know."

"Good." Willow stood and walked around to the other side of her. She wrapped her arms around Lily's upper body and gave her a squeeze. "So, I can leave you with your grandfather and Aunt Indina and not have to worry about you getting picked up by the cops while your dad and I are in Italy?"

Lily let out a loud groan. "Yeeesss." She dragged the word out. Their eyes met in the mirror that stood above the dresser. They both smiled, but then Lily's turned downward. It wrenched Willow's heart to see the sadness clouding those beautiful eyes.

"I want Daddy to move back home," her daughter said. "Can you guys please just get back together?"

"We're working on it," Willow said. "I promise, baby." She pressed a kiss to the top of her head, grateful that her voice didn't crack over the words. She rubbed Lily's arms and gave them a pat before releasing her. "Now, get to bed. You have school tomorrow."

"No, I don't."

"Oh, yes, you do," Willow informed her. "You're going to *my* school."

Lily groaned.

"You thought you hated Calculus? Wait until this math and science nerd teaches it to you."

"Now I really regret that fight," Lily muttered.

Willow chuckled as she exited the room. As she crossed the hallway to the guest bedroom where she'd been sleeping these past few weeks, the dull ache that had become so familiar made its nightly appearance, settling into the depths of Willow's chest. Tonight's hurt cut even deeper after having Harrison in the house for much of the evening. Earlier, when they'd stood quietly together in the downstairs living room, she almost suggested he spend the night. But if she'd feared news that she and Harrison were going away for their anniversary would give the children false hope, having him spend the night definitely would.

Her phone chimed with a text message. Willow was almost afraid to look. Marcus hadn't responded to her last text. She'd been anticipating a follow up invitation for them all to get together once they got back from Italy.

The text wasn't from Marcus. It was Harrison.

Can you grab that brown leather duffle and leave it in the living room? Will try to find some time to pick it up before Saturday.

She went downstairs to the walk-in closet in their master bedroom and pulled the duffle from the top shelf. She carried it over to the foyer and set it underneath the tall console table so that it would be easily accessible when Harrison dropped by to pick it up. Her eyes fell on the car keys she'd dropped in the misshapen bowl Lily had made in Girl Scouts years ago, and, without giving it too much thought, Willow grabbed both the keys and the bag and took off for the garage, stopping in her bedroom for her purse. She texted Lily to let her know she was leaving the house for a bit and would be back in a half-hour.

The night air felt heavy with the imposing clouds that hung low in the sky. They'd hovered over New Orleans all day, threatening to unleash a violent downpour upon the city. The late hour meant virtually no traffic on the interstate, so Willow found herself pulling up to the curb in front of Campbell & Holmes's Law Offices in under fifteen minutes. The moment she got out of her car, a loud boom rent the air and a deluge burst from the sky above.

She ran up to the wooden porch that wrapped around the three-story colonial Jonathan had converted into his law office when he moved to New Orleans years ago. An old-fashioned gas lantern, like the one they'd installed at their own house, illuminated the front porch.

Figuring Harrison was on the third floor and probably wouldn't hear her knocking, Willow pulled her phone out and called him.

He answered with a simple, "Hey."

"I'm outside. Can you come downstairs?"

"You're here? Why? What's wrong?" She immediately heard the approach of his heavy footsteps. Apparently he hadn't been upstairs. Before she could answer any of his questions, the door swung open. "What's going on?" Harrison asked the moment he spotted her.

He stood before her in the blue plaid pajama pants she'd given him for Christmas, a green Tulane Law T-shirt, and bare feet. She loved the way her husband looked in a suit, but Willow preferred him like this. Relaxed. Casual. Sexy.

Goodness, but he was sexy.

She held up the bag. "Thought I'd bring this over. I

know you're going to be busy these next couple of days, and figured it would be difficult for you to drive out to Lakeview to pick it up."

Harrison arched one brow as he took the bag from her. "You came all the way here to bring me a duffle bag?"

She hunched her shoulders. "You have to pack."

Thunder cracked, and he took her by the wrist and tugged. "Come inside."

She hesitated. "I can't stay for long."

"You can't go back out there in this rain either," he rationalized. "It shouldn't last too long."

As she entered the law office, Willow realized that even though she'd been here dozens of times since Harrison started working with Jonathan, it had only been for a few minutes at a time. Why hadn't she taken a bigger interest? Was Harrison disappointed that she hadn't?

"Why were you down here?" She asked. "I didn't knock because I figured you'd be upstairs and wouldn't hear me."

He picked up the bowl he'd apparently set on the receptionist's desk on his way to the door. "I was heating up some left over Pad Thai. The microwave upstairs went out last week. I haven't had a chance to pick up another one." He held out the bowl. "Want some?"

"No. No. I'm still full from all the food Indina brought over."

The awkwardness that had become such a noticeable presence when they were together snaked its way around them, but she fought against it. This tension only took root because she allowed it to. This was her husband, her best friend. She would stop feeling so self-conscious around him.

"You mind coming up stairs?" Harrison asked. "I was just about to start pulling some clothes out for the trip. You can help me pick out my outfits."

"Help?" Willow asked, one brow peaked.

"Okay," he said, a grin creeping up the corner of his mouth. "Can you please come upstairs and pick out my clothes?"

Laughing, she followed him up the stairs to the small, converted room. Willow stopped at the threshold, her heart plummeting to the pit of her stomach.

The stark, sparsely furnished room was fine for a night here or there, but the thought of Harrison spending the past three weeks here made her physically sick. Especially when she thought about the home he'd provided for them, for her.

Guilt assailed her as she considered the mini-mansion she would return to once the rain let up. Meanwhile, Harrison would remain here, forced to sleep on a lumpy futon that looked straight out of a 1989 J.C. Penny catalog. The unfairness of it all was almost too much for her to stomach.

He didn't deserve this.

If anyone should be living in this little room, it should be *her*. Yet, she doubted it ever occurred to him that he had just as much right to their home as she did. After all, he was the one who'd paid for it.

Not that Harrison would *ever* bring up money with her. In all their years together, he'd never once tried to exert control over the money simply because he was the breadwinner.

It was in that moment that Willow decided, no matter what, she would figure out a way to fix her ailing marriage. She was one of the luckiest women in the world to have a husband like Harrison. She owed it to him to show just how much she appreciated him.

Chapter Six

He'd read two books on dealing with anxiety and tried every old wives' tale he could find online, yet Harrison's heart still raced like it was on crack as he and Willow made their way closer to the gate. There was a reason he never complained when Athens suggested Disney World every year for their family trip. It was within driving distance.

He hated flying. *Hated* it.

If this didn't show Willow how much he loved her, nothing he did ever would.

The excitement dancing in her eyes right now was almost enough to make up for the mind-numbing fear that had been building in his veins ever since he checked them into their flight yesterday. Harrison couldn't remember the last time he'd seen her smile so much.

"I downloaded an app that will translate words into English just by holding your phone up to the sign," Willow said as she settled back in one of the few chairs remaining at the gate. "In a way, I'm glad we waited to take this trip.

Technology makes it so much easier to travel internationally these days than it would have been seventeen years ago."

He simply nodded. His voice would probably squeak like a frightened five-year-old's if he tried to speak.

Willow played around on her phone while they waited for the passengers from the previous flight to deplane. Harrison fought the urge to pace, though he sure as hell would benefit from expending some of this pent up energy. The gate agent announced that boarding for their flight would begin in five minutes and Harrison immediately started praying the rosary. Didn't matter that they weren't Catholic. He'd take all the help he could get.

When the call for first class passengers was made, he sucked in a deep breath and tried to quiet his racing heart.

Willow looked back at him and smiled. "You ready?"

He swallowed and nodded. He had no doubt his fear showed on his face. That was confirmed when his wife's gaze softened. She reached for his hand and took it in hers.

"It'll be okay," she said. She stood on her tiptoes and whispered in his ear. "I won't let anything happen to you."

There wasn't a damn thing she could do if this plane started to go down, but just hearing those words from her released some of the tension tightening his muscles.

They took their seats in first class and were immediately served mimosas. He'd vowed to leave alcohol alone after those shots of bourbon had put him on his ass, but Harrison downed the champagne and orange juice in one gulp. He wondered how long he should wait before he asked for another.

Willow could barely keep still in the seat next to him. She was like a kid embarking on a wild new adventure, her eyes bright with excitement. She turned to him and smiled.

"Thank you for doing this," she said. "I wasn't sure

about the trip at first, but now that we're on the plane and ready to take off, it's starting to sink in that I am actually going to Italy! I'm so happy we decided to do this."

Happiness. That's what he saw on his wife's face. He would endure however many hours it would take to get them to Rome just to see that look on her face. It was worth it.

But that didn't mean he had to like what it took to put that look on her face.

He groaned when the plane started to pick up momentum on the runway. Willow reached over and took his hand again, bringing it to her lap and giving it a gentle squeeze. Harrison closed his eyes and relished in the comfort she offered. They used to hold hands like this all the time. Even on the short drive from his parents' house to their own, she would reach over and cover his hand on the gearshift while he steered with the other. When had touching become such an abnormal thing between them?

Their hands remained entwined for most of the flight, with Willow only letting go when they were served their meals. As she watched movies on the screen embedded on the back of the seat in front of her, or read on her e-reader, her hand rested comfortably in his.

Their layover in London wasn't nearly as long as Harrison had hoped, but he was still grateful when the wheels hit the tarmac.

She called the kids as soon as they deplaned.

"I'll give them another call once we land in Italy, and then that's it," Willow said. "No more kids." Harrison looked at her with a skeptical lift to his brow as she pocketed her phone. "Okay, fine. One five minute call a day, just to check-in."

He nodded. "Even if you weren't planning to call, I

would. We've got to make sure Lily isn't picking fights with everyone in the neighborhood."

Willow groaned before laughing, and the sound put him at ease.

Too bad it wasn't enough to allay his fears of getting back on a damn plane. After less than an hour, they were once again boarding. He'd just survived a ten-hour flight across the Atlantic, yet this two-and-a-half-hour flight down to Rome seemed just as daunting. Who in the hell thought sending a metal tube filled with people in the air was a good idea?

Once again, Willow's steady presence calmed him. Instead of reading or watching television, they talked. It wasn't the kind of talk they needed to have—one that would allow them to finally delve into the issues that had been plaguing their marriage this past year—but this wasn't the time for that discussion anyway. Instead, they talked like a normal husband and wife, the way they used to talk before everything started to change.

She filled him in on the discussion she'd had with Dr. Saul before he'd arrived at the school on the day of Lily's fight, and how she wasn't all that optimistic that Lily would be allowed to continue at St. Katherine's Academy. Harrison learned that Willow had already started looking at other schools that would possibly admit her.

"Who knew the teenage years would be so much harder?" he asked.

"Every person who has ever parented a teenager," Willow said with a laugh. "Your Mom warned me a long time ago that I needed to get ready. Whenever I bragged about how sweet Lily and Athens were as children, Diane would tell me not to get lulled into this fantasy that they would stay that way once they became teenagers. Apparently, she experienced the same with her kids."

"Not with me! She was probably talking about Indina and her smart ass mouth. She's always been the trouble maker. Still is."

"Stop talking bad about your sister." Willow laughed and pinched him on the arm. As far as Harrison was concerned, it was a kiss directly on the lips. He'd missed this playful banter they'd always shared. He'd taken past moments like this for granted.

He'd taken *so damn much* for granted. That life would always be easy. That his marriage would never have any bumps. That his children would always be healthy and trouble free. That both his parents would be around for him for years to come.

God, how things had changed in just a year. Everything in his world had been upended within a span of a few short months.

But it seemed as if things had started turning around. Working on plans for the foundation had finally helped to lessen some of the pain he felt whenever he thought about his mom. Athens was on the right track with his pre-diabetes. Things were still up in the air with Lily, but if they found an alternative to St. Katherine's there was still a chance she could recover from this fighting fiasco.

And then there was Willow.

A week ago, the thought of her holding his hand for hours seemed as improbable as him enjoying one of those *Real Housewives* reality shows Lily always had playing in the family room. Yet, here they were, hand-in-hand.

When they finally touched down at Rome's Fiumicino Airport, and he knew for certain that he would be on land for the next seven days, Harrison took his first true breath in over sixteen hours. Now all he had to do was try not to spend his entire week feeling anxious about the flight back home.

It shouldn't be too hard. After all, he had a week with his wife in one of the most romantic places on Earth to distract him.

Once they picked up their bags from baggage claim, Harrison started looking around for the taxi line, but Willow wanted to take the Leonardo. She'd read up on the high-speed train that took passengers directly to Rome's Termini train station, in the heart of the city. The train station was only a few minutes from the hotel where they would be staying, so it worked out perfectly.

As they boarded the train, Willow took his arm and wrapped hers around it.

"I'm having a hard time staying calm," she admitted. "Remind me that we have an entire week here and that I need to pace myself, because right now I just want to see and do *everything!*"

"We have an entire week. And the itinerary I have planned will allow you to see everything your heart desires."

The look he saw in her eyes when she looked up at him struck Harrison square in the chest. This woman still loved him. There was zero doubt in his mind. Whatever had been lost between them over this past year, it wasn't love. The love was there.

Her enthusiasm intensified with every mile the bullet train ate up on their way into the city. Once they arrived at Termini Station, they took a cab the short route to the Boscolo Exedra Roma. It wasn't the uber luxury hotel he'd wanted to book, but Harrison knew his wife would throw a fit if he'd spent over a thousand dollars a night on a hotel. It didn't matter how much money sat in their bank account,

Willow never seemed to shake off the frugality she learned as a child, growing up with a single mother who was barely able to make ends meet when her girls were young.

They checked into their room and Willow told him he could have first dibs on the shower. The urge to ask her to join him was so damn strong his body strained with it, but he fought it. The one thing he would *not* do on this trip was test the boundaries of this delicate situation they now found themselves in. Expecting Willow to jump into the shower with him would test those boundaries.

Once he was done, she took her turn. He pulled on an undershirt and the sweat pants he'd thrown into the duffle at the last minute, then he opened the curtains to the beauty of Rome. He'd read that their hotel sat in a square called the Piazza della Repubblica, but this looked more circular than square to him. At the center stood an ornate marble fountain with naked, nymph-like women playing in the water.

"That must be the basilica," Harrison murmured as he looked beyond the fountain. He'd also read that directly across from their hotel stood the Basilica of Santa Maria something or another, and the ancient Baths of Diocletian. It was the first stop on the itinerary he'd put together for tomorrow's sightseeing. *Tomorrow* being the operative word. Right now, it was time to crash.

He closed the curtain and moved over to the bed. When he stretched across the cool comforter, his eyes immediately closed. They popped opened what seemed like seconds later as Willow woke him up, pushing at his shoulder.

"No, don't sleep," she said. "Wake up."

"Why?" He looked over and found her standing next to the bed, a towel wrapped around her still damp body.

A tidal wave of lust crashed into him. It had been months since he'd seen his wife's bare thighs. It was yet another thing he'd taken for granted over the years. Having sex on a regular basis.

God, how he missed sex.

"I read that when it comes to preventing jet lag, the one thing you absolutely cannot do is go straight to sleep," Willow continued. "We have to stay on our normal schedule." She looked over at the clock on the bedside table. "It's only three p.m., so we need to stay up for at least another six hours or we're going to throw everything out of whack. We should go out and do something."

"I hadn't planned much for today because I figured we'd be too tired." Why hadn't he researched jet lag? He should have known they'd need to prepare for that.

"I'm not as tired as I thought I'd be," Willow said.

She unwrapped the towel as she searched in the suitcase for something to wear. Harrison's reaction to her unclothed body was immediate, his dick hardening as only one thought entered his mind.

"At the very least we should go eat," she said, clasping on her bra. She was oblivious to the party taking place below his waist. "Although, to be honest, I'm not all that hungry just yet. Can you believe all the food they fed us on those flights? Back home you're lucky if you get a pack of pretzels."

Why was she talking about pretzels at a time when his dick was trying to drill a hole in the mattress?

He reminded himself that he wasn't going to push for sex. Although, damn, wasn't that what vacation without kids was supposed to be about? It was the first time they'd gone anywhere without Athens and Lily in decades. They should be having sex every minute they were in this room.

Apparently, Willow didn't share those sentiments. Not

if the way she dressed without even throwing a casual look toward the bed was any indication.

Accepting that sex with his wife would not be happening in the next hour, Harrison pushed himself up and changed into gray slacks and a polo shirt. Twenty minutes later, they were on the sidewalk, facing the fountain and the jam packed traffic circle that surrounded it.

"So, what do you want to do first?" he asked.

"I still can't believe that *you* didn't plan anything for today. *You?* That's unheard of."

He shrugged. "Like I said, I assumed we'd be too tired. But we can still find something to do. With as many years as you've been wanting to come here, you must have a laundry list of landmarks you want to see."

"And knowing you, plans to visit all those landmarks are already set in motion."

His wife knew him well. "Of course they are," he answered. "Do you want to just stroll around the neighborhood and look at the architecture?" He stopped. "Hold on a minute." He pulled up the web browser on his cell phone. "Yeah, I knew I'd read this. The national museum is right over there. I didn't add it to the official itinerary because I knew it was close and figured we could dip in there if we found ourselves with some extra time."

She looked over at the pale yellow building, then shook her head. "As much as I love looking at art, it's not exciting enough to keep me awake. We need something that's going to invigorate us."

Tapping her finger to her chin, she turned in a slow circle, examining the area around them. Harrison watched as a smile curved up the corners of her mouth. "That."

He looked over his shoulder to where she was pointing. "What? The sightseeing tour bus?"

"What's wrong with that?"

"They're for tourists."

"Um, hello. We are tourists! Come on, it'll be fun."

She grabbed him by the wrist and tugged.

Their Roman adventure had officially begun.

As the double-decker bus navigated the city's narrow streets, Willow couldn't believe she'd ever—even for a moment—considered not joining Harrison in Rome. It was as if a long-held dream was coming to life in full Technicolor right before her very eyes. She was the one who'd insisted they sit in the bus's uncovered upper deck, so she refused to complain as they both braved the chilly, fifty-degree temperatures. It was worth it. The view from up there was spectacular.

She huddled against Harrison as the soothing, accented voice coming through the earpiece described the various tourists' sites along the route. He wrapped his arm more snuggly around her, and pulled her in even closer. She'd missed the sense of comfort that came from the feel of his solid body against hers. She closed her eyes for a moment just to bask in it.

When they hung the curve on Via del Cardello and the Coliseum came into view, Willow literally gasped at the breathtaking sight.

"Oh, my goodness," she whispered. "I can't believe I'm actually seeing this with my own two eyes." She turned to Harrison. "I can't thank you enough for putting this trip together. It's only been a few hours, and I already know this will be an adventure of a lifetime."

He lifted her hand to his mouth and placed a gentle kiss in the center of her palm. "I did this for you. Enjoy it."

Warmth radiated from the spot he'd kissed, spreading throughout her entire body. She clung to it. Wanted to bathe in it. She never wanted to let go of this feeling of being wholly loved and cherished. Harrison alone could make her feel this way.

When the bus pulled up to the Coliseum stop, Willow insisted they get off.

"It's on our list of places to visit tomorrow," Harrison pointed out.

"I don't care." She tugged on his wrist. "We don't have to go inside. I just want to take a few pictures to send to the kids."

They took silly selfies on the short hill just outside the gates of the ancient stadium, then hopped back on the next bus to finish their circuit of the city.

Willow settled in next to him again and tried to remember the last time she'd been so content to just relax with her husband. It felt like old times, like those days before they had five dozen obligations pulling at them from every corner of their lives. Before cheer camp and karate lessons and SAT practice sessions and dinners with high-paying clients. Before the mountain of commitments and responsibilities that required her to have a desk calendar, phone calendar and a whiteboard hanging on the back of the utility room door.

When had life gotten in the way of...life?

"You hungry yet?" Harrison asked.

"Famished," Willow said, still clutching his arm to her side. "I didn't realize just how hungry until you mentioned it."

He tipped his head toward the next stop, where a line of

people were waiting to get on the bus. He pulled out his phone and showed her a map. "If we get off here and grab something to eat, we can walk back to the hotel. It's only about five blocks."

She looked up at him and smiled. "Sounds perfect."

Warm tingles surged through her stomach at the sight of his answering grin. How had she managed to exist all these weeks without seeing that gorgeous face every day?

They descended the stairs, then ducked into the first restaurant they encountered. At this point, Willow didn't care where they ate, as long as she had something to fill her belly.

It turned out even the tiniest, hole-in-the-wall restaurant in Rome had better Italian food than any she'd ever dined in back home. She and Harrison shared an appetizer of the most incredible calamari she'd ever eaten, then sipped on delicious house red wine while they watched people stroll along Via Barberini.

"I cannot believe I'm eating Italian food, in an Italian restaurant, *in* Italy." Willow reached across the table and covered his hand. "I know how hard that flight was for you. Just the fact that you were willing to take it means so much."

"Holding your hand the entire flight made it bearable," he replied, turning his hand palm up and enclosing her fingers in his. They sat that way for several minutes, neither letting go of the other's hand until the waiter arrived with their meals, carbonara for her, lasagna for Harrison. As usual, they each set aside a small portion of their food for the other to try. But, instead of setting the forkful of pasta onto Harrison's plate, Willow made a spur-of-the-moment decision and held her fork up.

"Open up," she told Harrison, holding out the food for him.

He lifted one brow, an irresistible grin gliding across his lips. He opened his mouth and Willow slid the fork inside. His eyes closed and the moan that resonated from deep in his throat hit her deep in her belly.

"Amazing," he said.

Her focus centered on his mouth and the sheer perfection of it. She'd always loved that mouth, the way his lips were inexplicably soft and firm at the same time. Goodness, but the things she'd experienced courtesy of that mouth. A tremor of sensation quaked through her belly at the thought.

He reciprocated the gesture, holding up a forkful of lasagna for her to sample. Just as the tangy, slightly sweet taste of fresh tomato burst onto her tongue, Harrison's phone tolled with the sound of an incoming text. He looked down at it and cursed.

"What is it?" Willow asked, her mind automatically going to the kids.

Guilt flashed in his eyes. "I need to quickly check email. I told LaKeisha to only contact me if it's an emergency, so the fact that she texted means it must be important."

Willow sat back in her chair and tried not to fall victim to the frustration clawing its way into her psyche. She'd been married to him for too long to expect Harrison to remain true to that no work promise he'd made. Though, it would have been nice to have their very first day be work-free. That didn't seem like too much to ask.

"Dammit," he said.

"Is it bad?" Willow asked.

He looked up from his phone. "The work thing? No. But one of my surprises for you just fell through." He clicked the phone off and set it back on the table. "I just read in an email that the lead in the opera I wanted to take you to has the flu and won't be performing. Dammit."

The opera?

"But you hate that kind of stuff," Willow pointed out. "Especially the opera."

"Yeah, but you love it. This trip is all about you, remember?"

And just like that, her heart melted. The Harrison Holmes she knew would rather peel his own skin off than sit through an opera.

"It's okay, Harrison."

"No, it's not. We are supposed to have a science day and a culture day."

Willow perked up. "A science day?"

He nodded. "And a culture day. There's the opera, and I also set up a private tour of the Da Vinci Museum. It supposedly has all his experiments."

Yep. Heart melting here. *Could this man be any sweeter?*

"I appreciate the fact that you were even willing to go to the opera more than I would appreciate the actual performance." She reached over and trailed her finger across his jaw before tacking on, "But the Da Vinci Museum is a must-do."

"No doubt," he returned with a laugh as he picked up his glass of wine and took a sip. "You know what I was thinking about when I set up that private tour?" he asked, pointing the glass at her before setting it back on the table.

"Hmm?"

"The little science shows you used to put on for Lily and Athens when they were younger. You built those dioramas of the different ecosystems, and always talked about turning it into a TV show for kids. Didn't Ezra talk to an old friend from the paper who'd moved into TV and now works at the local PBS station? Why didn't you follow up with him?"

Willow did her best to stave off the instant resentment that seeped into her bones.

"Why didn't I follow up?" She heard the bite in her tone. "When was I going to follow up, Harrison? Between the twenty minutes I have after dropping Athens off at school and before I go to the grocery store? Where am I supposed to find the time to develop something for TV with two kids to take care of and a household to run?"

His head snapped back as if she'd slapped him, but now that she'd set off on this mini-tirade, Willow couldn't stop.

"There are PTA meetings, snack days at school, 'volunteering' for the spring bizarre and the library book sale and the dozen other things parents are told are volunteer-only, but that you're made to look like a bandit if you don't participate in. All of that stuff has to get done. When am I supposed to work on my little science show?"

Harrison looked as if he'd been bowled over by a raging tidal wave.

"I...I didn't know," he said. "I should have. I should—" He shook his head. "Damn, I'm sorry, Wills."

"No, I'm sorry," she said, her voice hoarse with guilt. "I didn't say any of that to make you feel bad. I just...I—" She glanced up at him and her heart broke at the remorse clouding his face. Her conscience prodded her into owning up to her own culpability. "Harrison, I said all of that because *I'm* the one who feels bad for not following up with Ezra's friend. The opportunity was right there and I let it pass."

"When would you have followed up? You just pointed out how you don't have a minute for yourself. You do so damn much and I don't know the half of it. I just know it all gets done."

Now *he* was making excuses for her.

She had no excuse. And she had no reason to complain. Absolutely none. How could she complain about having to make muffins once a quarter for her kid's school when Harrison sometimes spent weeks working eighteen-hour days?

Willow closed her eyes and took in a deep breath. This was not how she'd pictured things going at their first meal in Italy.

"Harrison—"

"We can look into getting someone to help out at the house again," he offered.

And here came another deluge of guilt.

He'd suggested hiring someone to clean the house more than once over the years, but Willow had always shot down the idea. Not because she couldn't use the help, but because her pride wouldn't let her accept any.

Once her own mother had finally gotten on her feet, she'd been able to raise three children while working a full-time job, going to school at night, and keeping a clean house. What would it say about her if Willow had to hire someone to clean her house when being a stay-at-home mother was her only job?

It didn't matter that her kids were into way more than she and her sisters had been into back when they were growing up. A trip to the library once a week was the extent of the Carter girls' extracurricular activities, while Lily and Athens had scouts, drama club, karate, drill team, study groups and a load of other interests that occupied the family's afternoons and weekends.

And Willow had to admit that she and her sisters had

been required to do more around the house than she required of her children. She was the one who'd decided to do it all on her own, despite Harrison's grumbles about the kids needing more responsibilities. Her kids were already under a mountain of pressure. Willow didn't want to add even more to their plates.

Twenty-five years ago, she wasn't competing with kids who fluently spoke four languages, spent summers building homes in Haiti, or were accomplished pianists and cellists. If Lily and Athens wanted to stand out on their college applications, being a black belt in karate and having a hundred community service hours would stand out much better than knowing how to fold a fitted sheet.

And that's why she couldn't entertain those long-ago ambitions to become the black, female equivalent of Bill Nye the Science Guy. Yes, she'd love to teach kids to enjoy science, but she couldn't do it all. No one could. She'd sacrificed her dreams in order to make sure her kids could follow theirs.

"I have no problem taking care of the house," Willow said. "That's my job."

"But it doesn't have to be," Harrison said. He hesitated for a moment before he added, "Have you ever thought that maybe...maybe this is why you're unhappy?"

He didn't know it, but he'd hit the nail on the head.

"I just need you to be happy, Willow," he continued.

The desperation in his voice tore into her soul. "Harrison, it isn't your job to make me happy."

"Like hell it isn't." His fiercely whispered words sliced through the air. "What good are all those hours I'm putting in at the office if we're not happy?" He impaled her with a look so full of hurt and anguish Willow felt it clear to the bone. "And if you're not happy, I'm not happy.

You are my happiness, Willow. Without you, there just isn't any."

She couldn't speak. What words could she possibly say?

"I just want to know what I can do to bring us back to the way we used to be," Harrison pleaded.

"I do too," she managed to utter past the lump in her throat. She closed her eyes. She couldn't face these emotions, not right now.

"I can't do this right now, Harrison."

"Willow—"

"I know," she said, cutting him off before he could say anything else. But he wouldn't back down.

"We can't keep putting off this conversation."

"I *know*." She opened her eyes, and with a soft plea in her voice, repeated, "I know. But this conversation deserves more than either of us can give it right now. We're dead on our feet. We can't talk about this when jet lag is creeping up on us.

"We *are* going to talk. Just not...not right now. Please, Harrison. Can we have these first couple of days to just enjoy ourselves? I want to enjoy this. Enjoy *you*! These last few hours have been so amazing. To think that this is just the start to our week makes me happier than I can even describe. I don't want this dark cloud hanging over our heads the entire time." She pleaded with him. "I *promise* we will talk."

His reluctance was palpable, but he didn't push her to continue. Willow's shoulders practically wilted with relief.

They finished up their meal in near silence, with Harrison occasionally commenting on passersby. Willow declined dessert—something she'd vowed she would not do while here in Italy—because fatigue from all those hours in the air had finally caught up with her.

As they followed the GPS's directions back to their hotel, Willow linked her arm in the curve of Harrison's and leaned her head against his upper arm. They'd only tiptoed around the edges of the conversation they needed to have, yet the little they'd discussed had been enough to drain her.

You're stalling.

No, she wasn't. She knew what she was up against. She knew they would have to delve much deeper if they were going to save their marriage. She just didn't have it in her right now.

What she wouldn't give to click her heels three times and return to the relationship she'd shared with Harrison for the nearly two decades they'd been together.

You're in Rome, not Oz.

Repairing her marriage wouldn't be that easy. Nothing worth fighting for ever was.

By the time they arrived back at the hotel, Willow was dead on her feet. But her exhaustion took a back seat to anxiety the moment she opened her suitcase and encountered the satin and lace nightgowns Jade had bullied her into buying. Why had she listened to her sister? Why hadn't she anticipated the reality that now lay before her, the fact that she and her husband were about to share a bed for the first time in over two months?

Goodness, *two months!*

It had started back when Athens caught a stomach bug that had been making its way around his school. Willow spent the night in his room, and even though it had turned out to be only a twenty-four hour virus, she'd felt uneasy leaving Athens alone the following night. Not wanting to disturb Harrison the day before his first big meeting with the Delmonicos, she'd slept in the guest room upstairs so that she could check in on Athens throughout the night.

Then the next night. Then the next. And the next.

A few weeks later, she and Harrison had made the decision to take a break and he'd moved out.

But they were together now. And they were about to slide underneath the covers and share this big, comfortable bed.

Would he expect them to do *more* than just sleep? Why wouldn't he? A healthy sex life had been one of the most enjoyable elements of their relationship. Reaching over in the middle of the night and climbing on top of her husband was as normal as breathing.

But there was nothing normal about the atmosphere between them these days. And engaging in any kind of physical intimacy tonight would be nothing more than putting a temporary Band-Aid on the various scars currently marring their marriage.

The bathroom door opened, and Harrison walked out wearing forest green pajama pants and nothing else.

Then again, it had been a long time since she'd had sex, and her body could use some.

His bare chest beckoned, enticing her with all that smooth skin and those firm muscles that fit exquisitely underneath her cheek. He didn't have the chiseled, washboard abs he'd had in his twenties, but that had never been her definition of perfection. The perfect male body was the one standing before her. She was married to one of the sexiest men she'd ever encountered. Hands down.

"The bathroom is yours," he said, knocking her out of her lust-filled daze.

"Oh." Willow shook her head. "Thank—thank you."

Even though she'd showered before they left, Willow needed another after being out all afternoon. She didn't want to take too long, though. Given how tired she was, she was afraid she'd fall asleep under the spray. When she exited the bathroom ten minutes later, she found Harrison standing at the window, looking out over the piazza below.

"Beautiful, isn't it?" Willow said, coming up behind him. She fought the urge to wrap her arms around his middle and rest her cheek against his bare back.

He looked over at her and grinned. "I have to admit, I didn't do half bad with the location."

He turned and gestured with his chin to the seating area. A bottle of red wine and a slim, rectangular tray of fresh fruit covered in plastic wrap sat on the small round table. "That arrived while you were in the shower. Maybe we can have some dessert after all."

The sight of the fruit and wine instantly conjured memories of their fifteenth wedding anniversary. Harrison surprised her by sending the kids to his parents' for the night and turning their house into a den of seduction. He'd gone all out, having food from her favorite restaurant delivered, followed by a couple's bath and a night of nearly continuous lovemaking. The next morning, he'd greeted her with breakfast in bed, which included fruit that made it to places that caused Willow to blush even now.

She wondered if he'd had that night in mind when he ordered these from room service.

"It's courtesy of the management," he said, sticking a pin in the tantalizing thought bubble her imagination had concocted.

"Oh," she said. "Well, that was nice of them."

Her eyes darted to the bed, then back to the fruit.

"You're ready for bed, aren't you?" Harrison asked. He slipped the tray into the small refrigerator Willow hadn't even realized was hidden behind a panel on the dresser. "This should keep until tomorrow."

Then he rounded the other side of the bed—*his* side of the bed. He got in and pulled up the covers, tucking them underneath his arms and turning onto his side.

Willow just stood there like a tree stump.

After a few moments, Harrison looked over his shoulder. "What's wrong?"

"Uh, nothing." She shook her head to clear it. "Nothing. I'm fine. I'm good."

But she wasn't good.

Willow wasn't sure what she'd been expecting, but it wasn't for her husband of seventeen years to simply go to sleep after getting in bed with her for the first time in two months. Maybe it was the romance of the city, or the way he'd held her close on the tour bus and their walk back to the hotel, or the emotion she'd witnessed in his eyes as he ardently proclaimed his desire to make her happy. Whatever it was, it had set up an expectation of...well...*some*thing to happen tonight.

Willow struggled to suppress her confusion as she climbed in next to him. She turned out the light on the gooseneck lamp above her side of the bed, plunging the room into darkness.

She drew the duvet over her shoulders, then pushed it down a minute later. She twisted onto her right side, then onto her left. No matter how hard she tried, she could not get comfortable.

"Willow, what's wrong?" Harrison asked.

"Nothing," she quickly said.

Liar. There was definitely something wrong. And she knew exactly what it was.

She was horny for her own damn husband!

All this time she'd been trying to figure out how to gently let Harrison down when he undoubtedly tried something tonight, yet *she* was the one who had to resist climbing over to his side of the bed and trailing her lips along all that smooth, bare skin.

A groan escaped her throat.

"Willow?" Harrison repeated.

"Don't mind me," she said.

I'll just be over here wondering how I'm supposed to sleep in a bed with you all night and have that be the only *thing we do.*

Chapter Seven

Willow woke up with one leg wrapped around Harrison's solid thigh, the top half of her body draped over his. His large hand possessively palmed her ass, while a thick, telltale bulge pulsed deliciously against her inner thigh. The temptation to slip her hand inside his waistband and wrap her fingers around his hardening length was almost too strong to fight.

But she fought it. She'd come to the realization overnight that it was better if she and Harrison didn't become intimate again without at least addressing some of their issues, and she didn't want to send any mixed signals that could be misconstrued. An early morning hand job definitely fell into the mixed signals category.

So instead of giving in to the urge to make all kinds of wicked love to her husband, she carefully levered herself off him and climbed out of the bed. As she stared down at Harrison sprawled across the rumpled linens, Willow questioned her good judgment. What sane woman would walk away from all the pleasure that strong, solid body would provide? All she had to do was ask and Harrison would be hers for the taking.

Why not do it? What was the harm in pretending, just for this week, that everything between them was normal?

"You know why," she whispered.

With a sigh, she left him in bed and went into the bathroom to get ready. When she walked out ten minutes later, she found Harrison standing over a map of the city he'd spread across the foot of the bed.

"Want to hear today's game plan?" he asked.

As he gave her a rundown of his hour-by-hour itinerary, Willow suppressed her annoyance as best she could. She'd expected this. She knew her husband well enough to know he'd planned this vacation down to the very breaths they would take.

What she wouldn't give to see him act impulsively just once! To say to hell with schedules and appointments and minute-by-minute itineraries. But he'd hesitated at visiting the Coliseum yesterday because it wasn't part of his carefully laid plans, even though they were right there. Could she truly expect him to throw caution to the wind and be spontaneous?

"How's all that sound?" Harrison asked, excitement dancing in his eyes.

"It sounds like a lot," Willow said. "But we've got a lot to see," she quickly added. She didn't want him to think she didn't appreciate the work he'd put in to making this trip special.

The smile that once lit up her entire world broke out across his face. He nodded toward the bathroom. "Give me just a few minutes in there and we'll get started."

A half-hour later, Willow was ready to take back every unflattering thought she'd had about Harrison's meticulous planning. They seemed to be one step ahead of the crowds at every tourist site they visited. When they entered the Pantheon, the temple was practically empty. As she stood underneath the opening in the ancient structure's magnificent dome, Willow clutched her fists tight and fought the urge to scream with glee. She was positively giddy as the sun shone down on her head.

"I can't believe I'm actually here," she whispered to Harrison.

"I can't believe they built this thing almost two thousand years ago. We have to come back here with the kids one day. Athens would be blown away to see something like this still standing."

She whipped around. "Come back? Have you forgotten about that long flight you'd have to take?"

"I'm not saying we come back next week. I'll need some recovery time. But yeah, I'm willing to take that flight again so the kids can see this."

Willow grinned. "You're just determined to live up to that #1 *Dad* T-shirt Lily gave you, aren't you?"

"Damn right."

They left the Pantheon and headed east, walking past several galleries, yet another basilica, and numerous restaurants. Willow picked up the pace when she heard a faint rumbling sound that gradually grew louder the further they walked. They turned the corner and she gasped.

"Oh, my God." She stood stock-still for a second before turning to Harrison. "Do you know what this is?"

He held up the map he'd taken from the hotel's front desk, but Willow could tell he wasn't looking at it. The smile on his face stretched from ear to ear. "According to this it's called Trevi Fountain." He looked up at her. "Is it supposed to be famous or something?"

Willow burst out laughing as she grabbed him by the arm and tugged him toward the guardrail. They snapped a couple of selfies for the kids and then accepted an offer from a fellow tourist to take their photo. A heady sensation enveloped her as they posed for the camera, Harrison's arm wrapped around her middle, his chin tucked against her neck. She didn't have to look at the picture to know that this one was frameable. She already had the perfect spot on the mantle for it.

"Not bad," Harrison said, holding the phone up to her. The happy couple staring back at her on the phone's sleek screen filled Willow with a sense of hope that had been missing from her life this past year. For the first time in a long time, her smile wasn't fake. That was true happiness in her eyes.

They did the customary coin toss over their shoulders and into the fountain, but when Harrison started to walk away, she stayed him, grabbing his wrist.

"Not yet," Willow said. "Can I have just a few minutes to soak this all in?"

His eyes softened with his gentle smile. "Of course," he said. "Take all the time you want."

She squeezed his hand. "Thank you."

Willow focused her attention on the iconic fountain, absorbing the momentousness of the moment, allowing it to seep into her soul. How many times had she dreamed of this? To be standing here right now, hearing the water rushing over the polished travertine and marble. It was unlike anything the little eight-year-old who'd been obsessed with Audrey Hepburn and Gregory Peck ever dreamed she would experience.

When she turned from the fountain, she found

Harrison standing a few feet away, holding his phone up to her.

"Are you recording me?" Willow asked.

"I had to. I needed to capture the look on your face right now." He lowered the phone and stared at her, naked adoration emanating from his tender gaze. "You're breathtaking, Willow."

Her heart swelled as a fierce yearning surged through her, tearing through the dense web of excuses she'd weaved around herself over the past year. How could she ever question the love staring back at her? How could she think—even for a moment—that she and Harrison weren't meant to be?

This man was her soul mate. It didn't matter that their relationship was no longer the storybook fairytale she'd thought it would always be. It was still, without question, the absolute best part of her.

Willow reached for his hand.

"This takes my breath away," she said. "All of it."

She stood on her tip toes and placed a delicate kiss against his lips. She wanted to do more. She wanted to push her tongue inside his mouth and devour him. Lust carved a path through her bloodstream, baiting her like the call of the sirens found in marble statues all around this city. It was a seductive force, tempting her to ignore the problems plaguing their marriage and lose herself in the romance of the moment.

But she couldn't. There was still too much unsaid—too much they needed to work through. A simple kiss would have to suffice. For now.

Harrison requested an Uber to take them to the Museo Leonardo da Vinci for their private tour. As they progressed from one fantastical invention to another, Willow reverted back to that bright-eyed little girl who fell in love with learning how things worked. She was blown away as she viewed the Renaissance genius's sketchbook, marveling at the way da Vinci's mind worked.

"I think you're right," Willow said. She looked over her shoulder at Harrison. "We have to bring Athens and Lily to see this. I want them to love science the way I did—the way I *do*," she corrected.

He held up his phone. "All it takes is a call to the travel agent. But that's for later. This time, it's for us to enjoy alone." He looked at his watch. "Speaking of enjoying ourselves, there's something else I had on the itinerary that I thought would have to wait until later in the week. But since this tour took less time than I'd anticipated, we can do it now."

They exited the museum and Harrison hailed a cab. Less than ten minutes later, they were dropped off at the base of the famed Spanish Steps.

"I wondered if we'd get the chance to see this," Willow said as she jumped out of the cab. "Do you think we have time to visit the church at the top?"

Harrison pulled something up on his phone. "We still have hours to kill. Our tour of the Vatican and St. Peter's Basilica isn't until four."

"Good! Because after this I want to walk through the Villa Borghese gardens. Let's go!"

Less than half way into their climb, Willow started to regret all those spinning classes she'd skipped. By the time they reached the church at the pinnacle of the steps, it felt as if the fires of hell were licking at her thighs. She took a moment to catch her breath and vowed to add a couple of extra aerobic days to her workout schedule as soon as they returned home.

The crowd on the steps' top landing was thicker than those they'd encountered at the other sites they'd visited today, but as she looked out over the balustrade, Willow understood why everyone congregated here. The view was like something out of a dream.

"Stand right there," Harrison said. "Don't move."

"What are you—" Willow watched as he walked over to an old man selling roses to tourists. He returned with a single stem. Before handing it to her, he pulled out his phone and swiped across the screen with his thumb. He held up the phone as he finally handed her the rose.

"You saw this picture a few years ago of a woman standing on the Spanish Steps looking out at the city below."

Willow gasped. "You remembered that?" She stared in amazement at the photo he'd taken from a magazine advertisement for perfume. "Where'd you even find this picture?"

"I've had it in my phone for years. You refused to throw away that copy of *Essence* magazine. Sometimes I would catch you staring at it with this faraway look on your face." He hunched his shoulders. "I could see how much you longed to be here." He handed her the rose. "I wanted you to have this moment."

Could a heart actually burst with gratitude? Everyone standing here was about to find out, because Willow doubted her heart could contain the emotions filling it right now.

She mimicked the model's pose, holding the soft petals up to her nose as she stared out at the city stretching in front of them. After capturing the picture, she and Harrison went over to the Trinità dei Monti, but discovered the church was closed to tourists at the moment.

"Do you want to wait until it reopens?" Harrison asked.

Willow shook her head. "I want some time to see the Villa Borghese."

They left the Spanish Steps and strolled along the Piazza Trinita dei Monti, the small stretch connecting the Piazza di Spagna to one of the entrances to the Borghese family's famed villa.

"So we're just going to walk around some old Italian family's gardens?" Harrison asked.

"I promise you'll love it," Willow insisted.

"Is it as nice as my backyard landscaping?"

She held her thumb and forefinger a few centimeters apart. "Maybe just a little."

"Just a little huh?" Harrison said fifteen minutes later as they ambled along past the marble busts that lined the Pincio Promenade.

"Hey, don't sell yourself short. We do okay, but we don't have Borghese money."

Harrison looked around. "I doubt the entire state of Louisiana has Borghese money."

Her loud burst of laughter interrupted the tranquility of the quiet gardens, but she couldn't help it. Harrison had always been a genius at putting a smile on her face.

He squeezed her hand. "It feels good to hear that sound again," he said. "It's been too long since I heard you laugh."

Willow dipped her head. She could feel a blush forming on her cheeks. "Not all that long."

"Long enough," he countered. "I'm not talking about the occasional laugh when Athens cracks one of his corny jokes. I'm talking about a *real* laugh. The kind I used to hear often. And a real smile, like the one you're wearing now." His voice took on a solemn note. "I'm sorry I haven't been able to put a smile on your face, Willow."

Sadness, laden with guilt, settled within her chest. It

was unfair to allow him to assume responsibility for the state of their marriage when she was just as much to blame. Willow took him by the hand and guided him to one of the wooden benches lining the walkway. Once seated, she flattened her palms on her thighs and stared at the tour group huddled around Embriaco's water clock, where she and Harrison had just visited.

"None of this is entirely your fault," Willow finally spoke. She looked over at him. "You know that, don't you?"

"You keep saying that, but it doesn't change the way I feel." His earnest gaze sent another arrow of guilt straight through her chest. "I live to make you happy, Wills. That's why this past year has been so damn hard. Sensing you weren't happy and not knowing how to fix it; it's been driving me crazy."

"If it were as easy as you fixing it, we would have been fixed months ago. *Fixing* things is what you do." She reached over and took his hand. "But there is no easy fix for this."

"What *is* this, Willow? What broke between us?"

She turned more fully toward him, bringing one leg up on the bench. She caught sight of a small orange insect creeping along the bench's edge and let it crawl onto her finger. As she observed the bug, Willow tilted her head to the side and said, "Did I tell you Jade was in New Orleans a few days ago? She had speaking engagements at Tulane and Loyola." Willow watched as the bug flittered away. "She was only in the city for the day, but she and I had the chance to hang out and talk."

"Okay," he said, dragging the word out a little. "So, what did Jade have to say?"

Turning her attention to him, she continued. "Well, you know my sister. She isn't one to play Monday morning quarterback when it comes to her profession. But we talked about some of the big life changes that have taken place over the last year, and how those things can affect a family, both positively and negatively. We've had a lot of those this year, Harrison. The biggest being the loss of your mom."

He sucked in a breath and let it out slowly. "Yeah, that's a blow that's still being felt."

"And it will continued to be felt for a long, *long* time. I loved your mother so much. She was truly one of my very best friends."

The corner of his mouth tipped up in a small smile. "Everyone used to say if she had to choose between the two of us, she would have chosen you."

A crack of laughter shot out of her mouth. "You know that's not true."

He shook his head and rubbed the light stubble shadowing his jaw. "I'm not too sure about that. Mama loved her some Willow."

She laughed, but then sobered, staring out once again at the 19th century clock.

"It's still so hard for me to accept that she's gone." She fought against the swell of sorrow that attempted to overwhelm her. "But Diane's death is just the tip of the iceberg. There have been so many changes—stressors, as Jade referred to them. You transitioning to partner in Jonathan's law firm, compounded with Athens's pre-diabetes diagnosis, and now this thing with Lily." Her shoulders slumped as the weight of everything once again settled into her bones. "Jade believes I may be suffering from something called situational depression. And after reading up on it, I think she may be onto something."

"You're depressed?"

"Well, yes," she said. "Think of all the things I just

listed. Does it really come as a shock that it would lead to me feeling a bit depressed?"

"So that's why we're separated?"

"The depression isn't what caused us to grow apart, Harrison. I think it's a result of us growing apart. It's not a chicken or egg kind of thing. It's fed into this feeling."

He clamped his hands together and stared straight ahead. After a few moments passed, he asked, "Did Jade offer suggestions about how to fix it? Do you need to be on antidepressants or anything?"

"No." Willow shook her head. "At least I don't think so. Jade did recommend I talk to someone. She gave me the name of a doctor she knows back home. I plan to call him once we get back."

"Okay," he said with a nod. "That's good. If this is what you think you need in order to feel better, let's do it."

"Honestly, I think I'm starting to come out of the depression. As more time passes, and some of the stress starts to subside, it'll get better."

"But there will always be stress, Wills."

"Yes, but not to this level. Not only did we experience really huge stressors, they all seemed to pile up at once. But Athens's health has taken a turn for the better. Things are still a bit chaotic at the law practice, but it isn't nearly as bad as it was when you first became a partner. And while we're nowhere near over losing Diane, it feels as if we're finally starting to heal. Establishing the foundation has helped with that."

A smile drew across his face. "It has," Harrison said. "She would be proud of what we've done."

"So proud," Willow agreed.

He looked over at her. "What about *us*? Are *we* starting to heal?"

Willow mulled the question over for several long moments before finally answering.

"Yes," she said. "I think so." She regarded him with a thoughtful smile. "We needed this. We needed this time together to just talk. The more we can talk things through, the more we can continue to heal what's broken."

Harrison held his hand out to her. She captured it, entwining their fingers as they continued their stroll. They visited the Temple of Diana, then moved on to the Borghese Gallery. They hadn't booked tickets ahead of time so they couldn't view the artwork inside the museum, but Willow was happy to simply walk around the outside of the beautiful stone building and admire the amazing architecture.

"Maybe I shouldn't have kept this trip a surprise," Harrison said. "If I knew this was a place you wanted to visit, we could have ordered tickets ahead of time."

"Don't." Willow placed her hand against his chest. "This is perfect, Harrison. Every detail is just...it's perfect."

The tender yearning she witnessed in his steady gaze sent an arrow of longing straight through Willow's heart. He lifted the hand she'd placed on his chest and pressed a delicate kiss to the center of her palm. Then, with aching gentleness, he lowered his head and treated her lips to the same show of affection.

It was an innocent kiss, even more so than the kiss they'd shared at Trevi Fountain. Yet that strange concoction of emotions—fear, excitement, panic, desire—churned through her once again. What did she think would happen? That he would demand they go back to living together without addressing the issues in their marriage simply because she let him kiss her?

The irrationality of it struck her like a slap to the face. This was *Harrison*, for God's sake. If she made a list of all the people in the world she should fear, Harrison Holmes would be last on the list. He wouldn't even be *on* the list.

Where had this feeling come from? When had this started?

There wasn't a particular time or incident she could point back to. There had been a gradual build-up, like everything else that had led them to this point. Guilt over her dinner with Marcus, the mundane routineness that came with seventeen years of marriage, the general stress of life—all of it had contributed to this unfamiliar distance between them.

Willow reined in the anxiety his kiss stirred within her. The first step in finding their way back to each other would be to return to being the affectionate couple they once were. When he started to pull away, she slipped her hand behind Harrison's head and drew him in for another kiss. A deeper kiss. A kiss like the ones they used to share.

His shoulders went rigid for a moment before relaxing into the kiss. He captured her jaw in his palm and held her steady, tilting their heads and deepening the kiss. His mouth opened wider and he sucked her tongue inside. Willow leaned in closer, relishing the solid feel of his chest, its strength so familiar, so comforting.

She backed him up against the marble building and flattened her front to his. They stood there kissing like a couple of teenagers experiencing fresh, new love. But for Willow this *did* feel new. It had been so long since she and her husband had just existed like this, sharing the deep, soul-stirring love that had always been the cornerstone of their union. She could barely contain the myriad emotions swirling through her as she once again felt Harrison's love wash over her.

How she wished this kiss could be the balm they

needed to mend what was broken between them. If only it could vanquish the discontent that had built up over these months they'd spent gradually growing apart.

They'd forgotten how to be a couple. Everything in their lives revolved around the kids, or the family, or his work. None of it was about them anymore. A marriage couldn't thrive—it couldn't survive—if the focus was constantly centered on things outside of it, without ever looking within.

But, for the first time in a long time, it felt as if they'd turned a corner. She and Harrison had talked more in the day and a half they'd been in Rome than in the last two months. They would find their way back to each other. The certainty of it filled her with a sense of hope she'd been lacking for far too long.

When Harrison finally released her lips, the smile on his handsome face felt like a ray of sunshine on a dark and gloomy day. He pressed a kiss to her forehead before resting his against it.

"God, I've missed that," he whispered.

"Me too," Willow said.

He captured her face in his palms, caressing her cheeks with the soft brush of his thumbs. "So why haven't we done it more often, Wills? Why did we stop?"

"That's what we need to figure out," she said.

"Are you ready to do that?" he asked.

Willow knew what her answer would signify. It would be a promise to reveal things she'd kept hidden for nearly a year.

She should have done so a long time ago.

She nodded. "Yes. I'm ready. Understanding how we got here is going to help us find our way back to what we used to be." She cupped his jaw. In a desperate whisper, she said, "Because that's what I want, baby. I want my husband. I want my marriage. I want *us*." She caressed the side of his face with the pad of her thumb. "I love you, Harrison."

His expressive eyes brimmed with relief and gratitude.

"I love you too," he said. He brushed his mouth against hers. Their lips still touching, he said, "Not that long ago, I thought all it would take is the two of us saying those words to each other to make everything okay. But I realize now that it won't be so easy."

"No, it won't be easy," Willow said. She lifted her face and looked him in the eyes. "But it will be worth it."

You need to get up and out of this bed.

Harrison knew what he *needed* to do. He'd been looking forward to this day in particular ever since he and his travel agent finalized the itinerary for this trip. He had one goal today: to blow Willow's mind. It would all start with a private tour of a winery by a local guide who was scheduled to pick them up in another hour. Which is why he needed to get out of bed and start getting ready.

But how in the hell was he supposed to leave this?

For the second morning in a row, Harrison found himself waking up with his wife's luscious, petite body draped across him. Her breasts spilled temptingly out of the top of the lacy gown she wore—a gown he'd never seen before. A gown she must have bought specifically for this trip. From the moment he'd first laid eyes on it, he'd started reading way more into that silky nightgown than he should have.

Was she trying to tell him something with her tempting

choice of sleepwear? Or had she simply gone shopping because she was due for a new gown?

He wanted it to be the former, but Harrison was too afraid to ask. If he did ask and found out it was the latter, his fucking heart with shatter into a million pieces. It's the same reason he'd suffered through a second night of unquenchable lust, but hadn't made any attempt to satiate himself. If he tried to become intimate with Willow and she rejected him, Harrison knew it would crush him for the rest of the trip.

Yet, things had taken a turn yesterday. Not only did Willow *not* shy away from his touch, she *initiated* a fair amount on her own. Just thinking about that kiss in the gardens caused his blood to stir. The way her tongue pushed into his mouth, as if she couldn't get enough of him. The way her body melted against his, as if she wanted to lose herself in him.

But there was a big difference between holding hands and a few kisses, and what he wanted to do in this bed right now. It would be a mistake to assume that Willow would be open to sleeping together again simply because of what happened yesterday.

As he stared up at the ceiling and listened to the cadence of her delicate breathing, Harrison tried to recall back to when the act of making love to his wife had become such a foreign concept. That trip to Philadelphia had been the biggest turning point in his mind, but as he thought back on it, Harrison recognized that it hadn't happened overnight. It had been a gradual shift.

Maybe there was something to those stressors Willow mentioned yesterday. He'd undergone those same life events, why hadn't he ever considered their effect on him? He'd spent so much time and energy worrying about his dad becoming depressed that he hadn't taken the time to look inside.

Although, for him, it wasn't depression as much as it was body-numbing anxiety and stress. And, if he were being honest, he could admit that it had started well before his mother's death. It was even before he'd transitioned to partner at the law firm. For him, the earth shifted underneath his feet the moment he made the decision to leave Bossier, Guidry & Associates.

During his ugliest time at Bossier, sex had been his greatest stress reliever. Back then, knowing his wife was waiting for him at home was the only thing that got him through the day. He would turn to Willow five, six times a week, desperate for the escape he found in her arms.

After a while, the stress had started affecting him in a way he'd heard about from other men, but based on the healthy sex life he and Willow had always enjoyed, had never in a million years thought would apply to him. But the responsibility of juggling multi-million dollar mergers and keeping up with the younger, hotshot lawyers trying to make a name for themselves in the firm had definitely had an adverse impact on him. The desire had been there, but after a while, the pressure of his job wouldn't allow him to use sex as a distraction. It had consumed every hour of his day.

Harrison didn't have any performance anxiety to contend with right now. If he had even the smallest indication that his advances would be welcomed, he'd say to hell with the winery and spend the entire morning tearing up these sheets with his wife.

His hips lurched upwards. He ached with the need to bury himself in Willow's warm, welcoming body. To feel her soft thighs caressing his face as he feasted on the paradise between her legs. He could still taste her, even after all these months. Her flavor was imbued on his tongue.

But just because he was eager to get back to the exuberant sex life they'd once shared, that didn't mean Willow was ready. Even before they left home, Harrison had mentally prepared himself for this reality. The thought of sex not happening when they had an entire week without the threat of children walking in on them for the first time in years was enough to make him cry, but that's where they were. Willow had to be the one to make that call.

God, please let her make the right call.

He let out an audible groan and tried his best to ignore his aching cock.

"Hmmm?" Willow's low murmur reverberated across his chest as she nestled against him.

"Hey," Harrison whispered. "Are you awake?"

She looked up at him. Her sleepy, sexy grin took the situation in his pants to an entirely new, painful level. His pajama bottoms were seconds away from full-on tent status.

She shifted, settling her chin on his chest. "Yes, I'm awake," she answered. "One thing you can say about these Italians, they don't skimp when it comes to the mattresses in their hotels. I haven't slept this well in ages."

Or maybe it had something to do with the fact that she was back in his arms again. Did she even consider that?

"So, what's on the agenda for today?" she asked, her eyes bright with excitement.

"It's a surprise," he said. She pinched his side. "Hey!"

"Tell me," she demanded.

"Can't a man surprise his wife without her attacking him?"

She pinched him again. "Tell. Me."

He peered down at her, one brow raised. "Or what?"

A mischievous smile curved up the corners of her mouth. "Or I start biting." She nipped the spot just below his breastbone and Harrison nearly jumped clean off the bed.

Sweet mother of God.

"Come on, Harrison. Tell me."

Did she really expect him to speak? Could she not feel how hard his dick was right now?

"I...uh...I hired a car—" he started, but then his phone rang, shattering the playful mood.

"Is it the kids?" Willow asked, pushing herself up. "What time is it back home?"

"The kids should still be sleeping," Harrison said as he reached for the phone. He frowned at the screen. "It's a local number. Hello?" he answered. As he listened to the raspy voice struggling to speak on the other end of the line, he sensed all his plans crumbling like a wall of ancient bricks. Served him right for scheduling a trip during flu season.

"I understand," he said with a sigh. He ended the call and tossed his phone on the bed. "Shit."

"What's wrong?"

"Our driver has the flu."

"Driver?"

Harrison pitched his head back against the headboard. "I hired a driver to take us on a private tour of the countryside today," he said. "We're supposed to visit a winery and have a picnic at his family's small vineyard. But the entire clan is sick." He slammed his hand on the mattress. "First the opera singer, and now this."

"It's okay," Willow said as she drew up alongside him. "I love the thought behind it. That's what counts."

"No, what counts is touring the damn Italian country-side and drinking wine like I planned for us to do."

"Well, why can't we still do that?" She scooted off the bed and grabbed hold of his wrist, tugging him into a sitting position. "I know how much you love following your little plans, but things don't always go the way we want them to go."

"My little plans?" He huffed out a laugh. "Thanks, Wills."

She returned his smile. She was so damn gorgeous, even with remnants of sleep crusting around her eyes.

"To be fair, I would be lost without your schedules. They keep me sane. But we're on vacation, let's be sponta-neous for once. Why don't we rent our own car and tour the countryside on our own?"

"Hmm," he mused. "That idea has some merit."

She rolled her eyes and tugged his arm again. "Would you come on?"

"What about the picnic?"

She threw her hands up in the air. "We'll put together our own picnic!"

Harrison had to fight the urge to laugh at her impa-tience. God, she was cute when she was ready to strangle him.

"I don't know about this," he said.

"Come on! That little convenience store on the next block has better meats and cheeses than high-end grocery stores back home. We'll buy a couple of bottles of wine and just drive. Where was the vineyard?" Willow asked.

"Umbria?"

"Ah, you see! If we're going to venture outside of Rome, I'd rather drive down to the Amalfi Coast. This is a blessing in disguise. Let's go!"

This time he let her pull him up. Even though the thought of renting a car and driving without having a clue as to what they were going to do was as appealing as getting a root canal without Novocain, Willow's enthusiasm lessened his anxiety.

Harrison knew she only tolerated his regimented way of thinking because she loved him. It wouldn't hurt to be spontaneous and carefree for once, would it? Even if it did, it wasn't as if he hadn't worked his way through a panic attack or two in his life.

He called down to the hotel's concierge, who called back in less than twenty minutes with news that he was able to secure a car. An hour later, Harrison and Willow settled in their rented Fiat convertible, armed with a GPS, an overnight bag, and the hotel's phone number in case they got lost.

"You ready?" Willow asked, smiling from her place behind the wheel.

"I'm ready," Harrison answered. "Let's get this adventure started."

Willow had demanded she drive once the valet pulled the rental up to the curb. They'd looked at the Fiat a few months ago when shopping for a car for Liliana. The plan was to give it to her for her high school graduation, but after this fighting business, Harrison wasn't sure she deserved a new car. That little sedan she got from Ezra would have to do for now.

They headed south, following the GPS's directions out of Roma proper. Twenty miles into their journey, Willow pulled onto the shoulder and turned over the driving duties to him.

"As much as I love driving this cute car, I don't want to

spend the entire trip concentrating on the road ahead," she said.

Harrison took over, grateful for the clear skies and slightly warm weather. He had an appreciation for once-in-a-lifetime experiences, and driving through the Italian countryside with the top down and his awed wife at his side was one he never imagined he'd have. An hour outside of Rome, he ignored the GPS's directions to continue on E45, turning east instead toward the village of Valle Fioretta. He pulled up to a roadside market and bought fresh fruit for them to snack on, then continued on toward the coast.

The highway led them to the town of Terracina.

"Have you ever heard of this one?" Harrison asked Willow.

She shook her head. "No. It looks interesting, though, doesn't it?" She reached for his phone. A minute later, she read from whatever website she'd pulled up. "There's a cathedral that was once dedicated to St. Peter. Should we go?"

Harrison shrugged. "Why not? That's the point of being spontaneous, right?"

Willow's face lit up with her bright smile. "I'm so proud of you," she said. She leaned over and kissed his cheek. "I told you being spontaneous could be fun."

They found the ancient cathedral and spent more than an hour touring it. In the most surprising role reversal of the trip so far, it was Willow who had to convince *him* that it was time to leave. He could have spent hours looking at the amazing frescos and stunning architecture.

They continued their drive, journeying along the highway that hugged the coastline, but after just twenty minutes Harrison found himself pulling to the side of the road yet again. There was barely enough space for the little

Fiat in the space he'd parked in on the mountain side of the road, but it would have to do.

"What's wrong?" Willow asked.

He shut off the ignition and opened the door. "If I don't take a minute to enjoy this view I'm going to drive us off the cliff. Let's go."

They got out of the car and, grabbing on to each other's hands, darted to the other side of the highway. There was just enough space between the roadway and the guardrail for his peace of mind. He needed to enjoy this without worrying about a car sideswiping them.

Harrison stood there for a moment, just taking it all in. Colorful homes dotted the mountainside, rising up from the shore and along the face of the mountain.

"This looks like something from a postcard," he said.

"Can you imagine waking up to this view every day?" Willow asked. "It's absolutely breathtaking."

"Yes, it is," he said, his eyes focused solely on her. He'd been waking up to her breathtaking beauty for nearly twenty years. He'd never imagined a time when her gorgeous face wouldn't be the first thing he saw when he woke up in the morning.

He couldn't go back to waking up alone.

"Willow—"

She turned to him. "How much longer until we reach Naples?" she asked, cutting off the plea Harrison was about to make. It was just as well. Bringing up the issues that plagued their marriage would ruin the relaxed, carefree atmosphere they'd enjoyed so far. They deserved at least one day without their marital problems intruding on their fun.

"According to the GPS, we should be there a little

before two o'clock," he said. "That is, of course, if we don't stop again."

"Soooooo, you're saying we should be there by four?" Willow asked with a laugh.

"If we're lucky." Grinning, he hitched his head toward the car. "Come on, we still have a lot of coastline to see."

They meandered along the winding mountain road, which afforded a stunning view of the Tyrrhenian Sea. It was like something out of a travel magazine. That agonizing plane ride was worth every anxious, nerve-wracking minute just for the chance to witness this spectacular view.

"So, are you still upset that your plans to visit the winery fell through?" Willow asked.

Harrison shook his head. "Not even a little bit. I don't care how nice the pictures were on their website, there's no way that vineyard could match what we've seen today."

"Told you," she said. She twisted in her seat and rested her head against the smooth leather, a small smile playing across her lips. "There's something to be said for just going with the flow, especially when on vacation."

"I guess so."

"Oh, you guess so." She laughed. She ran her hand up and down his arm. "You should treat all our vacations like this. It too often turns into a job for you."

"What are you talking about?" He glanced over at her. "I don't treat vacations like a job."

"Really?" she said with a snort. "How about that trip up to Chattanooga a few years ago? Are you saying you didn't go just a wee bit overboard?"

"I wouldn't say I went overboard."

Her burst of laughter echoed through the car. "Oh, please. We didn't even touch the board games we brought to play in the evenings. You had so much planned during the day that the kids were exhausted by the time we got back to the cabin."

"I just wanted to make sure they saw everything, that's all," he said with a shrug.

Willow shook her head, still laughing. "Admit it, Harrison. You're a control freak."

He wouldn't deny it. He *couldn't*. And she knew that he couldn't. She'd known him too long.

"Maybe a little," he finally conceded.

"Maybe a lot," Willow returned. She patted his arm. "That's okay. It's one of the things I love about you. Usually," she tacked on. "I just wish you would relax more, baby."

Her hand remained on his arm, moving up and down in a slow caress.

"You know I've never been good at just relaxing, but I guess I can try a bit harder," he said. "And if today is what being spontaneous results in, I can learn to do that more often too."

"That's what I've been trying to tell you," she said, her voice taking on a raspy, slightly seductive tone. Her fingers traveled the length of his arm. "A little spontaneity can be a good thing every once in a while."

Instead of reversing course at his wrist, her hand continued downward, moving to his thigh. She spread her fingers out, gently kneading the muscle. Harrison's dick twitched in his pants.

When she moved for his zipper, he sucked in a breath. He glanced over at her. "Wills, what are you doing?"

"Really, Harrison?" Her low chuckle reverberated along his skin. "I know it's been a while, but I didn't think I'd have to spell it out."

She tugged his zipper down and reached inside his pants.

"Willow," Harrison said in a warning tone.

"Hmmm?"

"What are you doing?" he asked again.

She moved her seatbelt aside, leaned across the seat, and whispered, "It's called being spontaneous."

She maneuvered her fingers inside the flap of his boxer briefs, which were already having a hard time containing his steadily growing erection. He damn near came in his pants the minute he felt skin-on-skin contact.

He clenched his teeth. "Do you want me to wreck this car?"

"Um, no. That wouldn't be good." She brushed the backs of her fingers along his erection before closing her hand around it and giving him one smooth pump. Harrison sucked in his stomach, along with another swift breath. His hips jerked upward, seeking more of her touch.

She started to move her hand in earnest, squeezing gently on the way up, then harder on the way down. She rubbed her thumb around the head, coating him with the droplets of moisture that collected at the tip of his cock. Harrison followed the motion of her hand, lifting his hips nearly off the seat with every pull.

He looked around, taking a sharp left and pulling into a small cutout on the side of the mountain. He released the seatbelt and quickly moved his seat back.

"Your mouth. Please," he begged.

With that subtle, seductively wicked smile he'd come to love so much over the years, Willow unbuckled her seatbelt and leaned over to his side of the car. When her soft, warm lips closed around his dick, Harrison was certain he wouldn't survive the next five minutes. No one could sustain that amount of pleasure without succumbing to it.

She flattened her tongue along the underside of his

cock, then trailed it upward, repeating the motion over and over and over again. Then she sucked him in deep, swallowing his entire length, until he hit the back of her throat.

Harrison gripped the steering wheel so hard he thought he would break it. He trembled as Willow relaxed her jaws on the way down, and then hallowed them out on the way up, creating a suction that drove him out of his mind with need. He shoved his fingers in her hair and helped to guide her head up and down his cock, taking control of the rhythm.

"Just like that," Harrison choked out past the lust clogging his throat. He pumped his hips, fucking her mouth with fevered thrusts, surging and surging and surging, until he couldn't stand it anymore. He felt the orgasm building at the base of his spine and figured he had no more than ten seconds before he erupted.

It only took five.

When Willow sucked hard once again, he exploded, his body releasing every drop of the pent-up desire he'd been storing away for months. She continued to hold him in her mouth, drinking him in until there was nothing left.

Harrison fell back against the seat, his chest heaving with the deep breaths he drew in.

"Wow. That felt like old times," Willow said. She looked over at him and grinned. "I can't believe I just blew you parked along a roadside in Italy. I need to put that on my bucket list just so I can check it off."

Harrison would have thought he was too spent to laugh, but he managed a brief chuckle despite his fatigue. He looked over at her and wrapped his hand around her neck, bringing her to him and devouring her mouth. When he finally released her, he continued to hold on to her head, massaging the muscles of her neck with his fingers.

"What just happened here, Willow?"

"Is an explanation really necessary?" she asked, a skeptical arch to her brow.

"I know *what* happened," he said. "But I need to know if I'm reading more into it than I should. Not that I don't appreciate the roadside blowjob, but is that all that was, just a blowjob?"

She lifted her shoulders in a meek shrug. "Do we have to put a label on it?"

"Willow—"

"I don't know, Harrison. I just... I wanted to touch you." Her eyes softened as she reached over and cupped his jaw in her palm. "I miss touching you."

He stared into her eyes. What he saw there revived some of the optimism his life had been lacking lately.

"You really do still love me, don't you?" he asked.

"Yes," Willow said. She brushed her fingers along his jaw. "I will say it again and again and again until you believe it. In the midst of everything that's gone sideways this past year, that is the one thing that has remained true. I've never stopped loving you, Harrison."

The intense joy her words produced left him breathless as he leaned over again and connected his lips with hers. A part of him was afraid to trust the hopefulness cascading through his veins. But trust it he would. Finally—*finally*—he'd encountered a crack in the dome of uncertainty that had been hovering over their marriage. He wouldn't stop until they'd shattered it to pieces.

A brisk wind filtered through the dense green leaves of the lemon trees that grew all around them, releasing a fresh burst of pungent citrus into the air. Willow drew in another deep breath, savoring the fragrant aroma. They'd once visited an orange grove in Florida while driving to Disney World a few years ago, but she didn't recall it being this potent. There was a vibrancy to the air here in Sorrento that she couldn't compare to anything she'd ever experienced.

Or maybe she was just seeing things differently now.

After that remarkable drive down the coast with Harrison this morning, the entire world seemed more vibrant, more full of life. Colors appeared brighter. The air felt lighter. For the first time in months, the knot that had been a constant in her stomach had started to untwine.

Harrison's strong fingers clutched more securely around her hand as they meandered along the dirt path that sliced through the shady copse. He'd held onto her hand since they arrived, letting go only long enough to pay their entrance fee into the lemon grove. Holding hands seemed like such an insignificant thing, but the comfort it provide seeped into her bones, filling Willow with a sense of peace she hadn't felt in far too long. No one else could ever make her feel this way. Only Harrison. He'd been the one constant in her life she could always turn to when she needed to feel safe.

She leaned in closer to him, wrapping her arms around his waist and giving him a squeeze.

"Thank you for indulging me yet again," Willow said. "I know it isn't the vineyard you'd wanted to visit today, but I'm loving this."

"As long as you're enjoying yourself. That's all that

matters." He kissed the top of her head, then lowered his mouth to her ear and whispered, "So, is walking through lemon groves another bucket list item you never told me about, or are we being spontaneous again?"

"A little bit of both," she answered with a smile.

They'd stopped in Naples for a late lunch, but when Willow realized Sorrento was just another hour's drive down the coast, she insisted they continue on to the tiny coastal town, notable for the limoncello produced from its groves of lemon trees.

"It's another of those things I've always wanted to do. We were so close. Why miss the opportunity?"

"You don't have to convince me," he said. "After our little roadside excursion on the side of the mountain, I'm all in when it comes to being spontaneous."

A tremor of satisfaction coursed through her at the memory of what they'd done a few hours ago. When it came to making love to him with her mouth, it was all about how powerful it made her feel. She controlled every sigh he made, every lift of his hips. Watching Harrison receive pleasure, sensing how much he enjoyed it, had always meant more to her than the act itself.

Their flirting over these past couple of days harkened back to the time when they'd first started dating. Harrison may not remember it, but he'd been spontaneous back then too. Or maybe he'd been willing to do whatever she asked in hopes that it would lead to sex. Whatever the case, it had made for such romantic, carefree days. Their sole focus had been on making the other happy.

How long had it been since her husband's happiness resided at the top of her priority list?

Too long.

Willow had slowly come to realize that her trepidation

over this trip had been groundless. This wasn't about finding a temporary fix for their broken marriage. It was a reminder of all she and Harrison *used* to share. Of what their love looked like before they allowed the stress of everyday life to creep in and suck the joy out of their marriage.

They'd grown apart because they'd allowed themselves to grow apart. It was as simple as that. She'd heard stories over the years from girlfriends and neighbors about how much work they had to put in to keep their relationships above water. She'd felt so lucky, smug even. She and Harrison never had to *work* at their marriage. It was perfect. Easy. No additional effort required.

Oh, how wrong you were.

No marriage was perfect. It had just taken theirs much longer to show wear and tear.

But being here with Harrison, having this time away for just the two of them in this incredibly romantic part of the world, it provided the first tiny step to getting back to the love that had always been there between them. It would take work, but as long as they were both willing to do their part, they would eventually get there.

The sound of birds chirping rang out, and for the third time in less than an hour, Harrison slipped his free hand in his pocket and pulled out his phone. He read whatever was on the screen, frowned, and slipped it back in.

"What's going on?" Willow asked.

He sighed, then said, "Nothing."

"Don't even try that on me. That's the third text you've gotten since we've been here. What time is it back home? Around nine a.m.? It must be pretty important if they're texting you already."

"It's just work stuff," he said.

"I figured that much," she said, trying to keep the frustration from her voice. "I thought you told LaKeshia to contact you only if it's important?"

"I did."

"So?"

He released another sigh and took his phone out again. He quickly typed up a message, hit send, and stuffed the phone back into his pocket.

"There," he said. "I told her to let Jonathan handle anything else that comes up."

Willow didn't know LaKeshia Lawrence all that well, but she knew the woman was sharp as a tack. If she thought this emergency was something Jonathan could handle, she wouldn't have bothered texting in the first place.

She nearly told him that she didn't mind if he called the office, but then thought better of it. She *did* mind. This was *their* time. The nature of his job required he work more than the average forty-hour work week, but he too often worked twice that many hours. To be honest, Willow was shocked that he'd managed to remain unplugged these past couple of days. If Harrison was willing to leave work behind, why would she allow it to intrude upon their vacation?

He'd always been a workaholic, especially back in those early days at Bossier, Guidry & Associates. Foolishly, Willow assumed his work life would become less chaotic when he joined Jonathan's smaller firm. Until she realized how much the workload increased when it was dispersed between two lawyers instead of two hundred.

Yet, despite the ridiculous hours he sometimes put in at the job, he never skimped when it came to making time for his kids. Whether it was scouts with Athens or helping Lily with her English homework, she could count on Harrison to be there when their kids needed him.

But there were only so many hours in the day. And when he and Jonathan decided it was time to officially become partners, he'd started to devote even more of them to the job, which meant less time for just the two of them.

Her resentment over the time he put in at the office had been a source of conflict in her for so damn long. Guilt over it ate her up inside.

She *knew* Harrison was under a lot of pressure to perform. She also knew exactly what she was getting into when she married him. Her husband's insatiable drive was one of the things that had first attracted her to him. He pushed himself harder than anyone she'd ever met, including her own mother, one of the hardest working people Willow had ever known. Her mother had worked hard all those years out of necessity. Harrison did it out of pure determination to succeed. It was part of his DNA.

Diane had once told her a story about a time a ten-year-old Harrison had been caught lying to the school librarian, claiming his father would take the belt to him if he didn't get all A's in school. It had been a bald-faced lie. He'd wanted extra time in the library to study and figured the librarian would take pity on him if she thought he'd get a whupping.

How could she resent his unrelenting ambition when the fruits of it provided such a comfortable roof over her head? It was her husband's drive that put food in their children's mouths, paid for the ridiculously expensive private schools they both attended, sent them on annual family trips and allowed them to donate to others in the community. Harrison's uncompromising resolve to be the absolute best had provided a life for her that, as a young girl, Willow could never imagine she would be living. What right did she have to complain?

But what was the point of having this nice, comfortable life if they couldn't enjoy it together? She'd so often considered telling him that she was willing to give up the big house and fancy car if it meant having him home more.

Willow had always thought it was selfish to want more of his time, but these past couple of days showed her that it wasn't selfish. It was *necessary*. It was part of the work they would have to start putting into their marriage if they wanted it to last.

They returned to the entrance of the lemon grove and were treated to another shot of limoncello by the owners. They purchased several bottles of the tangy liqueur to bring back as gifts, then asked for recommendations for dinner. The owner's daughter suggested a restaurant just up the road in the tiny city of Sant'Agnello.

Once there, they opted for an outside table, despite the chilly air rolling off the Bay of Naples. The breathtaking view of the bay and Mount Vesuvius was worth a few goosebumps.

After their hour-long dinner, Harrison suggested they be spontaneous again and check into the adjacent hotel instead of navigating the winding, narrow coastal roadway to the hotel Willow had looked up as a potential placed to stay on their drive down.

"You are doing well with this lesson in spontaneity, young grasshopper," Willow teased as they made their way to their room.

"I'm trying to impress my lovely teacher," Harrison answered, placing a kiss on her lips before holding the keycard up to the sensor on the door.

The moment they entered the room, Willow sensed

that things were different. An unmistakeable expectation permeated the air, a confirmation of the shift that had taken place between them over the course of the day. Ignoring its significance would be foolish. Denying what she knew would happen tonight was pointless.

So she made the first move.

Without saying a word, Willow took the overnight bag from Harrison's hand and dropped it onto the floor next to the door, then she guided him to the bed and pushed against his shoulders, urging him to sit.

Harrison looked up at her. "I guess we're not easing into this, are we?"

"Nope." She straddled his lap and wrapped her arms around his neck. "It's been too many months since I had you inside of me. I'm not easing into anything."

She seized hold of his mouth, claiming it with a possessive hunger that left no question as to what she wanted.

Him. She wanted him.

Her heart pounded ferociously as searing need, sharp and fervent and all-consuming, pulsed through her veins. She wanted to devour him, to reacquaint herself with every inch of this amazing body she hadn't explored in far too long.

She traced the seam of his lips before coaxing them open with her tongue, licking her way inside and feasting on his decadent flavor. Willow ground her pelvis against the growing bulge in his lap. She undulated her hips while pressing downward, groaning with the need to take her husband inside. Anticipation danced across her skin, her body primed for what was to come.

Harrison palmed her ass, gripping it a little too roughly, the tinge of pain quickly turning to pleasure as he smoothed his hands over her backside and along her hips. A familiar warmth began to spread throughout her body as his fingers inched inside her shirt and fanned across her belly. He moved upward, pulling the cups of her bra down and closing his hands over her breasts.

A strangled moan escaped as he pinched and plucked and drove her out of her mind. When he lifted the shirt over her head and closed his lips around her nipple, Willow had to clutch his shoulders to keep herself from falling clean off his lap. She pitched her head back and thrust her chest toward him, welcoming every tender nip and decadent suck.

She could already feel an orgasm building. Months of pent-up desire and need coalesced like kindling in her veins; hit her with the barest spark and she would go up in flames. As Harrison continued his pleasurable assault on her breasts, he unbuckled her jeans and pushed them down her hips. He fingered the lacy edge of her underwear before dipping his hand inside and brushing his thumb across her plump clit.

Willow's blood caught fire.

He played with her swollen flesh, alternating between feather-light caresses and deepening strokes. When he eased two fingers inside her rapidly dampening center, Willow nearly lost it. She held his wrist steady as she rode his fingers hard, pumping her hips like a piston, taking him in as far as she could. Moments later she shattered around him, her climax hitting her with breath-stealing power.

Harrison wrapped his arm around her waist and twisted around on the bed. He quickly undressed her, then undressed himself before climbing on top of her and burying his face against her throat. He kissed his way up her neck and along her jawline, the caress of his soft, yet firm lips triggering tiny, pleasurable explosions all along her skin.

When he closed in on her mouth, she practically inhaled him. She couldn't get enough of his kiss.

Harrison wedged his hips between her thighs as he hungrily explored her mouth, his tongue hard and searching. Willow reveled in it all. The demanding thrusts of his tongue, the familiar, delicious burn in her thighs as she stretched her legs wide to make room for him, the intoxicating anticipation as she waited for the moment when his body would enter hers.

With his intense gaze holding her hostage, Harrison entered her with one smooth stroke.

A bolt of unrestrained pleasure shot through her, sending delicious tremors along her nerve-endings as sensual gratification seeped into her bones. Willow crossed her ankles at the small of his back and lifted her hips up to meet his thrusts. Every skillful, plunging stroke set off a new round of exquisite sensations.

Desire for her husband consumed her. Willow clutched him to her, sinking her nails into his back as she held on for dear life.

God, she'd missed this!

Every delicious slide of his thick, stiff flesh sparked a barrage of delicious memories. Years of generous, giving, selfless lovemaking. Years of Harrison being focused solely on her pleasure. How had she gone so long without this?

His mouth closed around her nipple as his deep, demanding strokes pushed her closer to the exquisite ecstasy that awaited her on the other side. He tempted and taunted her, bringing her so close to completion, only to pull back before she could reach it. She was at war with herself, aching for the release she knew he could give her, yet wanting this to last forever.

"Please," Willow pleaded, unsure of what she was asking for.

Her husband knew.

He dipped his hand between them and ground his thumb against her center as his hips continued to pump. The intensity of the sensations crashing through her were unbearable. Willow teetered on the precipice of an orgasm, her stomach clenching as that feeling built up yet again.

With one final thrust, Harrison sent her over the edge. Pleasure exploded within her, her limbs trembling as powerful aftershocks coursed through her veins.

The moment overwhelmed her. Her love for her husband, for the life they shared, for the future she wanted them to have together, it all coalesced in a mass of emotion that refused to be contained.

Harrison kissed the tears that trailed down her cheeks.

"Please stop crying," he whispered.

"I can't," Willow choked out in a hoarse voice. "I miss this. I miss *us*."

"I know, baby," he said. "I know. I miss us too." He smooth a tear from her cheek. "But we're here. I'm not going anywhere. I don't care what happens, Willow, I'm not letting you go without a fight."

"You promise?" she asked.

He molded his palm to her cheek and held her prisoner with his intent, steady gaze. The fervent love in his eyes stole the breath from her lungs.

"I promise."

Chapter Eight

A s he looked upon his sleeping wife's breathtaking face, Harrison had to talk himself out of saying to hell with the plans he'd made for today. At the moment, he couldn't think of anything he wanted to do more than spend the next twenty four hours in bed reliving the night he and Willow had shared. He wanted to relive it over and over and over again.

But today was *the* day. It was the day he'd been looking forward to from the moment he began planning this trip. The surprise he had in store for his wife was one she would cherish for decades to come.

So, instead of snuggling against her warm, naked body, he'd gently snuck out from under the covers and forced himself to get dressed. Their impromptu drive down the coast had blown his plans way off course, so he let Willow sleep while he contacted the travel agent and made new arrangements. He'd spent the past twenty minutes just standing there, watching the rhythmic rise and fall of her slender back as she slept. She looked so beautiful, so peaceful. Gone was the stress and tension he'd noticed on her face for the past few months. *This* was the Willow he knew.

Harrison hated to disturb her, but if they didn't get out of here soon they'd never make it to his surprise. He tickled the bottom of her foot. She quickly pulled it back under the covers.

"Wills," he said in a hushed voice. "You need to wake up."

She groaned and twisted around, hauling the pillow over her head. The thin bedsheet pulled taut over her breasts and Harrison had to remind himself that stripping out of his clothes and diving back in bed with her wasn't a smart idea.

Tempting, but not smart. The smart thing to do would be to treat Willow to this mind-blowing day. They could have a repeat of what they did last night anytime.

God, please let us have a repeat tonight.

"Come on," Harrison said. "We need to get going."

She moved the pillow a few inches to the side and peeked at him. "Do we have to?"

"Yes. Our flight leaves at eight thirty and it'll take us at least an hour to get to the airport in Naples."

She flung the pillow off her face and sat up in the bed. "Flight? What flight?"

"The one I just booked," he said. "Our spontaneous trip took us well south of where we were supposed to be today, so we won't be able to take the train to our next destination. I had to buy a couple of last-minute airline tickets." He shook his head. "I can't believe I have to get on a plane again."

"Where are we going?"

"It's a surprise."

"Harrison?" she said in that warning tone.

He remained silent.

"Give me a minute while I channel my stubborn ten-year-old son," she said, crossing her arms over her chest. "I'm not moving from this bed until you tell me where we're going."

His brow arched in amusement. "Does that ever work for Athens?"

"No, but I'm not Athens," she said. "Tell me."

Harrison shook his head, chuckling at her cute, defiant pout. "Fine. I'll give you a hint." He leaned forward and braced his hands on either side of her hips. "We're going to a place where the streets are a little wetter than usual."

Confusion flashed in her eyes before they brightened with excitement. "Venice? We're going to Venice!"

"Yes." He kissed her on the nose. "And I refuse to change any of the plans for today, so get up and get dressed."

She jumped out of bed and was dressed quicker than Harrison could remember in their seventeen years of marriage. They drove the thirty miles north to the airport in Naples where they were able to leave their rental car and hop on a plane to northern Italy.

The train ride from Rome would have taken just under four hours. By flying, they reached Venice two hours earlier than his original itinerary had them arriving. He'd pre-booked a private water taxi to take them into the city center based on the time they were supposed to arrive, but Harrison wasn't willing to waste time milling about. Instead, he had the driver take them to the port.

Once there, they boarded a vaporetto—a water bus—to take them across the Venetian Lagoon. By the time they arrived at one of the docks of the Grand Canal, Harrison was sure the smile on Willow's face would be permanently etched there.

"If I'd known you were this excited about seeing Venice, I would have planned for us to spend more than just a day," he said.

"I thought it was too far from Rome to even consider coming up here. I just didn't think we'd have the time." She turned to him. "I cannot believe you were able to pull this off, Harrison. It truly is a trip of a lifetime."

"And just think, we still have a couple of days remaining."

"I know!" Her face beamed. "So, what do you have planned for today?"

"Everything," he said. "Everything you could possibly want to do in Venice."

"We're taking a gondola ride, right?"

He looked at her as if she'd lost her mind. "Do you really think I'd bring you to Venice and not get you alone in a gondola while some old Italian guy sings off-key in our ears? Come on, Wills. You know me better than that."

She pitched her head back and laughed, the sound sweeter than honey to his ears. He'd missed his wife's laugh so damn much.

Once they arrived on the island, they set out to explore, walking through San Marcos Square and the ornate basilica that stood as its focal point. Strolling along the square's perimeter, they watched as mimes performed and small school children fed the birds swooping down from the red clay rooftops above. They meandered through the narrow alleyways and across the various bridges connecting the city's many islands, dipping into shops that sold colorful Murano glass and intricate, handmade jewelry.

A stray rain shower sent them scurrying into a tiny

pizza shop where he and Willow spent a full two hours dining on the best pizza he'd ever eaten. Harrison feared the rain would put a damper on his plans, but it seemed as if God was in his corner today. Just as they were finishing off the bottle of wine they'd ordered with lunch, the rain clouds dissipated and the warm sun began to stretch its fingers through the restaurant's slender windows.

"Just in time," Harrison said as he paid for their meal and left an inordinate tip for occupying the table for the past two hours.

"Just in time for what?" Willow asked.

He stood and held a hand out to her. "I do believe I promised you a ride in a gondola."

Their private gondola was waiting for them by the time they arrived at the dock, just to the left of the Bridge of Sighs. They boarded the long, flat-bottomed boat, and were handed two glasses of champagne.

"I'm not sure if I should have any more to drink," Harrison said. "Those two glasses of wine with lunch was more alcohol than I usually drink in a month."

"But you're in Venice," Willow said with a wistful sigh. "When will you ever get another chance to drink champagne while cruising these beautiful canals?"

He held his glass up. "Point taken." Willow clanked her glass against his and took a sip of champagne before settling against his chest. Satisfaction thrummed through his veins as their surprisingly talented gondolier softly serenaded them.

Nearly a year ago, when he'd first decided to book this trip, this is the scene that immediately popped into his head. He'd pictured this moment, imagining how it would feel to have his wife snuggled against him as they gently listed from side to side. The picture became murky as things started to sour between them over the past year, to the point where Harrison wasn't sure they'd even make it into this gondola. But they were here now. And it was more magical than anything he'd dreamt up.

He'd never been good at shutting out the rest of the world, but he forced himself to push thoughts of all the things that had been causing him stress to the side so that he could just exist in this moment with his wife. He wanted to relish this. They deserved this time together.

His vibrating phone pulled him out of his relaxing lull.

Shit.

He would not answer this phone. He'd caught Willow's resigned, disappointed look yesterday when those text messages came through. He'd promised her he wouldn't work while they were here. He couldn't renege on that promise, especially while enjoying this romantic moment he'd been looking forward to for so long.

But this was a *call*, not a text. What in the hell could have happened for LaKeshia to *call* him? What if it wasn't LaKeshia? What if it was Jonathan? Or Luca Delmonico himself? He couldn't just leave his client hanging. Some other client, maybe, but not this one.

Didn't matter. He wouldn't answer. Even though it raked across his skin like a bad rash to think about something going wrong that he wouldn't be there to handle, Harrison refused to give in. Being here with his wife, doing all he could do to save their marriage. *This* is what was important.

The phone stopped vibrating, but started again just a few seconds later.

"Answer it," Willow said.

"What?"

"Someone's calling you."

"How can you tell? My phone's on silent." And there was no way she could feel it vibrating from where she sat.

"You tense up whenever it rings." She lifted off of his chest. "Just answer it, Harrison. If you don't you'll spend this entire time wondering what's going on back at the office. Find out so you can truly put it out of your mind."

He gave her another look, asking if she was sure.

She answered with a nod.

Harrison tried not to seem too eager as he pulled the phone out, but he needed to know what the heck was going on. He had three missed calls from Michael Delmonico.

What the hell?

"Hello," Harrison answered, not bothering to lessen the harshness in his voice. If it had been Luca, sure, but the man's son was a pain in the ass.

He impatiently listened while the younger Delmonico rattled on about a surprise counter Phillip MacMahon had offered them today. Harrison cursed underneath his breath. Knowing Phillip, he'd probably been waiting for the chance to spring this on Michael because he knew he could easily manipulate the twenty-something year old.

"No." Harrison's firm replied halted Michael's rambling. "No more emails between you and their lawyers for the rest of the day. Don't reply earlier than eleven a.m. tomorrow morning. Any earlier and you give MacMahon the upper hand. This way he'll think you had more important issues to handle before getting back to him. And when you *do* get back to him, tell him the answer is no and all other communication will be handled through your attorney.

"Now, please, don't call again, Michael. I'm on vacation. If anyone from Bossier, Guidry & Associates, or Bayou

Landing Dredging contacts you, direct them to Jonathan Campbell at Campbell & Holmes."

Harrison ended the call before Michael Delmonico could take up any more of his time.

"I'm sorry, Willow," he said. "That's the last time I'll let that happen. And, just to make sure, I'm cutting the thing off completely. If Dad or Indina needs to get in touch with us about the kids they'll call your phone anyway."

He started to power his phone off, but Willow caught his wrist.

"Don't do that. You have the navigation app. Here, give it to me." She took the phone from his hand. "I'll turn off the vibrate. Now the only way you'll see an incoming call is if you're looking at the phone. Don't look at the phone."

She handed it to him and Harrison slipped it back into his pocket. When he returned his attention to her, there was an impish smile turning up the corners of her mouth.

"What?" he asked.

"I forgot how sexy you are when you're being a badass, hotshot lawyer."

He huffed out a laugh. "The acquisition of a dredging machine company. Not the sexiest subject matter."

"It is when you talk about it," she said. She leaned against his chest again. "But thank you for turning the phone off. You need this vacation just as much as I do. *More* than I do." She looked up at him. "I know your job is important, but there's more to life than just work."

"I know that, Wills."

"Do you?" The earnest sincerity in her eyes surprised him. "I worry about the stress of it all, Harrison. High stress jobs can lead to bad things happening."

Harrison knew she was thinking of her own mother. A few years ago, Rachel had been rushed to a hospital in

Houston with what her colleagues thought was a stroke. It turned out to be symptoms of stress that only presented as a stroke. Even though his mother-in-law had fully recovered and was back to kicking ass and taking names, the incident had been a wake-up call.

"I'd never allow the stress of the job to get to the point where it causes harm, Willow."

She snorted. "I'm sure that's what everyone in a high-stress job says." She flattened her palm against his chest. "I don't want you to think for a second that I don't appreciate how hard you work for me and the kids, Harrison. You put in all those hours at the office and still make time to be there when Athens and Lily need you, but it doesn't leave much time for *you*," she said, pressing a finger to the center of his chest. "The sacrifices you make are noble, but I don't want you to look back in another twenty years and realize you've sacrificed your entire life. I'd be willing to give up some of the comforts you provide if it means you don't have to work so hard."

He cupped her jaw in his palm and smoothed his thumb back and forth across her silky skin.

"You don't have to worry about me, baby."

But even as the words left his mouth, Harrison was self-aware enough to acknowledge that her concern had merit.

His first panic attack happened back when he was in law school, sitting alone at a table at three in the morning in the twenty-four hour law library. The next one happened in the men's restroom at the federal courthouse a few years after he'd started practicing law. Both times he thought he was having a heart attack.

He'd learned to spot the signs and calm himself down before things got out of control, but he had yet to master the art of taking it easy every once in a while. He didn't know how *not* to work hard. And as he grew older, this all-consuming drive only seemed to intensify. His compulsion to prove to Jonathan that he'd made the right decision in hiring him—to prove to himself that he'd done the right thing by leaving Bossier and Guidry—drove him to work harder than he ever had before. He kept telling himself that it was only temporary, but temporary had gone on for well over a year now. How much longer could he really use that excuse?

"It won't be as hectic in the future," he told Willow. "Things are starting to settle down at the law office."

Lies. More and more lies.

He and Jonathan were talking about expanding soon. If they made that move, there would be no settling down. Life at the firm would become even more chaotic, with him likely having to divide his time between two locations.

But Willow didn't have to know that yet. He would just make it a priority to do a better job at that work/home life balance thing they used to stress at Bossier, Guidry & Associates. Even though they knew no one paid any heed to it.

You can do this.

Hell yeah, he could do this. He could show his wife that she was the most important thing in his life while still proving he was the best damn lawyer Jonathan could have ever brought in as a partner.

As their gondola glided along the calm waters, Harrison pulled Willow in closer, and pressed a kiss to the top of her head.

"You know, in twenty years' worth of memories, this day may go down as one of my all-time favorites," he whispered.

"Mmm," Willow murmured. "That's saying a lot,

because there have been some pretty fine days during the last twenty years."

"Yeah, there have been," he said. Harrison felt her shoulders shaking as she chuckled. "What are you laughing about?"

"One of my favorite memories ever." She looked up at him, amusement flickering in her light brown eyes. "Stripper Barbie."

A sharp laugh shot from his mouth. "How did that get on your list of favorite memories?"

"Because it was funny as hell," she said.

"For you, maybe. I'm still mortified." Harrison shook his head as his wife continued to laugh at him.

The Stripper Barbie incident had become legendary. Liliana had fallen in love with Barney, the purple dinosaur, as a kid. One day, while Willow was sick with the flu, Harrison had stayed home to look after their daughter. He'd had no idea his poor wife's day was consumed by hours of watching that big, clumsy ass singing dinosaur. By the end of the day, he'd been ready to throw out the TV.

Willow being Willow, she'd hired a singing telegram to surprise him at his job the next day. But instead of hearing *Barney*, the guy on the other end of the line heard *Barbie*. And the only Barbie the company employed was the one who usually got called out to bachelor parties.

When the bleached blonde showed up at his office and began to strip out of her costume, he'd wanted to melt into the floor.

"I became pretty popular at the law firm after that," he said.

Willow cackled.

"The bosses weren't too happy, though."

"I was so afraid you were going to lose your job."

"Yet it's still one of your best memories, huh?"

She nodded, wiping tears of mirth from her eyes. "I'm just sorry I wasn't there to see your face. Jessica, your old office assistant, told me how horrified you were. You have no idea how much I would have loved to see it."

"Want to know what my favorite memory is?" Harrison asked.

"Hmm?"

"Three years ago. July Fourth weekend."

"Yeeeesssss." A blissful smile stole across her lips.

"Your mom drove in from Houston that Thursday evening and took the kids back with her for the weekend."

"We bought a bunch of food and didn't leave the house for two days."

"Not only did we not leave the house, we didn't put any clothes on either," Harrison reminded her.

She nestled her head underneath his chin and released a dreamy sigh. "We made love more times that weekend than we have in the last six months." She looked up at him. "We never should have allowed things to get to this point, Harrison. We've been too damn good together for too damn long to let things fall apart the way they have."

"But we're fixing it," he said. "And we're not broken. A little bent maybe, but nothing can ever truly break what we have, Willow. Our bond is too strong."

He pressed a gentle kiss to her lips. And for the first time in a long time, life was starting to feel normal again.

It was almost midnight when he and Willow arrived back at Termini Station. They were fed only a drink and light snack on their three-hour high-speed train ride from Venice, so they were both famished by the time they made it back to Rome. When Harrison discovered the lights on at the tiny, four-table restaurant just off the Piazza della Repubblica where they'd eaten a couple of nights ago, he was prepared to offer the man behind the bar an extra hundred dollars if he could get the chef to whip them up something quick to eat.

In keeping with the giving nature of the people they'd encountered here in Italy, the chef was all too happy to make them a dish and keep the restaurant open while they ate, encouraging them to take all the time they needed while they enjoyed their late meal.

"Two times on the same trip. I guess we can call this *our* restaurant," Harrison said as he twirled spaghetti onto his fork. "We'll have to make sure we eat here every time we visit."

"Every time?" Willow's brow rose. "So, does that mean I won't have to force you to take that long, long flight again?"

"It wasn't all that bad." He shrugged. "What's a little blood-chilling anxiety when you compare it to the fun we've had? Totally worth it."

"I agree," she said with a laugh. "It's worth it for the fun *and* the food." She forked a piece of veal from her plate and held it out to him. Harrison closed his lips around the tender meat and pulled it into his mouth.

"Divine," he said.

Willow's exuberant grin relaxed into a slow, secretive smile. Her eyes grew heavy with desire as she continued to stare at his mouth, and Harrison's hunger for their meal abruptly took a back seat to a different kind of craving.

"Are you done?" he asked. She nodded. "Good."

He called for the check and, surprisingly, had the bill squared away within a matter of minutes. The short, two-block walk to their hotel felt more like twenty. They couldn't move fast enough to satisfy the urgency pumping through his blood. His skin burned with the need to get his wife alone and savor every delectable inch of her mouthwatering body.

Taking her by the hand, Harrison led her into their hotel room and straight to the bed. They stripped out of their clothes, but before he could lean her back on the covers, Willow put a hand to his chest.

"It's been a long day and we're both grimy. We need to shower before we get to doing this."

Harrison chuckled, shaking his head at her practicality. They climbed into the shower, which was barely big enough for the both of them. Yet, they somehow made it work. As he washed her back, he ran his tongue along the slope of her neck, nibbling just below her ear. He rubbed his soapy hands over her breasts and down her stomach, slipping them both between her thighs and cupping her. Willow gasped as he spread her open and teased the ridged knot of nerves there, rolling it between his fingers, pinching and plucking until her legs started to shake.

"Okay, that's enough," she said in a strangled voice. "We're clean. Let's go."

"About damn time."

They attempted to towel themselves dry as they rushed out of the bathroom, but instead of joining her in bed, Harrison hoisted her up and wrapped her legs around his waist. Palming her incredibly grabable ass in both hands, he carried her over to the table next to the windows. He hoped no one could see them through the sheer curtains, but making love to his wife with Rome's romantic skyline as their backdrop was an experience Harrison wasn't willing to pass up.

He dropped to his knees and tugged her forward before wedging himself between her thighs and draping her legs over his shoulders. Then, with his hands gripping her waist, he dipped his head between her legs and feasted.

She tasted better than any of the delectable dishes he'd eaten this past week. He rolled his tongue around her clit, flicking it across the taut nub, lapping up her delicate flavor with deep, leisurely licks. Willow braced one hand on the glass tabletop and wrapped the other around his head, pulling him closer to her, pumping her hips to the rhythm of his tongue's movements. Her low, erotic moans of pleasure shot straight to his dick.

Harrison couldn't hold out much longer. The need to be inside her, to connect his body with hers, pressed against him like a raging bull, straining to burst through its cage. With an urgency he hadn't felt in longer than he could remember, he stood, lifted Willow off the table, turned her around and thrust into her from behind.

Her back bowed as she spread her fingers flat on the tabletop and pushed back against him.

"Oh, God. Harrison. More. *More*."

He met her demanding cry with longer, deeper thrusts. They rocked against each other, with Willow pushing back as he plunged forward, the erotic rhythm of their love-making sending him close to the edge. Too close.

Harrison pulled back before he could reach the point of no return. Because he wasn't nearly ready for this to end.

He turned Willow around and hoisted her into his arms once again. She let out a yelp of pleasure as she caught his face between her hands and drove her tongue into his mouth.

Balancing her with one hand cupping her ass and the other cradling her back, Harrison carried her to the bed and deposited her face down on the covers. He explored the small of her back with his tongue, trailing it along her smooth skin.

"Turn over," Harrison whispered. When she did, he settled between her thighs and connected her mouth to his. Taking his erection in his hand, he guided it into her warm, inviting heat, plunging with renewed ambition, desperate to make her body quake around him as it had last night.

Harrison braced his hands on either side of her and drove into her over and over again, quickening his pace, then holding back, repeating the pattern again and again, until he felt her thighs quiver against his hips. Unable to withstand his body's demand for release, he once again slipped a hand between them and brushed his thumb back and forth over her clit.

She surrendered completely, her body shattering underneath him. The sight of her losing herself was so hot it drove him straight over the edge. After only three more strokes, Harrison exploded in an orgasm so intense he thought he was sure to die. It traveled from the top of his head to the tips of his toes and all points in between.

His arms gave out. He collapsed on top of her, his body too spent to support him a second longer. He quickly rolled to the side, pulling Willow on top of him.

"Good Lord," she breathed against his chest. She looked up at him and gestured her head toward the window. "We need to get us a table like that for home. It's the perfect height."

Harrison's laugh rumbled in his chest. "I'll ask the concierge for the name of the manufacturer."

She laughed and yawned, lowering her cheek onto his chest once again. "Baby?"

"Yeah?" Harrison asked.

"I hope you don't take it the wrong way when I fall asleep in the next thirty seconds. Today was epic, but you wore me out."

He smooth his hand up and down her back. "Well, when you think about it, we pretty much covered the entire country today, from South Italy, to the north, and back to the center."

Willow's answer was a light snore.

He chuckled, drawing the bedding over her back. But as his wife drifted into a peaceful slumber, Harrison lay restless, staring up at the ceiling. Even as he replayed their conversation in the gondola over in his mind, he had to fight the urge to reach for his phone and check his email. It was as automatic as breathing. But how much was it really costing him?

He'd been so sure that he was killing it when it came to being the all-around family man. So maybe he went some nights with only a couple hours sleep. As long as he was there to shoot hoops with his son, teach is teenage daughter how to drive, and satisfy the hell out of his wife when they slipped into bed at night, what did it matter?

But it *did* matter.

There was something to be said for taking a bit of time for himself. This trip had shown him just how enjoyable life could be when he allowed it to slow down a bit. The Delmonico acquisition wasn't going to collapse in the next couple of days. He didn't have to know what was going on at all times back at the office.

And once they got back home and this deal was done, he would learn how to put work aside—truly put it aside—and enjoy his family. He was lucky as hell to have them. He'd always thought providing for their physical needs was the best thing he could do for them, but after his conversation with Willow today, Harrison now questioned his priorities. He'd sacrificed enough of himself for his career. It was time he focus on what really mattered in his life.

It wouldn't be easy. This drive to be the best had been a part of him for far too long. But he vowed to try. His family was worth it.

Chapter Nine

As the near scalding water rained down on her sore muscles, Willow luxuriated in the exquisite ache still humming throughout her body. It had been far too long since her inner thighs had experienced this delicious tenderness, the result of being spread wide for hours.

After Harrison led her on that sensual foray around their hotel room, she'd quickly fallen asleep, but just an hour later she'd awakened, ready for more. She'd used her hands and mouth to tease Harrison's body awake, stroking and sucking until he was hard and needy. Then she'd climbed on top of him and taken them both to paradise.

Goodness, but she'd missed sex with her husband. And, despite her soreness, she was ready to go again. They had a lot of lost time to make up for, and there was at least another hour before the National Museum opened. Surely they could spend some of that time making each other come.

Willow stepped out of the shower and toweled herself dry. Recalling how insatiable Harrison had been last night, she doubted it would take much to convince him to join her under the sheets for another round. Or maybe they could try the dresser this time? Up against the wall? All three places?

She wrapped the towel around her before exiting the bathroom.

And stopped short.

He stood with his back to her, stuffing clothes into his open suitcase, his phone tucked between his shoulder and jaw.

"I'm going to look for the earliest flight I can get. If I can fly out within the next few hours, I can be in the office by morning." He tossed a partially folded shirt in the suitcase. "Don't worry about my trip. I'll come up with an excuse for Willow for why we need to leave early."

Willow tucked the towel more securely underneath her arms and then folded them over her chest.

"Oh, you will?" she interrupted.

Harrison whirled around and stared at her, his eyes wide with shock and guilt. "Uh, Jonathan, I'll call you back." He tossed the phone on the bed and held up his hands. "Let me explain."

"You've come up with an excuse already? I'd have thought it would take at least a few minutes."

"Willow—"

She held up a hand. "Save your excuses. I don't want to hear it." She grabbed the bra and panties she'd left on the bed and pulled them on, then she plopped down next to his open suitcase and gave it a shove. "I just can't believe you, Harrison."

"Would you let me—"

"What has this entire trip really meant to you?" She looked up at him, trying to discern if she could even trust his words. "Was there any truth to anything you've said, or was this just your way of placating me? Whisk me off to Italy and maybe that'll shut me up for a while. Is that it?"

"No! Come on, Willow, don't do this. Not after the week we've had."

"It hasn't been a week!" she screeched. "That's my point! I can't get a full week of your time without you trying to cut it short because of some damn client. It shows me exactly where this marriage rates on the scale of what you consider important."

He threw his head back and dragged his palms down his face.

He had the nerve to be frustrated with her? Really?

"Are you going to let me explain, or am I just the bad guy here, no matter what?" Harrison asked.

"You're just the bad guy this time. Deal with it."

He released another of those irritated breaths. It only served to piss her off even more.

"I agreed to call my *children* only once a day while we've been here. My children! That's how important this trip was supposed to be to our marriage. Yet now we're cutting it short—going to the expense of buying last-minute airline tickets—because some high-maintenance client needs you?

"What if you died tomorrow? What would this client do? Do you think their entire business would implode? Newsflash! It wouldn't. They would just hire some new lawyer and go on about their merry way."

"Newsflash, I'm not dead," he countered. "I *am* their lawyer and an issue popped up that no one expected. I need to be there."

"We go home tomorrow, Harrison! Why can't Jonathan handle it until we get back?"

"It's not Jonathan's responsibility to handle it. This is *my* client."

"And I'm your *wife*! Where do I come in on your priority list?"

He spread his hands wide. "I booked this entire trip for you! I got on a fucking plane and flew across the ocean for you, Willow. You're telling me that's not enough?"

She folded her arms over her chest and pushed her shoulders back. Lifting her head in the air, she said, "I guess it has to be."

She snatched a sweater dress from the closet and went back into the bathroom. When she emerged five minutes later, Harrison was sitting at the table where he'd made love to her just last night, using an iPad she didn't even know he'd brought with him.

"Have you been working this entire time?" Willow asked. "What have you been doing? Tiring me out with sex then waking up in the middle of the night so you can work?"

"This is only my second time using this thing all week."

"Is that supposed to make me feel better?" She put her hand up. "Don't answer. I don't even care, Harrison. Text me when it's time to go to the airport."

He propped his elbows on the table and rubbed his temples. "Please don't do this."

She grabbed her purse and headed for the door.

"Willow!" he called, but she continued walking. She couldn't bear to even look at him right now.

She watched the door to their hotel room as she waited for the elevator, readying herself for the moment Harrison stormed into the hallway, determine to make her understand why he would allow his work to intrude on this time that was supposed to be just for them. The elevator door opened but their hotel room door didn't.

"Go on without me," she told the couple in the elevator. She hooked a thumb over her shoulder. "I just remembered I forgot something."

Willow turned toward their room and propped her hands on her hips. The pain in her chest intensified as each second passed with the door remaining closed, to the point where she could barely take a breath without wincing.

He had not come after her.

The elevator dinged its arrival. Willow glanced once again at the hotel room door before finally boarding the elevator. She felt numb as she made her way through the lobby and out into the chilly, overcast morning air. She turned right, retracing some of the same steps she and Harrison had taken this week. She walked along the old streets, peeking in the windows of the various shops, restaurants and gelatarias, her mind hardly comprehending what she was seeing.

How had he allowed her to just leave? How could he not even *try* to talk to her? To bring her back in that room and give her a solid explanation for why he so blithely tossed aside all the strides they'd made repairing their marriage this past week?

Hurt and anger encompassed her entire being, the bitter taste of it resting on her tongue, sinking into her bones.

With only a scarce idea of how she'd arrived there, Willow found herself back at the Trevi Fountain. She took a seat on the stone steps and mindlessly observed the tourists who walked up to the low gate surrounding the fountain. Kids pitched coins at the water, teens recorded short videos of themselves posing like the marble statues behind them, lovers stared into each other's eyes and kissed. Everyone looked so happy, so carefree. It made her feel guilty to have such agonizing thoughts flittering through her head while surrounded by such joy.

But sharing in their joy went beyond her capabilities at the moment. Willow's throat ached with disappointment as the reality of what this all meant gradually took hold.

Her marriage was over.

She wasn't ready to put voice to the words, but deep in her gut, she knew it to be true. Even if it wasn't immediate. Even if she and Harrison somehow managed to salvage their union for another couple of months or so, Willow just could not see them coming back from this.

Their time together over this past week had been a test, a way for her to see just where she fell on Harrison's list of priorities. To know that after seventeen years of marriage, after two kids and all the memories they had together, that he couldn't even give her a week where she didn't have to share him with someone else. Well, it was all the answer she needed.

And it hurt so, so much.

Maybe it was her fault for expecting him to change. Harrison had always been an overachiever. It was typical of him to work while on vacation. Just because she'd wanted this time to be solely for the two of them—because she'd decided to see it as a test of how committed he was to making their marriage work—that didn't mean he saw it that way.

"That's what you get for having expectations."

She wouldn't make that mistake again.

I nstead of trying to assuage the bitter ache pressing down on his chest with every breath he took, Harrison accepted it as punishment for the mess he'd made of things this morning. This misery was nothing less than he deserved.

What in the hell were you thinking?

One day! They had *one day* left to their vacation. And this was what he did?

This past week had been nothing short of magical. They'd made more progress in mending their broken relationship than he could have hoped for. Yet he went and ruined it with talk of cutting their vacation short. And for what? For the chance to show up that asshole Phillip MacMahon in front of a judge?

Who's the asshole now?

"What in the hell is wrong with you?" Harrison said in a harsh whisper.

Now, instead of being out there with his wife, enjoying their final hours in Rome on their actual wedding anniversary, here he was, staring out the window of their hotel room, watching as the world went about its business. His world had stopped the moment Willow walked out the door.

Why didn't he go after her? He'd started for her moments after she left, but then stopped, figuring she needed space.

But giving her space is what had gotten them in the state they were in right now. His moving out of the house had been his way of giving Willow the space she needed to clear her mind. He regretted that decision with every bone in his body.

He never should have left. He should have stayed in his

house and demanded he and Willow talk through their problems from the very beginning. The only thing his sleeping on that uncomfortable futon at the law firm had done was drive them further apart.

He hadn't learned a damn thing. If he had, he wouldn't have allowed work to intrude on their vacation and drive an even bigger wedge between them.

Harrison picked up his phone and reread the text he'd sent her. He'd needed to know she was okay, and to apologize. He'd written a damn novel, explaining that he was wrong to suggest leaving early. She'd replied with a simple, **Okay. I'm fine.**

That had been over an hour ago.

Harrison texted again. **You still okay?**

His chest grew tight as one minute passed. Then another. Then another.

After five minutes, he texted again. **Wills, just let me know you're okay.**

The electronic lock on their hotel room clicked open. "I'm fine," she said as she walked through the door.

The relief that crashed through him nearly took him out at the knees. "God, Willow."

Harrison made it to the bed on shaky legs as the built-up adrenalin of the past hour rushed from his body.

"I didn't mean to make you worry," she said. "I was just...frustrated."

"I get that," Harrison said with a nod. She came to sit next to him on the bed, but left at least a foot of space between them. It could have just as well been a mile. That's how distant she felt from him.

"I'm sorry, Willow," he said. "This isn't how I wanted our vacation to end."

Her shoulders lifted in a half-hearted shrug. "It is what it is."

Harrison reared back slightly. Had she really just hit him with the *it is what it is* line? She knew he hated that phrase. The defeatist sentiment behind it went against everything he believe in.

"Expecting you to spend an entire week unplugged was asking too much. I understand that now," she said. "Your work is important."

"It isn't more important than you."

Her composed, impassive expression signified the depths to which he'd fucked up. Anger and regret twisted in Harrison's gut. Anger at himself. After all the ground they'd made up this week, they were back at square one. It was written all over her face.

"Willow—"

"It's okay, Harrison." She turned to him, her eyes void of any real emotion. "You've worked hard on this case. It's not in your nature to leave a client hanging." She hunched her shoulder. "Besides, we can always come back to Italy, right?"

Her smile didn't reach her eyes.

"I'm sorry for ever taking those calls from the office," Harrison reiterated.

She gave him another of those bland half-smiles before expelling a tired breath and clamping her hands on her thighs. She looked around then turned to him with a quizzical frown. "Where are the bags?"

"In the closet."

Her brows rose. "Aren't we flying home today?"

He shook his head. "No. Jonathan is going to handle this issue with the Delmonicos. And whatever he can't handle, it'll just have to wait until we get home."

Her eyes brimmed with resigned acceptance. "Harrison, I told you I understand."

"We're not leaving, Willow. We're going to the museum and to that shopping district you wanted to visit and wherever else we can think of. It's our anniversary. Let's enjoy it."

The caution in her expression ate a hole in Harrison's gut. It was as if she wasn't sure she could trust him. But then she smiled, and this time it actually made it to her eyes.

Hours later, they found themselves strolling through the grounds of the Villa Celimontana. The peaceful gardens resided on a small hill overlooking the city. Its numerous, well-kept pathways wound their way around the gardens, with marble sculptures and bounteous foliage lining either side. He and Willow lucked upon a bench overlooking the city. The sight of the ancient ruins and modern life intermingling continued to fascinate him.

They sat for several long moments with neither of them speaking. For the thousandth time today, Harrison had to fight the urge to kick his own ass. He would never forgive himself for making such a mess of this. There had to be a way to make this right.

You know what you can do.

A cold chill raced through him as that voice that had harassed him all day once again poked at his conscience.

There was one thing he could do. He could tell his wife something he'd never shared with her before. Something he'd never shared with anyone. He had no idea if it would make a difference, but maybe if she understood the motivation behind why he worked so damn hard, she'd be willing to forgive him when he made an asshole move like the one he'd made this morning. It was worth a shot.

He stretched his arm across the back of the bench and

released a lazy sigh. "I've never told you how I became such a workaholic, have I?"

She looked over at him, an incredulous dip to her brow. "What?"

"I know I put in too many hours at the office, Wills. I thought I was doing a good job at balancing my work time and family time, but I was wrong."

"Harrison, you don't have to do this."

He touched her shoulder. "I do," he said. "I need you to understand where I'm coming from. This drive...this crazy need to always be at the top of my game? It's not an intrinsic quality I was born with or anything like that. It was, in fact, born out of a very specific incident."

The spark of interest that flickered in her expressive eyes provided the encouragement he needed to continue.

"Back when I was ten years old, I decided I wanted to play baseball. Alex was on the junior varsity team and, like every one of us Holmes boys, I wanted to be just like my big cousin Alex. I begged Mom and Dad to let me play for this neighborhood league that had just started up.

"One weekend we had a retreat at a campground over on the Northshore. I guess it was supposed to be some kind of team building thing, although that's not the term they used for it back then." He shrugged. "In addition to sports, they also wanted to help us grow as young men.

"For one activity, the session leader gathered us all in a group. We had to go around in a circle stating what we wanted to be when we grow up. When I said I wanted to be a lawyer, he laughed."

"Excuse me?" Willow said in her "oh no he didn't" voice.

"Yeah." Harrison huffed out a humorless grunt. "He laughed at me. Then, in front of the entire group, he told me that I needed to pick something more realistic for boys like me. Football or basketball or some other kind of sport. He said boys like me didn't have what it took to be lawyers."

"That bastard," she growled.

"He thought he was saving me from being disappointed when I didn't reach the lofty goal I'd set for myself."

"He should have encouraged you to dream big. That's what adults in that position are supposed to do."

"Not when that adult looks at you and doesn't see someone with potential, based solely on your outward appearance."

Willow's lips thinned with her angry frown. "And this happened to you at ten years old? My goodness, Harrison, that's Athens's age."

"I've already had 'the talk' with Athens," he said. Her eyes widened and her mouth dropped open. Harrison spoke before she could. "I won't let my son exist in this world without preparing him for what he has to face, Willow. As much as it hurt to hear those words back then—to learn what that counselor really thought of me—I'm not sorry it happened. It was my first window into seeing how people viewed me as a young black boy.

"I had to put up with shit like that throughout high school and college, and beyond. People look at my size and skin color and think I'm good for nothing but running a football. As if being a professional athlete doesn't require intellect. You think just anyone can learn all those plays they have to master?" He shook his head. "That's beside the point. I talked with Athens when he joined the Scouts. I wanted him to be prepared for the moment he had to face something like what I faced with that camp counselor, because he *will* eventually face it."

"It happened to you at Disney World," Willow said on

an awe-filled whisper. "Do you remember? The front desk person asked which team you played for before he even asked your name."

"You remember that, huh?"

"Of course I remember."

"I can promise you he wasn't the only one in the lobby that day who thought I played professional ball. Because in their minds those are the only black men who can afford to have their families stay in the most expensive resort on Disney property. Believe me, Wills, I've gotten that kind of thing my entire life."

"I get it too," she admitted. "Do you know how many raised eyebrows I get at Whole Foods from folks looking at my full shopping basket?" She shook her head, then she reached over and covered his knee with her palm. "I can only imagine how much worse it is for you. Why haven't you ever told me about this, Harrison?"

He hunched his shoulders and stared out at the layout of the city before them.

"It's not something I think about. At least I *try* not to think about it." He looked to her. "But it's there, Willow. It's always there. That one incident shaped my entire world view. I quit sports and concentrated solely on my studies because I didn't want anyone ever telling me that I only had one path in life.

"I carry that experience with me whenever I walk into a courtroom or sit at a negotiation table. I've witnessed the surprise on an opposing council's face when it turns out I know some obscure precedent that they believe someone like me shouldn't know. I'm expected to fail by virtue of the color of my skin.

"It's why I work so hard now. Because I don't want anyone to think I don't know what I'm doing."

She scooted closer to him and Harrison's heart swelled to near bursting with relief and gratitude. They still had a long way to go. He wasn't foolish enough to assume he'd repaired the damage he'd caused this morning, but the compassion in her eyes gave him hope.

"I've spent my life doing all I can to be the very best I can be, no matter the cost," he continued. "But I see now that it's costing me you, and that's one price I'm not willing to pay. There is nothing in this world that's worth losing you over, Willow."

"You haven't lost me." She reached for his hand and enclosed it in both of hers. "I can't believe it took you all this time to tell me this." She stared into his eyes. "But I'm grateful you finally did. It explains so much."

"I shouldn't have held it in for so long. We always prided ourselves on never keeping secrets from each other. This isn't a secret in the usual sense, but it's still something that's been sitting here between us." He caressed her palm with his thumb. "I don't want there to be anything between us. Ever."

Something passed across her face that made the hairs on the back of his neck stand at attention.

"Wills? Is there something you want to tell me?"

She shook her head as if to clear it. "What? No," she said. "No. You're right. We can't expect our marriage to work if we're not honest with each other."

Harrison decided that flash of unease he thought he saw in her eyes was just the vestiges of this long, tension-filled day. He would put it out of his mind and focus on the ground he'd managed to recoup. They had a few hours left in Rome. Maybe they could salvage what was left of their vacation.

Chapter Ten

Their return to New Orleans wasn't nearly as nerve-wracking as the initial flight across the Atlantic, but only because he had too many other things weighing on his mind to worry about whether or not the metal box they were flying in would crash into the ocean. After a week together in Rome, his relationship with his wife had improved, but not enough to satisfy him.

Harrison considered himself a realist, so he knew things wouldn't automatically go back to being normal. Willow had warned him that this trip wouldn't be a cure-all. Yet, a small part of him had hoped that's *exactly* what it would be. In some ways, it had proven to be even *more* than Harrison had hoped for.

He and his wife had rediscovered what it felt like to be in love again. They'd recaptured the magic that always happened with they made love. For the first time in months, Harrison knew what it felt like to sit across a table from Willow and hold her hand while they shared an intimate meal and talked for hours about anything and everything. That's what this week in Italy had given them. It had reduced the size of the chasm that had grown in their marriage.

But it hadn't vanquished it completely. That became evident as soon as they touched down at the airport in New Orleans. The uncomfortable tension that had become so familiar began to throb between them once again. Harrison felt as if he was walking on eggshells as they deplaned and headed for baggage claim. The feeling only intensified as they made their way to the car.

A question hung in the air. Was he dropping her off at the house and going back to sleeping at the law office, or was he going to be welcomed back into his home? Into his bed?

Harrison came up against the same apprehension he'd experienced back when he was unsure if he should tell her about the trip. What if he asked her if he could come back home and she turned him down? What would it say about the progress he thought they'd made this past week? Would it mean they were back at square one?

And what about the elephant in the room?

He still didn't understand why things had fallen apart in the first place. There were hints and snippets and possibilities still playing out in his mind, but the crucial, definitive reason behind the implosion of his marriage remained a mystery. How could he work to prevent it from ever happening again if he still wasn't sure where everything had gone wrong in the first place?

It was time they finally had the discussion they'd been putting off for far too long.

Willow had called the kids as soon as they touched down on the tarmac, and learned that Indina had taken them out to dinner with plans to go to the movies afterward. That meant he and Willow had several hours in the house by themselves.

Per her usual post-vacation routine, the minute they arrived home Willow immediately unpacked and started separating the dirty laundry. Harrison took a cursory tour of the house, checking to make sure everything was in order, biding his time. He needed to ready himself for the conversation he planned to initiate.

When he returned to the kitchen, Willow called out to him.

"I can throw yours in with mine," she said. "I doubt Indina cooked seeing that she took the kids to dinner, so I can have something delivered while you wait for the laundry to finish."

Harrison walked over to the utility room and casually rested his shoulder against the door frame. "So, I'm waiting for laundry and then what? Am I going back to the little apartment above the law practice? Is that what's happening?"

She looked up at him, a startled expression on her face. The pajama bottoms she'd been about to sort fell from her fingers.

"I..." she started, but it was as if she'd forgotten how to speak.

Harrison pushed away from the entry and came into the room. He kicked the stray pieces of laundry from around her feet and closed the distance between them.

"When are we going to talk about us, Willow? You said we'd do so after the trip." He lifted his shoulders. "Well, it's after the trip."

"You want to do this *now*?"

"If not now, when? What's the excuse for putting it off? The kids are out, so we don't have to worry about them overhearing us. Now is as good a time as any."

Harrison watched her jaw constrict as she swallowed.

After another moment's hesitation, she said, "Okay." She looked up at him. "I guess we're doing this."

The gravity in her voice sent a surge of apprehension up his spine. For the barest second, he almost suggested putting it off until they'd both had a chance to rest. But postponing this discussion wouldn't make it any easier.

He motioned for her to walk ahead of him as they left the laundry room and went into the kitchen. He'd been in this room less than five minutes ago, but somehow the air felt different. Heavier.

Harrison tried to ignore the ominous cloud suddenly cloaking the room as he rested his backside against the edge of the kitchen island and crossed his arms over his chest.

"Well?" He lifted his shoulders. "What happened to us, Wills? How did we go from being a happily married couple to two people who can go an entire week barely saying a word to each other?"

"That's not true, Harrison. It isn't that severe."

"Yes, it is," he said. "At least it has been in the past, and you know it."

She dropped her head back and released an exasperated sigh. "You're going to bring up that week this past summer, aren't you?"

"Yeah, I will. Because we went three solid days without speaking more than ten words to each other. And when I pointed it out, you gave me all these excuses and said I was being irrational."

"Do you remember everything that was going on that week, Harrison? You were working crazy hours at the office and not getting home until late in the evening. Lily's drill team was preparing for their performance at the Saints opening season game, and had practice every single day." She threw her hands up. "And Athens had some kind of

Scouts thing that I can't even remember right now. I just remember that it was chaos."

"Three days, Willow. Three. Days."

"Well, I'm sorry if life gets so hectic sometimes that I barely have time to tell you good morning. I'll tell it to stop."

Her brackish, sarcastic response was exactly why Harrison had avoided this conversation for so many months. He refused to back away from it this time.

"You know there's more to it than that. Something broke between us, Willow. I want to know what."

She pinched the bridge of her nose before looking over at him. "We talked about this in Italy. It's normal for couples to go through rough patches. We're lucky that we were able to go seventeen years without hitting any of those rough patches, but it was inevitable, Harrison."

"No. Something happened." Harrison pushed away from the island and walked over to where she stood next to the refrigerator, stopping a couple of feet from her. "I get that things can get a little out of control with the kids' schedules and the hours I sometimes put in at the office, but there was a distinct shift. It happened the week I went to Philly for that conference."

Her shoulders stiffened. He pounced, knowing he'd hit the nail on the head.

"What is it?" he asked. "*Talk* to me, dammit."

She tucked her arms in close, wrapping them around her upper body. "Let's not do this right now, Harrison."

"No. Something happened that week. Or, at least I think *you* think something happened." He paused for a moment before asking the question he didn't want to know the answer to. "Do you think I cheated on you while I was away at that conference, Willow?"

Her eyes shot to his. The wariness staring back at him tore a hole in Harrison's heart.

"That's it, isn't it?" The depth of his hurt was unlike anything he'd ever experienced. How could she consider, even for a moment, that he would be unfaithful to her?

Yet, Harrison had known it had to be something like this. He'd thought back to that week, when he'd called several times to talk to her only to find his calls going to voicemail. He'd taken to calling Lily's cellphone, but she too had an excuse as to why her mother couldn't speak. He tried to remember if maybe he'd taken pictures with a colleague that ended up on Facebook, or something else that could have put such a ridiculous idea in her head, but he could never pinpoint exactly what had caused her unfounded suspicions.

It was time he laid them to rest.

Harrison grasped her shoulders and leaned forward, capturing her gaze. Staring into her tear-laden eyes, he said, "From the first day I met you, there has never been a single woman in this world who has been able to take my attention away from you. I have never wanted—never even *thought* about being with another woman."

A single tear streamed down her cheek and the pain in his heart intensified.

"How, Willow?" Harrison asked in a harsh whisper. "How could you ever *think* I'd be unfaithful to you?"

She sniffed and brushed at the tear running down her cheek.

"I've never questioned your faithfulness," she said, her voice shallow and raw. "I know you have never been unfaithful, Harrison." She lifted her head and looked up at him, her eyes brimming with hurt and guilt. "But I have."

Willow flinched at the quickness in which Harrison dropped his hands from her shoulders and backed away. A solid ten seconds ticked by with agonizing slowness as he just stood there staring at her, his brow marred with confusion. He blinked several times before asking in a raspy voice thick with disbelief, "I...what?"

She put her hands up. "I didn't cheat in the traditional sense of the word."

"The traditional sense—" He took an abrupt step back and turned away. A second later, he turned back to her, his eyes wide with confusion and something akin to panic. "Willow, what are you saying?"

"Just hear me out." She pushed her fingers through her hair and sucked in a deep, fortifying breath. It felt as if a million pins were dancing underneath her skin, pricking at her frayed nerve-endings. She'd dreaded this moment for months. Now that it was finally time to confront it, Willow wasn't sure she could.

But she had to. She owed him an explanation.

"Do you remember that dinner we had at Drago's about a year ago with the old gang from Xavier? It was to celebrate Marcus Ewing receiving the President's Award?" Harrison's head dipped in a curt nod. "Well, a few months later, Marcus came back to town on business. We went out to dinner."

Willow caught the moment realization dawned. His eyes widened, then narrowed in suspicion. "A few months later? Was this...?"

She nodded. "It was while you were in Philly."

His stoic facade crumbled. "My God, Willow." The words came out in a tortured whisper. He dropped his head back and stared at the ceiling as he paced in the tight space between the pantry and island. When he returned his attention to her, his eyes were filled with accusation. "What did you do? Did you fuck him?"

"No! Goodness, Harrison! It was nothing like that." She held her hands out, pleading for understanding. "It was only dinner. Other than a peck on the cheek when I arrived at the restaurant and another when I left, there wasn't even any real contact between us."

"So why did you say you cheated?"

"I didn't *physically* cheat on you," she said. "But I did emotionally."

He shook his head. "I don't even know what that means."

"It means that it wasn't about Marcus, or any man for that matter. It was about *me*." She slapped her hand to her chest. "It's about the way I felt that night. I wasn't a mother, or a wife, or the person the Ladies Auxiliary can count on to bring coconut macaroons for the church bake sale. I was Willow. I was the Willow who was the first in her class to successfully separate proteins using electrophoresis. The Willow who organized a sit-in at the university president's office when the school tried to cut student aid. It had been so long since I'd felt that way that I barely recognized that old person I used to be."

"I never asked you to change," Harrison said. "Did I tell you your only job was to take care of the kids and bake cookies? Correct me if I'm wrong here, but I believe *I'm* the one who encouraged you to apply to graduate school. More than once, Willow. I knew how much you loved your field and I didn't want you to let it go if you truly wanted to work in science."

"I know that, Harrison." She covered her face in her

hands. "That's what's so confusing about all of this." She brought her clenched hands to her chest. "I love being a mother to my children and I *love* being your wife. I wouldn't change that for anything in this world, baby." He flinched at the endearment, and Willow's heart broke in two.

"I'm sorry," she said. "I know you don't want to hear this, but you asked what happened and this is it. The night we all went to dinner together, everyone had all this amazing news to share. There was Cheryl going on and on about her new promotion at the lab where she works, and Tameka with her announcement that she planned to run for attorney general in Nevada, and Marcus receiving the top honor from our old university, and you making partner at your law firm.

"What was *my* big news? I was named Parent of the Month for Athens's scouts troop." She held up a finger. "And don't you dare say that I should be proud of that. Don't patronize me. I don't begrudge a single minute that I get to spend taking care of my children, but that night—" She shook her head. "Something happened that night. For a few hours I was reminded of the Willow that wanted to change the world. I didn't realize how much I'd missed her.

"And that's why when Marcus called to invite us both to dinner a few months later, I decided to go even though you weren't there. I wanted to recapture that feeling. I wanted to have just a glimpse of what life could have been like if I'd chosen differently."

"If you'd chosen not to marry me?"

"No! If I'd chosen to be something other than a house-wife!" Willow held on to her patience by the thinnest thread. "You know how I grew up, Harrison. You know I watched my mom struggle to make ends meet while also trying to better herself. And you know what it cost her.

"To this day, if you asked my mother what she considers to be her biggest regret, she'll tell you it's the four nights my sisters and I spent in that foster care home after the police found us sleeping in that old car. Those four nights are forever etched into my mind, and I vowed I would never put my children in a position to experience anything like that."

"Willow, you know there is no way in hell I'd ever let that happen."

"Yes, I know that, but it doesn't lessen the fear. It doesn't erase those memories of sitting in that pay-by-the-week motel, wishing that my mom was there to help me with homework instead of having to be at her second job. It doesn't take away the shame of being the only kid at my kindergarten graduation who didn't have a parent in the audience to clap for me when I walked across the stage clutching my little rolled up diploma.

"I promised myself that my children would never know that feeling, but it doesn't mean that I can't imagine what my life would have been like if I'd pursued other dreams."

He hunched his shoulders, a blank, impassive look in his eyes. "I don't know what I'm supposed to make of that, Willow. Because it sounds as if you're not happy with your life."

"That is *not* what I'm saying!"

"That's sure as hell how it sounds. If you were happy you wouldn't be going out to dinner with some other man so you can dream about how great your life would be if you didn't have a husband and kids at home."

"You know what, screw you, Harrison!" She stomped up to him and pushed at his unmovable chest. "Screw! You! You don't get to stand there and make me out to be the bad guy because I wanted to indulge, just for a moment, in thoughts of what my life would have been like if I'd chosen to work outside the home.

"What if you hadn't gone to law school? What if, for some reason, life sent you in another direction? Or if that camp counselor hadn't steered you away from playing baseball? You mean to tell me you've never thought about how it would feel to play in the major leagues?"

"This isn't the same thing."

"The hell it isn't! We all have things we could have done differently, different paths we could have chosen. It doesn't mean we regret the things we *have* done, or wish that our lives were different." She folded her arms over her chest. "But, given how I grew up, I guess you think I should just be grateful for this life you've provided for me, right?"

"That's not fair."

"Neither is it fair to accuse me of being unhappy just because I wanted to dream a little, Harrison."

He scrubbed his hands over his face. The exhaustion in his eyes reflecting what she felt.

"Can you understand why I'm upset, Willow? Think about it. You've been keeping this from me for nearly a year. I've been wracking my brain trying to figure out how I messed up, because this entire time I thought it was something *I* did. And then because, I don't know, maybe you thought I wasn't hurting enough, you tell me that having dinner with some other man made you feel things I haven't been able to make you feel."

"This had nothing to do with me wanting to hurt you, Harrison. How could you say that?"

"How? You went out with *Marcus Ewing*! Just the two of you. How—"

"This is not about Marcus! Why are you so damn determined to make it about something it's not?"

"You went out with your old boyfriend, Willow! The same motherfucker who took your virginity. I'm supposed to treat that as if it's no big deal?"

"So, that's why you're upset? Because twenty years ago I slept with Marcus before I ever even met you?"

He closed his eyes and drew in a deep, measured breath. When he opened them again, the hurt staring back at her crushed Willow's soul.

"I'm upset because my wife didn't think she could trust me enough to tell me how she really feels." A breadth of tortured emotions played across his face. In a voice thick with anguish, he said, "You're breaking my heart, Willow. That's something I never thought you'd do."

Agony ripped through her chest at the desolate look in his eyes. She pulled her quivering lip between her teeth.

"I never intended to hurt you," she managed to speak past the raw pain in her throat.

His gruff laugh didn't hold an ounce of humor. "That's the thing about intentions, they don't mean a damn thing when it's time to face reality."

Willow knew there was nothing she could say right now to ease the pain she'd inflicted upon him, but neither could she allow either of them to walk away from this discussion with so much up in the air.

She cleared the emotion clogging her throat before speaking. "So, where do we go from here? Now that you know everything."

"*Is* this everything?"

"Yes, Harrison. It is." She hunched her shoulders. "What do we do now?"

He closed his eyes again, and the skin over his jaw grew

taut, an outward manifestation of his internal struggle. Finally, he opened his eyes, and said, "I don't know." He shook his head. "I don't know how I'm supposed to process this." He appealed to her with eyes brimming with sadness and pain. "Tell me how I'm supposed to process this, Willow."

There had been so many times during her life that she thought she knew what it felt like to have a broken heart, but Willow now understood nothing she'd experienced before could hold a candle to the pain slicing through her at this very moment. Seeing the agony he was in, knowing she'd caused it, made hers even greater.

She started to reach for him, but jerked her hand back. She had to give him space. She'd spent the past year working her way through these feelings. He was entitled to at least a few days. Although, if she had to go days without knowing how much damage her revelation had done to their marriage she would go insane.

No. Your marriage will *survive this.*

Willow knew her husband. She knew he wouldn't allow this to permanently come between them. He couldn't. *She* wouldn't allow it.

She loved him too much.

Eventually, he would realize he felt the same way. She just had to be patient and wait for him to come back to her.

Chapter Eleven

"No, no, no. This is all wrong."

As Harrison reached for a red pen in the ceramic pen holder Lily made for him at camp eight summers ago, his elbow connected with his NCBL travel mug, knocking it over and spilling leftover coffee on his desk.

"Son of a bitch!"

He shot back in his chair to avoid getting splashed. Grabbing a fistful of Kleenex, he tried to staunch the flow of the tepid liquid before it reached the files on his desk. Half a box of Kleenex later, he tossed the soiled tissues in the trash, propped his elbows on the desk, and covered his face in his hands.

Maybe coming down to the office this morning wasn't the best idea.

In the past, he could always count on work to provide an escape when there was some kind of unpleasantness he was trying to avoid in his personal life. Hell, he'd single-handedly negotiated four separate multi-corporation acquisitions in those final weeks before his mom passed. But there was no escaping the misery he'd been going through since leaving his house last night. It was too raw, too potent to do anything but breathe his way through it. And try his best to survive it.

Call her!

That voice in his head had been nagging at him to pick up the phone and call Willow for the past sixteen hours, but every time Harrison even thought about heeding its demand, something stopped him. He wasn't ready. There were still too many emotions he needed to work through before he could face his wife again.

Anger? Yeah, he was angry, but not for the reason he'd assumed he would be. His pride wanted him to be angry about her having dinner with Marcus Fucking Ewing, of all people. But his common sense wouldn't allow anger over that particular event to stick. He knew his wife. He believed her when she said nothing happened between her and Marcus.

What infuriated him even more were thoughts of the entire *year* they'd spent growing further and further apart because of something that could have been solved if Willow had just come to him and told him how she felt. He'd probably gone through a dozen bottles of antacids this past year, trying to assuage the anxiety that had burned a hole in his gut, stressing over the state of his marriage. When all it would have taken was one conversation, something to clue him in.

As angry as it made him, more than anything he was...hurt.

Why had she kept it to herself all this time? Why hadn't she come to him? She'd been his wife, his lover, his best friend for the past seventeen years. To know that she no longer felt comfortable sharing something so important with him shot a lightning rod of grief straight through Harrison's heart.

He couldn't pinpoint exactly when it happened, but something *had* broken between them along the way. Ten years ago, he would have noticed something was off. He would have caught the warning signs that Willow was unhappy. Ten years ago, *she* would have told him so. But they were both so busy these days that they no longer took the time to talk about such things.

The kids, their extended families, his job, politics, community activism, the state of the world; that's the kind of things that dominated their conversations—when they could find time to have meaningful conversations. They'd allowed their marriage to succumb to life's endless intrusions. Harrison could only pray it wasn't too late to save it.

There was a knock on the door a second before Jonathan poked his head inside.

"Hey," he said. "I didn't expect to see you in the office after that long flight yesterday. You sure you're not too jet lagged to be here?"

Maybe that was the reason he was so discombobulated this morning? Harrison mentally slapped away that thought. Jet lag had nothing to do with this.

"Nah, I'm good," he said. He motioned for Jonathan to come in. "You here to go over the materials for the arbitration?"

His partner waved that off. "We can go over that tomorrow. It's not as if you don't know this stuff inside and out." He plopped himself in one of the high-backed chairs that faced Harrison's desk. "Tell me about Italy. I haven't been back there since I tried out for the European League."

Harrison's head snapped back. "I didn't know you tried

out for the European League. Was this after you left the NBA?"

He nodded. "I worked out for the teams in Bologna and Madrid," Jonathan said with a shrug. "I decided against it because I knew I'd miss home too much. But enough about that. How was Italy?"

"Italy was good."

"Just good?"

"Of course the food was amazing. And the history was... well...what can you say about a place with buildings dating back thousands of years? And the—" Harrison stopped at the incredulous look on Jonathan's face. "What?"

"I don't want to hear about old buildings. I want to know how things are between you and Willow. Did you two work things out?"

He drew in a long, labored breath, praying his voice didn't give away the anguish behind his next words. "A week in Italy isn't going to fix everything between me and Willow."

Jonathan grimaced. "Shit," he cursed. "I guess that means you slept here last night, huh?" One brow arched. "You want to talk about it?"

"No."

"Are you sure, man?"

Harrison nodded. "Don't worry about me. I'm good."

"No, you're not good. You haven't been good for a while." He sat back in his chair and settled his ankle on the opposite knee. "If you don't mind, I'm going to take a few minutes to offer a bit of unsolicited advice."

"And if I *do* mind?" Harrison asked.

"I'm going to offer it anyway," Jonathan said with a grin. But then he sobered, his expression earnest. "Take it from someone with enough regrets to fill this entire house. There is nothing worth losing the woman you love over, Harrison. Nothing."

The intense remorse in the other man's eyes revealed more than Jonathan probably meant to. For the second time in as many weeks, the curtain behind his casual, carefree mien lifted, giving way to the unhappiness his law partner tried so hard to keep hidden from the world.

"I'm not looking to lose my wife," Harrison said. And he meant that. Down to his very last bone. His pain was still raw, but he wasn't about to let this ruin his marriage.

Jonathan held his hands up, his easygoing grin returning. "I just thought it was something you needed to hear. Not that I have a wife—or want one—but I recognize the kind of woman who makes a good wife. You have that in Willow."

Harrison thought back to that night a few weeks ago, when he and Jonathan had indulged in a bit too much of that high-priced bourbon. The night that should have been the man's third-year anniversary to the woman who'd practically left him standing at the altar. Over the years Jonathan had gallivanted around New Orleans with an endless parade of women, each more beautiful than the last. But if he were a betting man, Harrison would wager his last penny that not a single one of them had made him happy. Those smiles his law partner so frequently displayed rarely reached his eyes.

He didn't want to become another Jonathan. He didn't want to be the kind of man who only *pretended* to be happy. Someone who flitted from one woman to another, trying to fill a void left empty by the woman he was supposed to spend the rest of his life with.

He'd found the woman he was destined to spend the rest of his life with twenty years ago. Sitting underneath the shady branches of an oak tree on the quad at Xavier University, he'd spotted that beautiful face and his life had changed forever.

Willow *was* his life. There was no living without her.

Suddenly, an unrelenting urge to go to his wife gripped him and refused to let go. Harrison pushed his chair back and pocketed his cell phone.

"I have something I need to do," he said.

The phone he'd just slipped into his pocket trilled with an incoming text message. He took it out and cursed. It was from Willow.

"What's wrong?" Jonathan asked, rising from his chair. Harrison did the same.

"It's about Lily." He grabbed his keys from the drawer and rounded the desk.

"Everything okay? She's not hurt, is she?"

"No. It's about whether or not she'll be allowed to stay at her high school." Jonathan frowned in confusion and Harrison realized he hadn't mentioned his daughter's ode to Dwayne Johnson back when he was still known as professional wrestler, The Rock. "Lily had a fight at school a couple of weeks ago. I'll fill you in on it later, but I need to get down there ASAP."

"Go," Jonathan said, ushering him out of his office. "Everything's under control here. If Michael Delmonico shows up I'll give him a Popsicle and tell him to sit in the corner and wait for you."

Harrison chuckled. "I'll be back as soon as I can."

"What did I just say? Don't worry about what's going on here. Go and take care of your family."

"Thanks, man." Harrison pulled him in for a one-arm hug before heading out to his car. He made it to the school in under twenty minutes, courtesy of the lucky string of green lights he managed to catch. He pulled into the parking spot directly across from Willow's SUV. When he arrived at Dr. Saul's office, he was hit with a wave of deja vu. Everyone sat in the same chairs they'd sat in when he came to this office a few weeks ago.

"Come in." Dr. Saul gestured for him to enter. "Thank you for coming in on short notice. I hate that we all have to meet once again under these circumstances, but I do appreciate you both taking the time out of your day to be here."

"It's not a problem," Harrison said. "I understand how important this is. We all do." He looked to Willow for agreement. She regarded him with a mixture of warm affection and cautious uncertainty in her eyes. After a moment she snapped to attention, as if remembering why they were here.

"Yes. Yes, of course. Education is a top priority in our household." She looked to Lily, who sat in a chair against the wall. "Right, Liliana?"

His daughter nodded. Harrison feared she would throw up any second now. He'd never seen her light brown skin looking so pale.

Dr. Saul shuffled some papers on her desk, but then set them down and folded her hands on top of them.

"As you all know, the disciplinary board finished up their review yesterday. A decision was made to officially expel Liliana from St. Katherine's. I'm sorry."

Lily gasped, then burst into tears.

Willow rushed over to her. Perching on the arm of the chair, she wrapped Lily up in a hug as she addressed the principal. "We understand," she said. "We knew this was a possibility." She smoothed a gentle hand over Lily's hair. "It's okay, baby," she crooned in a soothing voice.

The disappointment he felt on Lily's behalf was overshadowed by the irrepressible love he felt for his wife right now as she comforted their daughter. Harrison had no doubt she would make a kickass scientist one day, but nothing could ever match her skills as a mother.

"Here is something for you to keep in mind," Dr. Saul continued. "Privacy laws dictate that student records remain strictly confidential, including disciplinary hearings. Therefore, if you are able to get Liliana into one of the other schools in this area, her record here at St. Katherine's will not be shared."

"Wait." Harrison leaned forward. "So you're saying we don't have to tell them why she was expelled?"

"You don't have to mention the expulsion at all. As far as any other school should be concerned, you wanted to give Liliana a new environment in which to learn." Dr. Saul smiled. "Good luck. Despite how it ended, it has been a joy having you Holmeses as a part of the family here at St. Katherine's."

When he'd walked through these doors a half hour ago, Harrison never imagined he'd be filled with such hope when he exited them. The situation wasn't ideal. Just thinking about the hassle and cost associated with getting Lily into a good school made him want to down a shot of that fine bourbon back at the office, but there was reason to feel optimistic.

Now if he could carry this optimism into the next important meeting he needed to have today, he would be set.

He trailed behind Lily and Willow as they made it to the SUV. After kissing Lily on the cheek and assuring her that everything would be okay, Harrison rounded the vehicle. He tapped on the driver's side window and waited for Willow to lower it.

"Can I come over?" he asked.

Her brows arched. "Tonight?"

"No." Harrison shook his head. "Right now. I don't want to wait to talk about this. About *us*. We need to put this to rest, Wills."

Cautious hope filled her eyes. "Okay," she said. "Follow me home?"

"I'm right behind you."

Harrison took off for his car and followed the black SUV out of the parking lot.

It was time they fixed their broken marriage, and he wouldn't be satisfied until they mended every single crack.

W illow made the left onto Argonne Boulevard, her heartbeat escalating with every inch that brought her closer to their house. She'd dropped Lily off at her friend Amina's, who'd suffered a broken wrist in a volleyball tournament while she and Harrison were in Italy, and had stayed home from school today.

The parenting experts out there would probably frown upon her choice to allow Lily to spend the rest of the day hanging out with her best friend after just learning that she'd been expelled from her high school, but Willow saw no reason to punish her further. There was nothing they could do about the decision of the disciplinary board at St. Katherine's. Besides, she didn't want her daughter to bear witness to the conversation set to take place at home.

The significance of it settled on her chest, a crushing weight that refused to ease up. What transpired over this next hour would determine what happened with her marriage, with the rest of her life. Willow gripped the steering wheel and tried to ignore the anxiety twisting in her belly.

She turned into the driveway and found Harrison's Mercedes parked in its usual spot. Her breath caught as a wave of bittersweet nostalgia washed over her. Her throat ached with the knot of emotion pressing against it, the result of a powerful sense of longing that suddenly gripped her. In that moment, Willow knew what she had to do.

She had to convince her husband to come home.

She had to convince him to come home because she now recognized that these last few weeks without him had been some of the most miserable of her life. She recognized that this break they'd taken—this foolish decision to try living apart—had done nothing but show her just how much he belonged in that house with her and the kids. Willow didn't care what it took. She was willing to walk through fire to make her marriage work.

But first she had to walk through that door.

Taking a deep breath, she climbed out of the SUV and made her way up the stone pavers. She was still several yards away when the front door opened and Harrison stepped out onto the landing.

"Where's Lily?" he asked, looking toward the SUV.

"I dropped her off at Amina's," Willow said as she climbed the stairs. She explained about Amina being home from school, and how Lily could use the time with her best friend after the rough day she'd had.

"Was Lily doing okay?" Harrison asked.

Willow nodded. "She's upset, but more with herself for ever getting into that fight."

They were stalling. Willow was tempted to go along with it, but it would only temporarily delay the inevitable. The time for playing games was over.

She motioned for Harrison to follow her inside. They moved past the foyer and into the living room. Willow set her keys and purse on the tall console table that butted against the wall, and then turned to him.

Without preamble, she said, "I want you to come home."

Several significant moments ticked by with nothing but the sound of water draining from the dishwasher she'd set before leaving for St. Katherine's. An angsty charge filled the air, fraught with foreboding and another unnerving, troubling quality she couldn't quite describe.

The longer he wordlessly stood there, the more Willow's trepidation grew.

"I...uh...I know it isn't that simple," she stuttered. "But I figured I'd start there and we can work our way through figuring out how to make it happen." When he still didn't speak, she held her hands out and pleaded. "Goodness, Harrison, say *something*."

His head jerked back as if startled, bewilderment emanating from his shocked gaze.

"I'm—" he began, but then he stopped. He kneaded his brows as he shook his head. "I'm trying to figure out what to say, Wills. I mean...I thought *I* would be the one saying those words, not the other way around."

Her knees buckled, relief surging through her. Willow slumped against the wall as the pent up tension rushed from her limbs. She started for him, but her steps faltered when Harrison held a hand up and took a couple of steps back.

"Hold on, Wills. We still have a lot to talk about."

His words stopped her cold. "Okay," she said. She fidgeted, not knowing what to do with her hands. "Okay, yes. Yes, we do."

Harrison reached for her, taking her by the wrist and

tugging her toward the sofa. He sat on the arm of the loveseat and pulled her into the space between his spread out knees.

"The same way that week in Italy wasn't the solution to our problems, that's the same way us agreeing that I should move back home isn't the answer either. Before I drive back to the office and pack up my bags—" He stopped and dropped his head back, releasing a gush of relieved breath. "Thank *God* I get to do that soon. I never want to see that damn futon again."

Willow hiccuped through a tearful laugh. "I'm sorry about that," she said.

He shook his head. "The bed isn't important. What's important is determining how we got here in the first place so that we never, *ever* find ourselves in this position again." He ran his hands up and down her arms before settling them at her waist. "I know how much it drives you crazy when I come up with my lists and strategies, but I think this is one time it would benefit us to use them. We have to figure out the best way to proceed in this matter."

Willow's mouth tipped up in a smile. "You're laying the lawyer speak on me."

The warmth of his throaty laugh washed over her like a soothing balm. "I'll try to be more conscious of it."

"No. I miss it," she admitted.

Tender remorse stole across his face. A pregnant moment passed before he spoke again, his voice hushed and filled with meaning. "What happened, Wills?" he asked. "Talk to me."

She lifted her shoulders in a pensive shrug. "It's like I said yesterday, that dinner earlier this year made me take stock of my life, and I—"

"No, I know what you said yesterday. I understand that

part, and it's something we'll need to discuss. In fact, it's the next thing on my mental list." One corner of his mouth lifted in a half smile. "What I can't figure out is how we got to the point where I didn't learn about how you felt until after I moved out of the house? Why did it take something that drastic, Willow?"

She bit the inside of her cheek as she stared into his eyes, her heart welling with emotion.

"I don't know," Willow honestly confessed. "I have no idea what we thought would be accomplished by you moving out, but whatever it was failed miserably. The only thing your leaving brought into this house was heartache, Harrison. You never should have moved out."

"I've felt that way from the first day I left," he said.

"I did too. From the very first day." She shook her head in disbelief. "If we both felt this way, why didn't we say anything? Have we always been this bad at communicating?"

"I think it's the opposite," Harrison said. "For so long, we've been so in tune with each other that everything just came naturally. I never had to wonder what you were thinking. I just seemed to know. And vice versa."

She nodded. "But something changed. It's as if the kids hit a certain age and life just got turbocharged, and suddenly, we stopped being in sync with each other."

He tightened his grip on her waist. "That's why I'm no longer leaving things up to interpretation, or operating as if we're both mind readers. I want you to *talk* to me from now on, Willow. And I'm going to listen. *Really* listen. I'm not going to just do what I think you want, or what I think is best. I want us to make time to talk to each other, and when we do, we only talk about these two people," he said, motioning between the two of them. "Deal?"

"That's a deal," Willow said. She leaned forward and placed a gentle kiss upon his lips. When she tried to pull away, Harrison closed his hand on the back of her head and held her to him for a few seconds longer, his soft yet firm lips opening over hers. He brought his other hand up to cup her cheek, and gently coaxed her mouth open with his thumb. Willow let him inside, her skin warming as the tip of his tongue tangled playfully with hers.

"Damn, I've missed that," he said when he finally released her lips.

"So, so much," Willow agreed. She rested her forehead against his, a smile stretching across her lips. "We have a lot of lost time to make up for. I hope you're ready."

He sucked in a swift breath. "Have mercy."

She choked on a laugh.

Harrison sat back, his hands returning to her waist.

"Okay, now that we've covered that, it's time to move on to the next item on the list."

She arched a brow in inquiry.

"I want you to think back to that night when we all had dinner," Harrison continued. "What do you wish you could have said that night, instead of talking about the kids?"

Willow's first instinct was to refute his insinuation that she wouldn't have wanted to talk about her kids. Those children were her pride and joy. She would never tire of boasting about their accomplishments. It's what a good mother did.

But she knew that's not what Harrison was getting at. She challenged herself to be honest about her feelings.

She didn't have to think too long before answering.

"I wish I could have talked about the hundreds of little girls who once hated science but now love it after attending my weeklong science camp," she said.

His eyes widened. "A science camp, huh?"

She nodded.

"Only a week long?"

"It's very hands-on, you see. Which requires a small class size. I figure if it's only a week long, more girls can attend throughout the summer."

Harrison tipped his head to the side, a contemplative look in his eyes.

"What?" Willow asked.

"Nothing. Just thinking."

"Just thinking about what?" she prodded.

"I'm just thinking about Brooklyn's *Dynamo Diane* comic," he said. "You read through it, right? You know how it's Mama who comes to the rescue of a bunch of little girls who're told they shouldn't be studying science because they're girls?"

Willow nodded. "Yes," she said, wondering if he was thinking what she *thought* he was thinking.

"Well, maybe there can be some truth to what Brooklyn thought would only be fiction."

"What are you saying, Harrison?" Her chest tightened with excitement as she anticipated his next words.

"I'm saying maybe we should go bigger when it comes to the foundation. Think about it, Willow. The Diane Holmes Foundation is geared toward encouraging young black girls to major in the sciences. I know the focus now is on helping those going to medical school, but once the foundation is off the ground, maybe we should think about expanding it to help girls get started at a younger age."

"Oh God, Harrison. Yes. *Yes*," she breathed. To honor her beloved mother-in-law's legacy while also helping young girls discover a love of science would be a dream come to life. "I would love to make this happen through the foundation."

"We'll talk to Indina and the guys, but you know they won't object."

Willow's shoulders slumped as reality reared its head. "The only thing is, I'm not sure if I'm qualified to help anybody right now. It's been a long time since I've studied science."

He shrugged. "So do what people do when they need to learn, go back to school."

"It's not that easy, Harrison."

"Yes, it is, Wills. If this is what you want, if it's what you think will make you happy—"

"Stop." She pressed two fingers to his lips. "Let's clear this up right now. I don't want you thinking I've been miserable all this time, because I haven't. I know how lucky I am, Harrison. I know there are millions who would kill for the life I've been blessed with." She wrapped her arms around his neck. "I promise you, I am more than happy."

"I'm not satisfied with you just being happy," he said. "I want you to wake up every morning fucking euphoric, Willow Holmes." He connected his lips with hers in a swift kiss. "Go back to school. It's almost time for Lily to start filling out college applications. You can do it together. It'll be a mother/daughter bonding exercise."

Willow threw her head back and laughed. "Walking around a college campus with her mother. Oh, I'm sure Lily would *love* that."

"I don't see why she shouldn't," Harrison said. "The only reason she's even here is because I saw you walking on a college campus and fell instantly in love."

Just like that, her heart was a puddle on the floor.

"Was it really instant?" Willow asked.

He nodded. "Absolutely. One look and I knew you were the woman I was meant to love and cherish for the rest of my life. And I will, Willow." He stood and pulled her flush against him. Capturing her cheeks between his palms, he looked into her eyes and said, "No matter what road bumps we hit along the way, I promise to love you for the rest of my natural born life."

Willow took his hand and brought it to her chest, placing it over her heart. "And I promise to do the same," she said. "As long as I have breath in me, I promise to love and cherish you for the rest of my life."

Chapter Twelve

It didn't matter how hard he tried to keep his smile in check, Harrison still found his lips splitting into a broad, ridiculously huge grin. A tidal wave of emotions washed over him as he turned the corner and, seconds later, pulled into his driveway. He had reason to smile.

He was home.

He collapsed back against the seat, his muscles sagging with relief. He tilted his head back and stared up at the car's ceiling; this time he didn't even try to suppress his deep, rumbling laugh. God, it felt good to be home.

His eyes roamed over the house and yard. It wasn't as if he'd expected anything to change in the five hours since he'd left earlier this afternoon, but it *felt* different. *He* felt different. He hadn't realized just how tense the act of pulling into his own driveway had made him this past year. For the first time in months, he didn't have knots in his stomach at the thought of walking into his house.

He looked over at the dinged up garage door he'd been meaning to replace. He'd considered its dents, courtesy of one too many basketballs bouncing off it, to be an eyesore.

They weren't. Those dents told a story. Each one signified a snippet of his son's childhood.

Those dents were going to hang around a while longer. He and Athens still had many more games to play in this driveway. There was *so* damn much he had to look forward to in this house. He couldn't wait to get started.

Just as he opened his car door, the front door of the house opened and Athens ran outside, with Liliana and Willow following behind. Harrison's heart expanded to the point where he could barely pull air into his lungs. How had he survived all these weeks without them?

He got out of the car and was nearly tackled to the ground by his son. He returned the bear hug, then tucked Athens in the crook of his arm and rubbed his head.

"How's it going, li'l man?"

"Mom says you're moving back!" Athens said, looking up at him.

Harrison hitched his head toward the trunk. "My suitcases are in the back."

"Yes!" Athens pumped his fists in the air. He slid his head out from under Harrison's hold and performed the silly touchdown dance he'd been trying to perfect for months now. Unfortunately, his son took after his father when it came to his dance moves.

Harrison peered over at the door and caught Lily regarding him, a hint of skepticism in her cautious stare. She'd long ago lost the guileless, childhood optimism her brother still possessed, but Harrison wanted to allay her suspicions and reassure her that he was indeed home to stay.

He climbed the steps and wrapped his arms around her. "How're you doing, baby girl?"

"I'm okay," she murmured against his chest. "Daddy, you're squeezing me too tight."

"I know," Harrison said. "I'll let go. Eventually." He released her a second later, but captured her shoulders in his hands and stooped down just a bit so he could look her in the eyes. "Are you sure you're okay?"

She nodded. "I am. I spent the afternoon at Amina's looking up schools. I found one on the Westbank that I think I can get into."

His eyes widened as he looked over Lily's head at Willow. His wife nodded and gestured toward the house. "We were just on the computer looking at the school's website. It'll be a bit of a drive, which means she'll have to get up at least an hour earlier every morning." She looked pointedly at Lily. "But if they admit her, we'll make it work."

He and Willow hadn't yet discussed whether or not to still give Lily the car they'd planned to buy her for her sixteenth birthday, which was just a few weeks away. As far as Harrison was concerned, this one mistake—despite the enormity of it—shouldn't change their plans. In the grand scheme of things, Lily had been a dream child over these sixteen years. She deserved that car.

But it wasn't his call alone. This was a decision both he and his wife would make together.

His wife. God, he was back with his wife!

Just the thought sent a crush of gratifying warmth crashing through him. He released Lily's shoulders and walked over to Willow. Capturing her chin between his fingers, he placed a faint, simple kiss upon her mouth. He heard Lily's loud groan behind him and smiled against his wife's lips.

"Welcome home," Willow said, a teasing laugh dancing in her eyes.

"Thank you. It's good to be back." Harrison hitched his head toward the front door. "Let's go inside before the neighbors start poking their heads out. They're all probably trying to figure out what's going on."

"Yes, I expect questions at the next Neighborhood Association meeting," Willow said. She looked over at Athens. "You, sir, have homework to do. Don't think I forgot about that in all the excitement. And you, ma'am," she directed at Lily. "You need to start working on the essay for the school's application." She looked to Harrison. "I'm pretty sure your application for law school was easier than the application for this high school."

"But it's so cool," Lily said as she led them all inside. "They have a Future Astrophysicists club. And their drama club takes *two* trips to New York each year. And their Languages Club traveled to China over the summer."

China? Harrison mouthed over her head.

Willow hunched her shoulders, amusement still sparkling in her brown eyes. The sight left him breathless. He loved this woman so damn much.

Harrison spent some time listening to Athens explain the newest comic books he'd bought with his leftover birthday money before insisting he start his homework. He then dropped in on Lily, and together they read through the application for the small, private high school she hoped to attend.

Once the kids were settled in their rooms, Harrison joined Willow in the kitchen, where the pungent aromas of tomato, garlic, and oregano signaled one of his favorite dishes.

"You're making lasagna," he said, coming up behind her

and placing a kiss on that spot behind her ear that he loved even more than lasagna.

"I figured it was a fitting welcome home meal. A little something to remind us of our time in Italy." She gestured toward the oven. "There's garlic bread too."

Harrison moaned with pleasure, although their upcoming meal had little to do with it. Every drop of the pleasure currently flowing through his veins had everything to do with the woman whose body stood flush against his.

He reached around her and took the salad bowl from her hands. "I can handle this," he said. "Why don't you open up a bottle of some of that wine you brought back from Rome and pour us each a glass?" He stopped. "On second thought, just pour a glass for yourself for now. I'll have my one glass with dinner."

She laughed as she slid the bottle from the built-in wine rack.

"Did you have a chance to talk with Jonathan?" she asked. "Is he okay with you working less hours?"

"One hundred percent," Harrison said.

As soon as he'd arrived back at the office this afternoon, he'd had a heart-to-heart with Jonathan about the time he'd been putting in at the law practice. Harrison had to admit that most of his work-related stress had been self-inflicted. Jonathan didn't pressure him to keep long hours; he'd made those decisions on his own.

But they'd talked about potentially expanding the law practice in the near future. If they followed through on those plans, it would likely require he work even more hours. That was something Harrison just wasn't willing to sacrifice anymore.

Jonathan assured him that if more man hours were needed, *he* would be the one to put in the work. Apparently, he had the time now that he'd broken things off with his latest girlfriend. It had been on the tip of Harrison's tongue to offer some of that unsolicited advice his law partner had volunteered earlier today, but he doubted Jonathan was ready to hear what Harrison thought about his numerous failed attempts to extricate himself from the memories of his ex-fiancée. The man would find his way to happiness. Eventually.

"Hey, can you grab the Romano cheese from the refrigerator?" Willow asked as she poured wine into her glass.

"Isn't it too early to add cheese shavings to the salad?" he asked on his way to the fridge.

"Who said anything about the salad? I want it to go with my wine."

He laughed as he opened the door and reached for the wedge of hard cheese. The footed bowl they'd gotten as a wedding gift seventeen years ago stood on the shelf next to it. It was layered with fruit, some kind of spongey cake and whipped cream.

"What's the occasion for the fancy dessert?" Harrison asked.

"Oh, that's a surprise for Athens," Willow said. "Just after you left, Dr. Fudge's office called. His test results came back. He's no longer in the pre-diabetic range."

Harrison whipped around, his eyes wide. "Thank God," he said. He walked over to Willow and wrapped his arms around her. "Thank God, thank God, thank *God*." He was seconds from tearing up and he refused to feel ashamed.

"I know," Willow said, tightening her hold on him.

"You did this, Wills. You made this happen. You've been so diligent, helping him to get better."

She shook her head. "Nope. We *both* did this." She

leaned back, her arms still around his waist. "We make a good team."

"Yes, we do." He kissed her on the nose. Just as he was about to release her, a thought occurred to him. Harrison frowned. "So, are we sure having dessert tonight is smart? Isn't it reinforcing the kind of bad habits we want the kids to avoid?"

"It was actually Dr. Fudge's suggestion that we celebrate with a healthy dessert. That way, we can show Athens that he doesn't have to give up everything good in order to eat healthy. It's berries, angel food cake, and light whipped cream. And it tastes *amazing*."

Harrison nodded his understanding. "Makes sense. I should know better than to question you."

"But that's what we're doing from now on, remember?" She pinched his butt. "It's called communicating."

Harrison huffed out a relieved laugh. "I'm just so damn happy he's going to be okay."

"We all will," Willow said. She tipped her head back, her eyes brimming with adoration and hope. "Now that you're home, everything is going to be okay."

Then she connected her lips with his. It felt like home.

"Mrs. Holmes, do you have any additional forms for the silent auction?"

Willow looked up at the young man dressed as Spider-man. "I'm sorry?" she said.

"The silent auction? We've once again run out of forms for the auction item pertaining to Ms. Jordan. Guests are getting a bit restless."

"Have you seen Catwoman walking around

anywhere?" Willow asked. "That's my sister-in-law, Indina. She said the event coordinator was going to get someone in the business center to make copies of the form."

Willow peered around the room packed with costumed guests, searching for her sister-in-law. The organized chaos of the past two hours had been enough to send them all running from the ballroom at the Windsor Court Hotel, but there would be no escaping tonight, not with the amount of money they were raising for the start of the Diane Holmes Foundation.

The silent auction alone had already raised more than Willow had anticipated they'd make for the entire gala, thanks in no small part to a surprise donation from R&B sensation Aria Jordan. The singer, whom Harrison's cousin Toby had discovered in a local club years ago and whose career he still managed, had donated dinner for twelve at one of the city's top restaurants, along with a private concert. When word got out on social media about the auction item, people who weren't even in attendance began calling in to place their bids.

Last Willow checked, the bid was at $27,000. Running a close second was a weeklong, all-inclusive vacation in the beach home Margo and Gerald owned in St. Marteen. The two had purchased the home several years ago after getting married there. That auction item stood at just over $15,000.

The buzz inside the ballroom had increased ever since they opened the doors and allowed people to enter the official kickoff party for the Diane Holmes Foundation. Hours earlier, the atrium had been packed with over five hundred comic book enthusiasts, some driving in from as far as Dallas and Pensacola. They'd paid $50 each just to view a collection of rare comic books that were on display. Some of those same comics, including those Margo had found in her attic, were also up for auction and pulling in a pretty penny.

It had been Brooklyn's idea to host the pre-gala event. Willow had to admit that they'd all been a bit skeptical at first that anyone would be willing to pay money just to look at old comics. Then again, they'd been a bit skeptical when Reid pitched his girlfriend's idea about a superheroes-themed gala as well. The entire family owed them all a huge debt of gratitude. As Willow looked around the packed room, she couldn't imagine a stuffy event with people in tuxedoes and ball gowns. This cheerful, jovial atmosphere spoke more to Diane's personality than any black tie affair ever would.

"You ready for a break yet, Ms. Lane?"

Willow turned to find Harrison approaching her in his pseudo-Superman costume. He'd refused to wear tights, no matter how much she'd begged. Instead, he wore black slacks, a button-down shirt with most of the buttons undone, and a Superman t-shirt underneath. And, of course, a cape.

Willow had gone all out herself as Lois Lane, donning a sharp black pencil skirt, white collared shirt, and the signature black-rimmed eyeglasses. She'd even flat-ironed her hair and curled it to recreate Lois's vintage deep waves.

"I don't think any of us will get a break until this thing is over. But I don't care because everything is going fabulously," Willow said. She turned and gave him a kiss. "Hey, have you seen your sister?"

Harrison tipped his head toward the wall of windows that faced the Mississippi river.

"Over there losing her shit over the decorator. He took it upon himself to change the color scheme for the photo area."

"Oh no," Willow groaned.

Harrison nodded. "Pretty sure he'll never make that mistake again."

"We need more forms for the auction," Willow said, but before she could go in search of them, Harrison grabbed her by the arm.

"Slow down a minute. Here." He produced a puffed pastry from behind his back. "I snuck this out of the kitchen for you. You've been running nonstop since this thing started."

"What else am I supposed to do?" Willow asked before stuffing the entire mini pastry in her mouth. She moaned in pleasure. "My God. Those two sisters are amazing. We should look into getting them for Lily's party."

"We can check. If they were able to take on a party of this size at the last minute, they can probably fit in something on a smaller scale with no problem."

She and Harrison had decided to go ahead with their plans to give Lily a car for her sixteenth birthday, but after witnessing her turnaround over the past couple of weeks, and taking into account how few problems she'd given them over the years, they'd agreed to up the ante by throwing her a surprise Sweet Sixteen birthday party, as well.

Ezra walked up to them. "Hey, where've you been?" He asked Harrison. "I've been looking for you two. Make sure you're around in the next ten minutes. We'll all need to be up on stage."

"For what?" Harrison asked.

"Just wait," her brother-in-law said.

Willow had a feeling she knew what was going on. Ezra came to the gala dressed as King T'Challa of Wakanda, but Mackenna told her earlier that he planned to do a wardrobe change halfway through the gala and emerge as the Black

Panther. However, having them all gather on stage for his big reveal was a bit over the top, even for Ezra.

"I need to go check in on Athens," Willow said. "I want to make sure he's not in the way." Her son had begged to join them at the gala, especially after learning about the superheroes theme.

"He's fine," Harrison said. "I just came from the back room where they all are. Alex hooked up a video game console. Athens, Jasmine and the twins are all back there playing on it. He's set for the night."

As if he'd been conjured by name, Alex appeared with his wife, Renee. Willow had already labeled them as winners of the costume contest planned for later in the evening. The couple, dressed as a black Dick Tracy and Jessica Rabbit, outshone just about everyone in the room.

Although, she had to admit Eli and Monica ran a close second. The physicians had opted to remain slightly in character, with Eli dressing as Purple Doctorfish from *Spongebob Squarepants* and Monica as Doc McStuffins from the Disney cartoon. Willow didn't even want to know what kind of money they'd spent on their costumes. She was just excited to see that so many had gone all in with the theme.

Toby joined them, one of the dozen or so in the crowd who'd opted for Spiderman tonight.

"This party is off the chain," Toby said. "I mean, look at this." He gestured around the decorated room with its floor to ceiling banners of Dynamo Diane, large balloon arches, and images of various superhero emblems flashing on the walls courtesy of numerous projectors around the room. Willow couldn't deny that Indina and her team had done a remarkable job putting this event together.

Jonathan stopped by dressed as Zorro, along with his

newest girlfriend who was dressed as what Willow could only surmise was a burlesque dancer. Or maybe a brothel owner? Willow couldn't remember the woman's name, but it didn't matter. She wouldn't be around for long. They never were.

Once Jonathan and his date left to get something to eat from the buffet that had just opened, Toby said, "Man, I'm happy Sienna decided to stay home with the kids tonight. She would be pissed to see him here with this new girl." He looked around. "But, then again, I'm sorry she's missing all of this. I need to take more video to show her what y'all managed to put together here. Aunt Diane would be proud."

Willow's chest filled with pride. Yes, her mother-in-law would be proud of what they'd done tonight.

"Can we get the children of Diane Holmes on stage please?" came the voice of tonight's emcee over the speaker system.

They all whipped around to the front of the room. Ezra had indeed changed into his Black Panther costume and stood on stage, his fiancée, Mackenna standing next to him.

"Oh, Lord," Harrison said. "What is this one up to?"

"I have no idea," Willow said. "You'd better get up there."

He caught her wrist. "You know what I told you. Mama would have picked you over me if she'd had to make a choice. You're just as much hers as the rest of us."

They joined the others who had already gathered on stage. Indina stood next to her husband, Griffin, with Reid and Brooklyn, standing opposite them.

"You too, Dad," Ezra called, motioning for Clark to come up on stage. Willow smiled at her father-in-law, looking as regal as he wanted to be as James Earl Jones's character from the '80s movie, *Coming to America.*

Ezra moved to the side, making room for Mackenna to step up to the microphone.

"Good evening, everyone," Mack began. "On behalf of the Holmes family, I want to thank you all for supporting this amazing event. I knew Diane for nearly twenty years. From the very first time I begged Indina to let me come down to New Orleans with her for Thanksgiving break back when we were both broke college students at Grambling, Diane welcomed me into her home and made me feel as if it was *my* home. She did the same for countless people around the neighborhood."

The room resonated with murmurs of agreement.

"Diane left us much too soon," Mack continued. "But with your help, her legacy will live on. And, to solidify that legacy, the city's illustrious mayor has a proclamation he'd like to share with you all. Mayor Carter?"

A buzz began to hum around the ballroom as Lucien Carter joined them on stage. Willow looked to Harrison, who hunched his shoulders in a gesture indicating that he had no idea what was going on either. Even Indina looked perplexed.

The mayor thanked Mackenna, then held up a linen folder emblazoned with the Mayor's Office's official seal.

"On behalf of the citizens of this great city, I, Lucien Carter, Mayor of the City of New Orleans, with gratitude for a life committed to community service, do hereby deem it an honor and pleasure to officially recognize this day as Diane Holmes Day in the City of New Orleans."

A roar of cheers went up as the mayor handed the proclamation to Clark. Willow tried to hold it together, but the moment she caught the sheen of tears sparkling in her father-in-law's eyes nothing would stop hers from falling. She wasn't the only one. Every single one of them on stage were teary-eyed as they shared hugs.

Soon after the proclamation, the brass band that had been entertaining the guests all night started up again, and a second line quickly formed. They all joined in the traditional New Orleans dance style, waving handkerchiefs and paper napkins as they high-stepped around the room.

Willow was seconds from passing out from exhaustion when Harrison pulled her out of the parade of costumed guests and steered her toward the drink station. It boasted a half-dozen elegant glass jar drink dispensers filled with fruit infused ice water, lemonade and sweet tea. He filled two cups with lemon-mint water and handed one to her.

"Thank you," Willow said after downing the water in one gulp. "I hate to say it, baby, but I think we're getting too old for this."

"I'd agree, but then look at that one." He nudged his head toward where the second line was still going strong. Her seventy-year-old father-in-law led the pack. "I think we're just out of shape. We need to join him on his morning jogs."

Willow laughed. "I think you're right."

He caught her by the shoulders and pulled her into him, then turned her around so that her back was flush against his chest. He wrapped his arms around her middle and nestled his chin against her neck.

"Hey," he spoke softly against her ear. "In another minute or so, look to the right, just beyond the tables where the auction items are on display. Tucked near the corner is someone dressed in a big, fancy dress like the kind in that movie you like with Mozart or somebody?"

"*Amadeus*," Willow said. "You're talking about the

Marie Antoinette in that beautiful cranberry and black gown? Or, at least, I'm guessing that's who she's supposed to be. I noticed her earlier."

"Yeah, there's something familiar about her. I've been trying to figure out who she is, but she has that lace mask covering most of her face. She seems pretty interested in Jonathan. She's been looking at him all night."

"Can't say I blame her," Willow remarked. "He's looking mighty fine in that costume."

Harrison turned her around and crossed his arms over his chest. Willow threw her head back and laughed. "But not nearly as fine as you, Superman."

"You're just saying that because you want me to help you with all that homework you're about to get once you start school."

She cocked her brow. "Are you saying you won't help me if I need it?"

"You know me better than that," Harrison said, wrapping his arms around her. "All you have to do is ask for it, my love. There's nothing I won't do for you."

She locked her arms behind his neck. "And that's just one of the reasons why I love you."

"Just one, huh?"

She nodded. "It would take the rest of my life to list them all. I'd rather spend my life *showing* you just how much I love you."

She tugged his head closer and claimed his lips in a slow, easy kiss. The kind of kiss they'd shared for years. The kind of kiss she planned for them to share for years to come.

Also by Farrah Rochon

The Holmes Brothers

Set in New Orleans, the Holmes Brothers series follows the lives of the men of the Holmes family as they find love in one of the world's most romantic cities.

Deliver Me

Release Me

Rescue Me

Chase Me

Trust Me

Awaken Me

Moments in Maplesville

Visit the sexy, sultry, small southern town of Maplesville in my *Moments in Maplesville* novella series.

A Perfect Holiday Fling (*Callie & Stefan*)

A Little Bit Naughty (*Jada & Mason*)

Just A Little Taste (*Kiera & Trey*)

I Dare You (*Stefanie & Dustin*)

All You Can Handle (*Sonny & Ian*)

Any Way You Want It (*Nyree & Dale*)

Any Time You Need Me (*Aubrey & Sam*)

Visit my BOOKS page to see my entire backlist!

Look for the long-awaited conclusion of Jonathan and Ivana's romance in **Return to Me,** *the final book in the Holmes Brothers series.*

Coming Fall 2018!

About the Author

A native of south Louisiana, Farrah Rochon officially began her writing career while waiting in between classes in the student lounge at Xavier University of Louisiana. After earning her Bachelors of Science degree and a Masters of Arts from Southeastern Louisiana University, Farrah decided to pursue her lifelong dream of becoming a published novelist. She was named *Shades of Romance Magazine*'s Best New Author of 2007. Her debut novel garnered rave reviews, earning Farrah several SORMAG Readers' Choice Awards. *I'll Catch You*, the second book in her New York Sabers series for Harlequin Kimani, was a 2012 RITA ® Award finalist. Yours Forever, the third book in her Bayou Dreams series, is a 2015 RITA® Award finalist.

When she is not writing in her favorite coffee shop, Farrah spends most of her time reading her favorite romance novels, traveling the world, and seeing as many Broadway shows as possible.

Find her through her website or your favorite social media platforms.